Great Trees I Have Known

Ruskin Bond is known for his signature simplistic and witty writing style. He is the author of several bestselling short stories, novellas, collections, essays and children's books; and has contributed a number of poems and articles to various magazines and anthologies. At the age of twenty-three, he won the prestigious John Llewellyn Rhys Prize for his first novel, *The Room on the Roof*. He was also the recipient of the Padma Shri in 1999, Lifetime Achievement Award by the Delhi Government in 2012 and the Padma Bhushan in 2014.

Born in 1934, Ruskin Bond grew up in Jamnagar, Shimla, New Delhi and Dehradun. Apart from three years in the UK, he has spent all his life in India, and now lives in Landour, Mussoorie, with his adopted family.

RUSKIN BOND

Great Trees I Have Known

RUPA

Published by
Rupa Publications India Pvt. Ltd 2023
7/16, Ansari Road, Daryaganj
New Delhi 110002

Sales centres:
Bengaluru Chennai Hyderabad
Jaipur Kathmandu Kolkata
Mumbai Prayagraj

P-ISBN: 978-93-5702-531-7
E-ISBN: 978-93-5702-532-4

First impression 2023

10 9 8 7 6 5 4 3 2 1

Printed in India

Contents

Introduction

During my lifetime, I have seen many things change—from tongas to cars and dhabas to malls. In a world yearning for constant change, trees are a much-needed, wise and grounding presence. Looking out my window, I often wonder how much life these trees have witnessed. From the flurry of squirrels and birds and the adventurous quests of the neighbourhood children to wars, famines and floods—they have seen the best and worst of this world.

Over the years, trees—majestic deodars, delicate willows, humming pines, glorious chestnuts, wizened old banyans and the generous jackfruit trees—have almost become recurring characters in my writing. *Great Trees I Have Known* is an ode to these trees. It brings together my stories and essays featuring the bountiful and stunning world of trees. In essays, like 'Growing up with Trees' and 'My Trees in the Himalayas', I recount all that I have gained from the trees around me. In stories, like 'The School among the Pines' or 'Dust on the Mountain', trees form the verdant backdrop against which my characters come alive. The collection also includes some essays, like 'The Friendly Oaks' and 'The Coconut Tree', marvelling at the wondrous qualities of specific trees.

I hope this book reminds you, dear reader, of the simple joy of lying down under the gentle shade of a tree, watching the leaves rustle in the quiet breeze. What more can one want from life?

Among the Maples and Oaks

It isn't many years since I left Maplewood, but I wouldn't be surprised to hear that the cottage has disappeared. Already, during my last months there, the trees were being cut and the new road was being blasted out of the Mountain. It would pass just below the old cottage. There were (as far as I know) no plans to blow up the house; but it was already shaky and full of cracks, and a few tremors, such as those produced by passing trucks, drilling machines and bulldozers, would soon bring the cottage to the ground.

If it has gone, don't write and tell me: I'd rather not know.

When I moved in, it had been nestling there among the oaks for over seventy years. It had become a part of the forest. Birds nestled in the eaves; beetles burrowed in the woodwork. Some denizens remained, even during my residence. And I was there—how long? Eight, nine years, I'm not sure; it was a timeless sort of place. Even the rent was paid only once a year, at a time of my choosing.

I first saw the cottage in late spring, when the surrounding forest was at its best—the oaks and maples in new leaf, the oak leaves a pale green, the maple leaves red and gold and bronze; this is the Himalayan maple, quite different from the North American maple; only the winged seed-pods are similar, twisting and turning in the breeze as they fall to the ground, so that the Garhwalis call it the Butterfly Tree.

There was one very tall, very old maple above the cottage, and this was probably the tree that gave the house its name. A portion of it was blackened where it had been struck by lightning, but the rest of it lived on; a favourite haunt of woodpeckers: the ancient peeling bark seemed to harbour any number of tiny insects, and the woodpeckers would be tapping away all day. A steep path ran down to the cottage. During heavy rain, it would become a watercourse and the earth would be washed away to leave it very stony and uneven. I first took this path to see Miss Mackenzie, an impoverished old lady who lived in two small rooms on the ground floor and who was acting on behalf of the owner. It was she who told me that the cottage was to-let provided she could remain in the portion downstairs.

Actually, the path ran straight across a landing and up to the front door of the first floor. It was the ground floor that was tucked away in the shadow of the hill; it was reached by a flight of steps, which also took the rush of water when the path was in flood.

Miss Mackenzie was eighty-six. I helped her up the steps and she opened the door for me. It led into an L-shaped room. There were two large windows, and when I pushed the first of these open, the forest seemed to rush upon me. From below, from the ravine, the deep-throated song of the whistling thrush burst upon me.

I told Miss Mackenzie I would take the place. She grew excited; it must have been lonely for her during the past several years, with most of the cottage lying empty, and only her old bearer and a mongrel dog for company. Her own house had been mortgaged to a moneylender. Her brothers and sisters were long dead.

I told her I would move in soon: my books were still in Delhi. She gave me the keys and I left a cheque with her. It was all done on an impulse—the decision to give up my job in Delhi, find a cheap house in a hill-station, and return to freelance writing. It was a dream I'd had for some time; lack of money had made it difficult to realize. But then, I knew that if I was going to wait for money to come, I might have to wait until I was old and grey and full of sleep. I was thirty-five—still young enough to take a few risks. If the dream was to become reality, this was the time to do something about it.

I don't know what led me to Maplewood; it was the first place I saw, and I did not bother to see any others. The location was far from being ideal. It faced east, and stood in the shadow of the Balahissar Hill; so that while it received the early morning sun, it went without the evening sun.

There was no view of the snows and no view of the plains. In front stood Burnt Hill. But the forest below the cottage seemed full of possibilities, and the windows opening on to it probably decided the issue. In my romantic frame of my mind, I was susceptible to magic casements opening wide. I would make a window-seat and lie there on a summer's day, writing lyric poetry…

But long before that could happen I was opening tins of sardines and sharing them with Miss Mackenzie. And then Prem came along. And there were others, like Binya. I went away at times, but returned as soon as possible. Once you have lived with mountains, there is no escape. You belong to them.

Rosebud: A Fragment

Jai had placed a chair on the beaten earth floor of the little courtyard, in the shade of an apricot tree. Apricots appeared to be the only trees that grew near the village. Their leaves were russet-red in the autumn sun. I felt sure that other fruit could grow here too—apples, pears, peaches. If I were living here, I thought, I could try them out. If I could get a message to McNulty he would send me saplings from the Saharanpur nurseries. And on the other side of the hill, where it was shadier and moister, there were plants that he would love to have. If I were living here—but I had no plans to stay.

Jai's village, in the next valley, was a warmer place. Here we were facing the snows—the mighty Srikanth peak towered directly above us. Two months from now the village would be under snow.

'Do you stay here through the winter?' I asked Gulabi.

She nodded, 'People come down from the Gangotri shrine to stay here during the winter. The temple priests and others.'

I looked down the mountain to where the river, green and gold, wound its way through sandbanks and rocky islets on which grew clumps of pine and maple.

'Why not live down there?' I asked.

'There is no land down there for fields,' she said. 'And sometimes the river is in flood and everything gets swept away.'

She seemed to give out some of the glow that was in her

face. I felt it pour over me. And this golden feeling did not pass, even when I went into the cool darkness of the house to join Jai in a meal prepared especially for us.

It can be hot in September, even in the mountains and by the time we climbed the steep path to Harsil, my companion and I were both very thirsty. I sat down on a low boundary wall, while Jai walked over to a small house to ask for water and enquire about his relatives.

It was one of those warm, humid afternoons when drowsiness is in the air, and the buzz of insects lulls one into slumber. I had closed my eyes and was half asleep when a footstep made me sit up. Someone was holding a tumbler of water before me, but the hands that held it were not Jai's. They were the hands of a girl—not very delicate, but firm and without blemish. I looked up into her face and our eyes met over the rim of the tumbler. I forgot to take it from her.

She was a fair girl, as fair as they come in the hills, and there was a tinge of pink in her cheeks. Her hair was black and glossy and lay open across her shoulders, for she had been drying it in the warm sun. Her clothes were plain but neat; her feet and hands were brown from sun and wind. Her lips were full and soft. Poppies in her cheeks and roses in her lips, I thought.

'You are thirsty,' she said.

I took my eyes off her for a moment, grasped the tumbler and drank till it was empty.

'Thank you,' I said. 'And who are you?'

'I am Gulabi.'

'Rosebud. A pretty name. It suits you.'

'These are my father's fields. Your friend is a cousin of mine. He is waiting for you in the house. Come inside and rest.'

What I liked about her was her smile. It dropped over her face slowly, like sunshine moving over brown hills.

How Far Is the River?

Between the boy and the river was a mountain. I was a small boy, and it was a small river, but the mountain was big.

The thickly forested mountain hid the river, but I knew it was there and what it looked like; I had never seen the river with my own eyes, but from the villagers I had heard of it, of the fish in its waters, of its rocks and currents and waterfalls, and it only remained for me to touch the water and know it personally.

I stood in front of our house on the hill opposite the mountain, and gazed across the valley, dreaming of the river. I was barefooted; not because I couldn't afford shoes, but because I felt free with my feet bare, because I liked the feel of warm stones and cool grass, because not wearing shoes saved me the trouble of taking them off.

It was eleven o'clock and I knew my parents wouldn't be home till evening. There was a loaf of bread I could take with me, and on the way I might find some fruit. Here was the chance I had been waiting for; it would not come again for a long time, because it was seldom that my father and mother visited friends for the entire day. If I came back before dark, they wouldn't know where I had been.

I went into the house and wrapped the loaf of bread in a newspaper. Then I closed all the doors and windows.

The path to the river dropped steeply into the valley, then rose and went round the big mountain. It was frequently used by the villagers, woodcutters, milkmen, shepherds, mule drivers—but there were no villages beyond the mountain or near the river.

I passed a woodcutter and asked him how far it was to the river. He was a short, powerful man, with a creased and weathered face, and muscles that stood out in hard lumps.

'Seven miles,' he said. 'Why do you want to know?'

'I am going there,' I said.

'Alone?'

'Of course.'

'It will take you three hours to reach it, and then you have to come back. It will be getting dark, and it is not an easy road.'

'But I'm a good walker,' I said, though I had never walked further than the two miles between our house and my school. I left the woodcutter on the path, and continued down the hill.

It was a dizzy, winding path, and I slipped once or twice and slid into a bush or down a slope of slippery pine needles. The hill was covered with lush green ferns, the trees were entangled in creepers, and a great wild dahlia would suddenly rear its golden head from the leaves and ferns.

Soon I was in the valley, and the path straightened out and then began to rise. I met a girl who was coming from the opposite direction. She held a long curved knife with which she had been cutting grass, and there were rings in her nose and ears and her arms were covered with heavy bangles. The bangles made music when she moved her wrists. It was as though her hands spoke a language of their own.

'How far is it to the river?' I asked.

The girl had probably never been to the river, or she may have been thinking of another one, because she said, 'Twenty miles,' without any hesitation.

I laughed and ran down the path. A parrot screeched suddenly, flew low over my head, a flash of blue and green. It took the course of the path, and I followed its dipping flight, running until the path rose and the bird disappeared amongst the trees.

A trickle of water came down the hillside, and I stopped to drink. The water was cold and sharp but very refreshing. But I was soon thirsty again. The sun was striking the side of the hill, and the dusty path became hotter, the stones scorching my feet. I was sure I had covered half the distance: I had been walking for over an hour.

Presently, I saw another boy ahead of me driving a few goats down the path.

'How far is the river?' I asked.

The village boy smiled and said, 'Oh, not far, just round the next hill and straight down.

Feeling hungry, I unwrapped my loaf of bread and broke it in two, offering one half to the boy. We sat on the hillside and ate in silence.

When we had finished, we walked on together and began talking; and talking I did not notice the smarting of my feet and the heat of the sun, the distance I had covered and the distance I had yet to cover. But after some time my companion had to take another path, and once more I was on my own.

I missed the village boy; I looked up and down the mountain path but no one else was in sight. My own home was hidden from view by the side of the mountain, and there was no sign of the river. I began to feel discouraged. If someone had been with me, I would not have faltered; but alone, I was conscious of my fatigue and isolation.

But I had come more than half way, and I couldn't turn back; I had to see the river. If I failed, I would always be a little ashamed of the experience. So I walked on, along the hot, dusty, stony path, past stone huts and terraced fields, until there were no more fields or huts, only forest and sun and loneliness. There were no men, and no sign of man's influence—only trees and rocks and grass and small flowers—and silence...

The silence was impressive and a little frightening. There was no movement, except for the bending of grass beneath my feet, and the circling of a hawk against the blind blue of the sky.

Then, as I rounded a sharp bend, I heard the sound of water. I gasped with surprise and happiness, and began to run. I slipped and stumbled, but I kept on running, until I was able to plunge into the snow-cold mountain water.

And the water was blue and white and wonderful.

The Joy of Water

Each drop represents a little bit of creation—and of life itself. When the monsoon brings to northern India the first rains of summer, the parched earth opens its pores and quenches its thirst with a hiss of ecstasy. After baking in the sun for the last few months, the land looks cracked, dusty and tired. Now, almost overnight, new grass springs up, there is renewal everywhere, and the damp earth releases a fragrance sweeter than any devised by man.

Water brings joy to earth, grass, leaf-bud, blossom, insect, bird, animal and the pounding heart of man. Small children run out of their homes to romp naked in the rain. Buffaloes, which have spent the summer listlessly around lakes gone dry, now plunge into a heaven of muddy water. Soon the lakes and rivers will overflow with the monsoon's generosity. Trekking in the Himalayan foothills, I recently walked for kilometres without encountering habitation. I was just scolding myself for not having brought along a water bottle, when I came across a patch of green on a rock face. I parted a curtain of tender maidenhair fern and discovered a tiny spring issuing from the rock—nectar for the thirsty traveller.

I stayed there for hours, watching the water descend, drop by drop, into a tiny casement in the rocks. Each drop reflected creation. That same spring, I later discovered, joined other springs to form a swift, tumbling stream, which went cascading down the hill into other streams until, in the plains, it became part of a river. And that river flowed into another mightier river that kilometres later emptied into the ocean. Be like water, taught Lao-tzu, philosopher and founder of Taoism. Soft and limpid, it finds its way through, over or under any obstacle. It does not quarrel; it simply moves on.

A small pool in the rocks outside my cottage in the Mussoorie hills, provides me endless delight. Water beetles paddle the surface, while tiny fish lurk in the shallows. Sometimes a spotted forktail comes to drink, hopping delicately from rock to rock. And once I saw a barking deer, head lowered at the edge of the pool. I stood very still, anxious that it should drink its fill. It did, and then, looking up, saw me and leapt across the ravine to disappear into the forest.

In summer the pool is almost dry. Even this morning, there was just enough water for the fish and tadpoles to survive. But as I write, there is a pattering on the tin roof of the cottage, and I look out to see the raindrops pitting the surface of the pool.

Tomorrow the spotted forktail will be back. Perhaps the barking deer will return. I open the window wide and allow the fragrance of the rain and freshened earth to waft into my room.

Sounds of the Sea

For years I had this large sea-shell, and by putting it to my ear I could hear the distant sob and hiss of the sea—or so I fancied, until this romantic notion was dispelled by twelve-year-old Mukesh, who told me that the same effect could be obtained by holding an empty cup to my ear. He was right, of course. In fact, the cup sounds better than the shell! And for years I'd gone on imagining that the sound of the sea was somehow trapped in my shell.... But I still cling to it, for it takes me back to Jamnagar, on the west coast of India, and memories of sea and sand, small steamers and large Arab dhows plying across the Gulf of Kutch.

My small hand in my father's, I explored with him the little port's harbour and beach, bringing home shells of considerable variety, and even, on one occasion, a small crab, which lived in a spare bathtub for several days and was forgotten—until a visiting aunt, deciding on a tub-bath after a long train journey, found it keeping her company among the soap-suds. Amidst much clamour and consternation, it was evicted from the house and dropped into a nearby well. But my aunt was convinced that I had deliberately placed it in the tub, and refused to speak to me for the rest of her stay.

A small British steamer was often in port, and my father and I would visit the captain, a good-natured Welshman who gave me chocolates, a great treat in those days, for Jamnagar was too small a place for a Western confectionery shop. I was ready to go to sea with Captain Jenkins, convinced that chocolates were only to be found on tramp steamers.

We left Jamnagar when the Second World War broke out and my father joined the RAF. It was to be some ten years before I saw the sea again, for I went to boarding school in the hills. I was still in my teens, but now bereft of my father, when I set sail from Bombay in the *S.S. Strathnaver*, a beautiful P&O liner, one of a fleet, its sister ships being the *Strathaird* and *Stratheden*. Those were the days of the big passenger liners, before fast air travel put an end to leisurely ocean voyages. It took just over a fortnight to reach Southampton or London, but there was never a dull moment on the voyage. Apart from interesting shipboard acquaintances—the sort of mixed company that gave Somerset Maugham material for his stories—there were also colourful ports of call: Aden, Port Said, Marseilles, Gibraltar. At Marseilles, I decided to miss the coach-tour and instead walk into the town. After three hours of walking along miles and miles of dockland, I finally reached the outskirts of the city—just in time to catch the coach back to the ship!

But later, living in London, I never tired of walking among the docks and wharfs along the Thames, for many of those places were associated with the novels of Dickens, which had inspired me to become a writer. Limehouse, Wapping, Shadwell Stairs, the Mile End Road, the East India Docks, these were all places I knew from *Bleak House, Dombey and Son*, and *Our Mutual Friend*. And there was the fog, a thick peasouper, that seemed to have lingered on from the fog that had enveloped the characters and the action in *Bleak House*, setting the tone for that masterpiece. London, I am told, no longer has fogs—they are dispersed by modern and scientific means—and although the air no doubt is cleaner and healthier now, I feel sure some of the magic has gone—along with the East End of old.

From London's dockland to the Channel Islands was a short trip but a considerable change. I lived on the island of Jersey for two years. It had a number of bays and inlets of great charm and beauty, and it was here that I learnt to watch the tides advancing and retreating, and discovered that the tides make different sounds in different places.

Every tide has its own music, and those who live near lonely shores soon learn to recognize the familiar ripple, throb, sob or sigh. And sometimes the tide comes up from the deep against four steep sand-bank and roars defiance.

The tide-rip which pushes through the Channel Islands off the Norman coast has a smoother thud than most, though it comes from the same Atlantic as the harsher-sounding waters among the Orkneys. The difference may be that the channel tides move through purple waters which have drifted up from sunny Portugal, while the other has a shiver from the coast of Greenland.

The music of sea waters is wonderfully varied. Every bay and headland and strait has its note which the local fisherfolk recognize even in time of dense fog; a note which guides them home or which helps them locate the place for their fishing.

For many years I have been living far from the sea. Sometimes I feel the urge to go down to the sea again, all the way from the Himalayas to Cape Comorin. And maybe I will one day.

Meanwhile, if I wish to listen to the sound of the sea, there's always my sea-shell—or Mukesh's tea-cup.

My Trees in the Himalayas

Living in a cottage at seven thousand feet in the Garhwal Himalayas, I am fortunate to have a big window that opens out on the forest so that the trees are almost within my reach. If I jumped, I could land quite neatly in the arms of an oak or horse chestnut. I have never made that leap, but the big langurs—silver-grey monkeys with long, swishing tails—often spring from the trees onto my corrugated tin roof, making enough noise to frighten all the birds away.

Standing on its own outside my window is a walnut tree, and truly this is a tree for all seasons. In winter, the branches were bare; but they were smooth, straight and round like the arms of an apsara. In spring each limb produces a bright green spear of new growth, and by midsummer the entire tree is in leaf. Toward the end of the monsoon, the walnuts, encased in their green jackets, have reached maturity. When the jackets begin to split, you can see the hard brown shells of the nuts, and inside each shell is the delicious meat itself. Look closely at the nut, and you will notice that it is shaped rather like the human brain. No wonder the ancients prescribed walnuts for headaches.

Every year this tree gives me a basket of walnuts. But last year, the nuts were disappearing one by one, and I was at a loss as to who had been taking them. Could it have been Bijju, the milkman's small son? He was an inveterate tree climber, but he was usually to be found on the oak trees, gathering fodder for his herd. He admitted that his cows had enjoyed my dahlias, which they had eaten the previous week, but he stoutly denied having fed them walnuts, saying they did not care for them.

Later, I found a fat langur sitting in the walnut tree. I watched him for some time to see if he was going to help himself to the nuts, but he was only sunning himself. When he thought I wasn't looking, he came down and ate the geraniums; but he did not take any walnuts.

It wasn't the woodpecker either. He was out there every day, knocking furiously against the bark of the tree, trying to pry an insect out of a narrow crack. He was strictly non-vegetarian and none the worse for it.

The nuts seemed to disappear early in the morning while I was still in bed, so one day I surprised everyone, including myself by getting up before sunrise. I was just in time to catch the culprit climbing out of the walnut tree. She was an old woman who sometimes came to cut grass on the hillside. Her face was as wrinkled as the walnuts she had been pinching. But in spite of her age, her arms and legs were sturdy. When she saw me, she was as swift as a civet cat in getting out of the tree.

'And how many walnuts did you gather today, Grandmother?' I asked.

'Just two,' she said with a giggle, offering them to me on her open palm. I accepted one, and thus encouraged, she climbed higher into the tree and helped herself to the remaining nuts. It was impossible for me to object. I was taken with admiration for her agility. She must have been twice my age, but I knew I could never get up that tree. To the victor, the spoils!

Last winter the PWD decided to take a new road past my doorstep, and the first casualty was the walnut tree. Along with a large number of different trees growing below the cottage, it fell to the contractors' axes.

Recently when I met the old woman on the road, I asked her, 'Where do you get your walnuts now, Grandmother?'

'Nowhere,' she answered stoically. 'That was the last walnut tree on the hillside.'

Unlike the prized walnuts, the horse chestnuts are inedible. Even the rhesus monkeys throw them away in disgust. But the tree itself is a friendly one, especially in summer when it is in full leaf. The lightest breeze makes the leaves break into conversation, and their rustle is a cheerful sound. The spring flowers of the horse chestnut look like candelabra, and when the blossoms fall, they carpet the hillside with their pale pink petals. It stands erect and dignified and does not bend with the wind. In spring, the new leaves, or needles, are a tender green, while during the monsoon, the tiny young cones spread like blossoms in the dark green folds of the branches.

The deodar enjoys the company of its own kind: where one deodar grows, there will be others. A walk in a deodar forest is awe-inspiring—surrounded on all sides by these great sentinels of the mountains, you feel as though the trees themselves are on the march.

I walk among the trees outside my window often, acknowledging their presence with a touch of my hand against their trunks. The oak has been there the longest, and the wind has bent its upper branches and twisted a few so that it looks shaggy and undistinguished. But it is a good tree for the privacy of birds. Sometimes it seems completely uninhabited until there is a whining sound, as of a helicopter approaching, and a party of long-tailed blue magpies flies across the forest glade.

Most of the pines near my home are on the next hillside. But there is a small Himalayan blue a little way below the cottage, and sometimes I sit beneath it to listen to the wind playing softly in its branches.

When I open the window at night, there is almost always something to listen to—the mellow whistle of a pygmy owlet, or the sharp cry of a barking deer. Sometimes, if I am lucky, I will see the moon coming up over the next mountain, and two distant deodars in perfect silhouette.

Some night sounds outside my window remain strange and mysterious. Perhaps they are the sounds of the trees themselves, stretching their limbs in the dark, shifting a little, flexing their fingers, whispering to one another. These great trees of the mountains, I feel they know me well, as I watch them and listen to their secrets, happy to rest my head beneath their outstretched arms.

Once Upon a Mountain Time

My solitude is not my own, for I see now how much it belongs to them—and that I have a responsibility for it in their regard, not just in my own. It is because I am one with them that I owe it to them to be alone, and when I am alone they are not 'they' but my own self. There are no strangers!

From *Confessions of a Guilty Bystander*
—Thomas Merton

The trees stand watch over my day-to-day life. They are the guardians of my conscience. I have no one else to answer to, so I live and work under the generous but highly principled supervision of the trees—especially the deodars, who stand on guard, unbending, on the slope above the cottage. The oak and maples are a little more tolerant, they have had to put up with a great deal, their branches continually lopped for fuel and fodder. 'What would *they* think?' I ask myself on many an occasion. 'What would they like me to do?' And I do what *I* think they would approve of most!

Well, it's nice to have someone to turn to…

The leaves are a fresh pale green in the spring rain. I can look at the trees from my window—look down on them almost, because the window is on the first floor of the cottage, and the hillside runs away at a sharp angle into the ravine. The trees and I know each other quite intimately, and we have much to say to each other from time to time.

I do nearly all my writing at this window seat. The trees watch over me as I write. Whenever I look up, they remind me that they are there. They are my best critics. As long as I am aware of their presence, I can try to avoid the trivial and the banal.

Ramesh, the son of the municipal cleaner, looms darkly in the doorway. He is a stunted boy with a large head, but has wide gentle eyes. His orange-coloured trousers brighten up the surrounding gloom.

'What do you want, Ramesh?'

'Newspapers.'

'To sell to the kabari?'

'No. For wrapping my schoolbooks.'

'Well, take a few.' I give him half a dozen old newspapers, the headlines already look meaningless. 'Sit down and wait for it to stop raining.'

He sits awkwardly on a mora.

'And what is your cousin Vinod doing these days?' (Vinod is a good-looking ne'er-do-well who seldom does anything apart from hanging around cinema halls.)

'Nothing.'

'Doesn't he go to school?'

'He has stopped going to school. He got a job at fifty rupees a month, but he left after a week. He says he will join the army in September.'

The rain stops and Ramesh departs. The clouds begin to break up, the sun strikes the steep hill on my left. A woman is chopping up sticks. I hear the tinkle of cowbells. Water drips from a leaking drainpipe. And suddenly, clear and pure, the song of the whistling thrush emerges like a dark sweet secret from the depths of the ravine.

Bijju is back from school and is taking his parents' cattle out to graze. He sees me at the window and waves, then grabs his favourite cow Neelu by the tail and tells her to hurry up.

Bijju is twelve, a fair, good-looking Garhwali boy. His younger sister and brother are very pretty children. The father, an electrician, is a rather self-effacing man. The mother is a strong, hard woman. I have watched her on the hillside cutting grass. She has the muscular calves of a man, solid feet and heavy hands; but she is a handsome woman. They live in a rented outhouse further up the hill.

Bijju doesn't visit me very often. He is rather shy. But one day I looked out of the window and there he was in the branches of the oak tree, smiling at me rather hesitantly. We spoke to each other across the three or four yards that separate house from oak tree.

'If I jump, I can land in your tree,' I said.

'And if I jump I will be in your house,' said Bijju.

'Come on then, jump!'

But he shook his head. He was afraid of me. The tree was safe. He put his arms round the thickest branch and held himself close to it. He looked very right in the tree, as though he belonged there, a boy of the woods, a tree spirit peeping out from a house of glossy new leaves.

'Come on, jump!'

'*You* jump,' he said.

In the evening his sister brings the cows home. I meet her on the path above the house. She is only a year younger than Bijju, a very bonny girl who is going to be ravishingly beautiful when she grows up, if they don't marry her off too soon. She too has the same timid smile. But if these children are timid of humans, they are not afraid in the forest, and often wander far afield with Neelu the blue cow and others. (And S, who is eighteen and educated at an English-medium private school, wouldn't go alone into the forest if you paid him!) But the trees know their own. They will cherish the wild spirits and frighten the daylights out of the tame.

The whistling thrush is here, bathing in the rainwater puddle beneath the window. He loves this spot. So now, when there is no rain, I fill the puddle with water, just so that my favourite bird keeps coming.

His bath finished, he perches on a branch of the walnut tree. His glossy blue-black wings glitter in the sunshine. At any moment he will start singing.

Here he goes! He tries out the tune, whistling to himself, and then, confident of the notes, sends his thrilling full-throated voice far over the forest. The song dies down, trembling, lingering in the air; starts again, joyfully, and then suddenly stops, as though the singer had forgotten the words or the tune.

Vinod, the ne'er-do-well, turns up with a friend, asking me to give them some work. They want to go to the pictures but have no money.

'You can dig up this slope below the house,' I tell them. 'The soil is good for growing vegetables.'

This sounds too much like hard work for Vinod, who says, 'We'll come and do it tomorrow.'

'No, we'll do it now,' says his more enterprising friend, and to my surprise they set to work.

Now and then I look out of the window. They are digging away with fair enthusiasm.

After about half an hour, Vinod keeps sitting down for short rests, to the increasing irritation of his partner. They are soon snapping at each other. Vinod looks very funny when he sulks, because he has a snub nose, and somehow a snub nose and a ferocious expression only reminds me of Richmal Crompton's William. But the work gets done by evening and they are quite pleased with their earnings.

Bijju is right at the top of a big oak. The branches sway to his movements. He grins down at me and waves. The higher he is in the tree, the more confident he becomes. It is only when he is down on the ground that he becomes shy and speechless.

He has allowed the cows to wander, and presently his mother's deep voice can be heard calling, 'Neelu, Neelu!' (The other cows don't have names.) And then: 'Where is that wretched boy?'

Sir Edmund Gibson has come up. He spends the summer in the big house just down the road. He is wheezing a lot and says he has water in his lungs—and who wouldn't, at the age of eighty-six.

'Ruskin, my advice to you,' he says, 'is never to live beyond the age of eighty.'

'Well, once ought to be enough, sir.'

He is a big man, but not as red in the face as he used to be. His Gurkha manservant, Tirlok, has to push him up the steep slope to my gate.

Sir Edmund was once the British Resident in the Kathiawar states. He knew my parents in Jamnagar, when I was just five or six. He is a bachelor and is looked after by his servants.

His farm at Ramgarh doesn't make any money and he will probably give it to his retainers.

When Sir Edmund was Resident, he was once shot at from close range by a terrorist. The man took four shots and missed every time. He must have been a terrible shot, or perhaps the pistol was faulty, because Sir E presents a very large target.

He also treasures two letters from Mahatma Gandhi, which were written from prison.

'I liked Gandhi,' says Sir E. 'He had a sense of humour. No politician today has a sense of humour. They all take themselves far too seriously. But not Gandhi. He took his work seriously, but not himself. When I went to see him in prison, I asked him if he was comfortable, and he smiled and said, "Even if I was, I wouldn't admit it!"'

Sir E's servant brings tea, but there isn't any milk. I think I have exhausted Bijju's supply.

Now it's dusk and the trees are very still, very quiet. Far away I can hear the *chuk-chuk-chuk* of a nightjar. The lights on Landour hill come on, one by one. Prem is singing in the kitchen. There is a whirr of wings as the king crows fly into the trees to roost for the night. A rustling in the dry leaves below the window. A snake? Field rats? Porcupines? It is now too dark to find out. The day has ended, and the trees move closer together in the dark.

We are treated to one of those spectacular electric storms which are fairly frequent at this time of the year, late spring or early summer. The clouds grow very dark, then send bolts of lightning sizzling across the sky, lighting up the entire range of mountains. When the storm is directly overhead, there is hardly a pause in the frequency of the lightning; it is like a bright light being switched on and off with barely a second's interruption.

John Lang, writing in Dickens's magazine *Household Words* in 1853, almost exactly one hundred and twenty years ago, had this to say about one of our storms:

> I have seen a storm on the heights of Jura—such a storm as Lord Byron describes. I have seen lightning, and heard thunder in Australia; I have, off Tierra del Fuego, the Cape of Good Hope, and the coast of Java, kept watch in thunderstorms which have drowned in their roaring the

> human voice, and made everyone deaf and stupefied; but these storms are not to be compared with a thunderstorm at Mussoorie or Landour.

Forgotten today, Lang was a popular writer in the mid-nineteenth century. He was also a successful barrister, who represented the Rani of Jhansi in her litigation with the East India Company. He spent his last years in Mussoorie and was buried in the Camel's Back cemetery. His grave proved to be almost as elusive as his books and I found it with some difficulty, overgrown with moss and periwinkle. Prem and I cleaned it up until the inscription stood out quite clearly.

Prem won't come home on a stormy night like this. He is afraid of the dark, but more than that, he is afraid of thunderstorms. It is as though the gods are ganging up against him. So he will spend the night in the school quarters, where he is visiting his mother who is staying there with relatives.

In the morning he turns up with a sheepish grin, saying it got very late and he didn't want to wake me in the middle of the night. I try to feign anger, but it is a gloriously fresh and spirited morning; impossible to feel angry. A strong breeze is driving the clouds away, and the sun keeps breaking through. The birds are particularly active. The king crows (who weren't here last year) seem to have taken up residence in the oaks. I don't know why they are called crows. They are slim elegant black birds, with long forked tails, and their call, far from being a caw, is quite musical, though slightly metallic. The mynahs are very busy, very noisy, looking for a nesting site in the roof. The babblers are raking over fallen leaves, snapping up absent-minded grasshoppers. Now and then, the whistling thrush bursts into song, and then all other bird sounds pale into insignificance. Bijju has taken his cows to pasture and now scrambles up the hill, heading for home; he is late for school, and that is why he is in a hurry. He waves to me.

Both he and Prem have the high cheekbones and the deep-set eyes of the hill people. Prem, of course, is tall and dark. Bijju is small and fair; but he will grow into a sturdy young fellow.

The rain has driven the scorpions out of their rocks and crevices. I found one sitting on a loaf of bread. Up came his sting when we disturbed him. Prem tipped him out on the verandah steps and he scurried off into the bushes. I do not kill insects and other small creatures if I can help it, but there is a limit to my hospitality. I spared a centipede yesterday even though, last year, I was bitten by one which had occupied the seat of my pyjamas. Our hill scorpions and centipedes are not as dangerous as those found in the plains, and probably the same can be said for the people.

Prem tells me that his uncle is immune to scorpion stings, and allows himself to be stung in order to demonstrate his immunity. Apparently his mother was stung by a scorpion shortly before his birth!

Azure butterflies flit about the garden like flakes of sky.

Learnt two new words: bosky = wooded, bushy (bosky shadows); girding = jesting, jeering (girding schoolboys, girding monkeys).

Poor old Sir E is in a bad way. He has diarrhoea, and little or no control over the muscles that play a part in controlling the bowels. The Gurkha servant called me, and I went over with some tablets. Sir E looked quite exhausted and was panting from the exertion of walking from his bed to the toilet. The Gurkha is very good—gives Sir E his bath, dresses him, helps him on with his pyjamas.

Grateful for my alacrity in coming over with some medicine, Sir E offers me a whisky-and-soda (the first time he has ever done this), and pours himself a stiff brandy. He dozes off now and then, but the laboured breathing won't stop. He is a tough old tree, but I think he is beginning to find his massive frame something of a burden.

I make an attempt at conversation. 'Were you at Oxford or Cambridge?'

'Oxford. I joined Oxford in 1905 and left in 1909. Came out to India in 1910.'

He has an excellent memory, unlike Mr Biggs (a retired headmaster) who is ten years younger but will repeat the same story thrice in ten minutes.

'And when were you knighted?' I ask.

'1939 or 1940.'

He is too tired to do much talking. I let him doze off, and give my attention to the whisky. The log fire burns well, the flames cast their glow on Sir E's white hair and hanging jowls. The stertorous breathing grows in volume. He wakes up suddenly, complains that the fire is too hot; Tirlok opens the window. I finish the whisky; he doesn't offer another. It is his supper time, anyway, and I suggest soup and toast. 'Call me in the night if you have any trouble,' I say. He looks very grateful. The loneliness must press upon him a great deal.

I go out into the night. The trees are bending to a strong wind. From the foliage comes a deep sigh, the voice of leagues of trees sleeping and half disturbed in their sleep. The sky is clear, tremendous with stars.

For the first time this year I hear the barbet, a sure sign the summer is upon us. Its importunate cry carries far across the hills. It can keep this up for hours, like a beggar. Indeed, its plaint—*un-neow, un-neow!*—has been likened in the hills to that of the spirit of the village moneylender who has died before he can collect his dues. ('*Un-neow!*' is a cry for justice!)

It is difficult to spot the barbet. It is a fat green bird (no bigger than a mynah, but fatter), and it usually perches at the very top of a deodar or cypress.

The whistling thrush comes to bathe in the rainwater puddle. Sir E is much better and is sitting outside in the shade of an old oak. They are probably about the same age. What a rugged constitution this man must have; first, to survive, as a young man, all those diseases such as cholera, typhoid, dysentery, malaria, even the plague, which carried off so many Europeans in India (including my father); and now, an old man, to live and battle with congested lungs, a bad heart, weak eyes, bad teeth, recalcitrant bowels and god knows what else, and still be able to derive some pleasure from living. His old Hillman car is equally indestructible. But, like Sir E, it can't get up the hill any more; he uses it only in Dehradun.

I think his longevity is due simply to the fact that he refuses to go to bed when he is unwell. No amount of diarrhoea, or water in his lungs, will prevent him from getting up, dressing, writing letters or getting on with the latest Wodehouse (a contemporary of his) or *Blackwood's Magazine*, to which he has been subscribing for the last fifty years! He was pleased to find that some of my own essays were appearing in *Blackwood's*. Nothing will keep him from his four o'clock tea or his evening whisky-and-soda. He is determined, I am sure, to die in his chair, with all his clothes on. The thought of being taken unawares while still in his pyjamas must be something of a nightmare to him. (His favourite film, he once told me, was *They Died With Their Boots On*.)

The cicadas are tuning up for their first summer concert. Even Mrs Biggs, who is hard of hearing, can hear them. Yesterday I met her on the road above the cottage and exchanged pleasantries. Up at Wynberg the girls' choir was hard at practice.

'The girls are in good voice today,' I remarked.

'Oh yes, Mr Bond,' she said, presuming I meant the cicadas. 'They do it with their legs, don't they?'

◆

A week in Delhi. It is still only early summer, but the heat almost knocks one over. Slept on a roof, along with thousands of mosquitoes. It cools off in the early hours, but only briefly, before the sun comes shouting over the rooftops. The dust lies thick on floors, leaves, books, people. May's golden dust!

Now, back in the hills, I am struck first of all by the silence. The house, too, makes itself felt. It has been here too long not to have acquired a personality of its own. It is not a cheerful-looking place, nor is it exactly gloomy. My bedroom is rather dark (because it faces the abrupt slope of the hillside), but there is a wild cherry growing just outside the window—a cherry tree which I nurtured ever since it was a tiny seedling, five or six years ago, and which has now grown so tall that the branches tap against the roof whenever there is a breeze. It is a funny sort of cherry because it flowers in November instead of in the spring like other fruit trees. Small birds and small boys willingly eat the berries, which are too acid for adult palates.

The sitting room, with its two big windows looking out on the forest, is a bright room. Most of the wall space is taken up by my books. The rugs are worn and tattered—they have been with the house right from the beginning, I think—and I can't afford new ones.

On books and friends I spend my money;
For stones and bricks I haven't any.

Sir E, quite recovered from his recent illness, has gone down to Dehra again to attend to his farm and the demands of his farm workers. He should be back at the end of the month.

The brilliant blue-black of the whistling thrush shows up best when the sun is glinting off its back, but this seldom happens, because the bird likes to keep to the shade where it is almost black. Hopping about, it reminds me of Fred Astaire dancing in tophat and tails.

Now that it's getting hot, my small pool attracts a number of afternoon visitors—the mynahs, babblers, a bulbul, a magpie. After their dip they perch in the cherry tree to dry themselves and I can watch them without getting up from my bed, where I take an afternoon siesta. I reserve the afternoons for doing nothing. 'Silence and non-action are the root of all things,' says Tao. Especially on a drowsy afternoon.

But I haven't seen the whistling thrush for several days. Perhaps he is offended at having to share the pool which he was the first to discover. I haven't heard his song either, which probably means that he has moved down to the stream where it is cooler and shadier.

Prem's mother and younger sister come for a few days. His mother is a very quiet woman and doesn't say much even to her son. She is quite handsome, although she looks rather worn and tired, due probably to her recent illness.

His little sister, about four, is a friendly little gazelle; not in the least pretty, but lively and intelligent. She will have to stay here for at least six months to be properly treated for her incipient tuberculosis. There is no treatment to be had in their village.

While I am resting, still exhausted from an attack of hill dysentery (who called this a health resort?), Sir E blows in, red-faced, as distressed as a stranded whale. His Gurkha servant has walked out, after quarrelling with his wife and mother-in-law, and has taken with him his twin sons (aged one and a half). I calm Sir E, tell him Tirlok will be back in a day or two—he is probably trying to show how indispensable he is!

Sir E takes out a cigarette and strikes a match, and the entire matchbox flares up, burning a finger. Definitely not his day. I apply Burnol.

'It's all that damned girl's fault,' he says. 'She has a vile temper, just like her mother. We were very wise not to marry, Ruskin.'

Wise or not, I seem to have acquired a family all the same.

◆

Hundreds of white butterflies are flitting through the forest.

When Prem told his mother that I kept a human skull in my sitting room (given to me by Anil, a medical student, and *not* pinched from the cemetery as some suppose), she told him not to spend too much time near it. If he did, he would be possessed by the spirit of the woman who had originally inhabited the skull.

But Prem, at the present time, is immune to spirits, having succumbed to the charms of his young wife who stays downstairs with his mother. They have only been married a few months. He leans over the balcony, chatting with her; advises her on how to keep the courtyard clean; then makes her a small broom from the twigs of a wild honeysuckle bush. She enjoys all the attention she is getting.

The sky is overcast this morning. Dust from the plains has formed a thick haze which hides the valley and the mountains. We are badly in need of rain. Down in the plains, over two hundred people have died of heatstroke.

I haven't seen Bijju for some days, but this morning his sister, Binya, was out with the cows. What a sturdy little girl she is; and pretty, too. I will write a story about her.*

---

*This story was called 'The Blue Umbrella'.

◆

'We'll take you to the pictures one day, Sir Edmund.'

'Yes, I must see one more picture before I die.'

So there comes a time when we start thinking in terms of the last picture, the last book, the last visit, the last party. But Sir E's remark is matter of fact. He is given to boredom but not to melancholy.

And he has a timeless quality. I have noticed this in other old people; they look more permanent than the young.

He sums it all up by saying, 'I don't mind being dead, but I shall miss being alive.'

A number of small birds are here to bathe and drink in the little pool beneath the cherry tree: hunting parties of tits—grey tits, red-headed tits and green-backed tits—and two delicate little willow warblers. They take turns in the pool. While the green-backs are taking a plunge, the red-heads wait patiently on the moss-covered rocks, coming down later to sip daintily at the edge of the pool; they don't like getting their feet wet! Finally, when they have all gone away, the whistling thrush arrives and indulges in an orgy of bathing, as he now has the entire pool to himself.

The babblers are adept at snapping up the little garden skinks that scuttle about in the leaves and grass. The skinks are quite brittle and are easily broken to pieces with a few hard raps of the beak. Then down they go! Babblers are also good at sifting through dead leaves and seizing upon various insects.

The honeybees push their way through the pursed lips of the antirrhinum and disappear completely. A few minutes later they stagger out again, bottoms first.

1 June

The dry spell continues. It is only before sunrise that there is any freshness in the air.

At dawn I said, 'Day, you will not begin without me.' I was up with the whistling thrush at five. The cicadas were tuning up, the crickets were already in full cry, and the whistling thrush was calling most sweetly. As none of these songsters could be seen, it was as though the forest itself was singing.

Feeling the dawn wind stir, I was happy that I had met the day at its very beginning.

When the sun came up, the day became sultry and oppressive. I had to walk two miles to Ban Suman and back. There was no shade anywhere along the road. But we are equipped with legs for the purpose of walking. As more and more people grow dependent on their cars, a new species of humans will evolve. Around the turn of the twenty-second century, I can see legless humans being born. By then, of course, there will be flying wheelchairs.

A pall of dust hangs over the mountain.

Someone asked Sir E if he could shoot a bird on his land at Ramgarh. The man wanted the bird for dissection in a biology lab. Sir E refused.

'It's in the interests of science,' protested the man. 'Do you think a bird is better than a human?'

'Infinitely,' said Sir E. 'Infinitely better.'

He goes down today to pay his farmhands. He will return in a few days unless it gets cooler in Dehra. He complains of being very bored up here, for he can't get about, and in Dehra he has his Hillman. 'I'm *rotting* with boredom,' he says.

Vinod, I hear, is laid low with a fever—the result of a day's hard work. He is now in retirement for the rest of the season.

Walked five miles down the Tehri road to Suakholi, where I rested in a small tea shop, a loose stone structure with a tin roof held down by stones. It serves the bus passengers, mule drivers, milkmen and others who use this road.

I find a couple of mules tethered to a pine tree. The mule drivers, handsome men in tattered clothes, sit on a bench in the shade of the tree, drinking tea from brass tumblers. The shopkeeper, a man of indeterminate age—the cold dry winds from the mountain passes having crinkled his face like a walnut—greets me enthusiastically, as he always does. He even produces a chair, which looks like a survivor from the Savoy's 1890 ballroom. Fortunately the Mussoorie antique dealers haven't seen it, or it would have been carried away long ago. In any case, the stuffing has come out of the seat. The shopkeeper apologizes for its condition: 'The rats were nesting in it.' And then, to reassure me: 'But they have gone now.'

Unlike the shopkeeper, the mule drivers have somewhere to go and something to deliver: sacks of potatoes. From Jaunpur to Jaunsar, the potato is probably the crop best suited to these stony, terraced fields. Oddly enough, it was introduced to the Himalayas by two Irishmen, Captain Young of Dehra and Mussoorie and Captain Kennedy of Shimla, in the 1820s. The slopes of Young's house, Mullingar, were known as his Potato Farm. Looking up old books, I was surprised to learn that the potato wasn't known in India before the nineteenth century, and now it's an essential part of our diet in most parts of the country.

As the mule drivers lead their pack animals away, along the dusty road to Landour bazaar, I follow at a distance, singing 'Mule Train' in my best Nelson Eddy manner.*

A thunderstorm, followed by strong winds, brought down

*Not Nelson's song originally, but he sang it better than anyone else.

the temperature. That was yesterday. And today, June, it is cloudy, cool, drizzling a little, almost monsoon weather; but it is still too early for the real monsoon.

The birds are enjoying the cool weather. The green-backed tits cool their bottoms in the rainwater pool. A king crow flashes past, winging through the air like an arrow. On the wing, it snaps up a hovering dragonfly. The mynahs fetch crow feathers to line their nest in the eaves of the house. I am lying so still on the window seat that a tit alights on the sill within a few inches of my head. It snaps up a small dead moth before flying away.

Sir E is back. He found it too hot in the valley. Even up here he has given up wearing a necktie. I'll have him wearing a kurta and pyjamas before long; the only sensible dress in summer.

At dusk I sit at the window and watch the trees and listen to the wind as it makes light conversation in the leafy tops of the maples. A large bat flits in and out of the trees. The sky is just light enough to enable me to see the bat and the outlines of the taller trees. Up on Landour hill, the lights are just beginning to come on. It is deliciously cool, eight o'clock, a perfect summer's evening. Prem is singing to himself in the kitchen. His wife and sister are chattering beneath the walnut tree. Down the hill, a kakar is barking, alarmed perhaps by the presence of a leopard. All the birds have gone to sleep for the night. Even the cicadas are strangely silent. The wind grows stronger and the tall maples bow before it: the maple moves its slender branches slowly from side to side, the oak moves its branches up and down. It is darker now; more lights on Landour. The cry of the barking deer has grown fainter, more distant, and now I hear a cricket singing in the bushes. The stars are out, the wind grows chilly, it is time to close the window.

◆

Bijju is very much an outdoor boy, even when he isn't grazing cows. He isn't very strong in the chest, but his legs are sturdy; he was having no difficulty in scaling the high retaining wall. He grinned down at me. He is rather like the whistling thrush—absent for days, then unexpectedly reappearing in the forest or on the hillside. Bijju sings too, although his voice is more vigorous than melodic.

And that reminds me of the story of the whistling thrush. The bird was once a village boy who tried very hard to play the flute in the same style as the god Krishna. When the god heard his favourite melody being plagiarized, he was furious and turned the unfortunate boy into a bird. The whistling thrush still tries to copy the divine melody, but somehow it always breaks off right in the middle of a stanza. There ought to be a moral here, especially in a land full of plagiarists. Or to be fair, I should say film-land…

The Whistler. This is my name for the youth who labours part-time in the school. He is something of a character—scatterbrained, carefree, easy-going. He is always whistling—loudly and quite tunefully (this time a bird turned into a boy?)—so that you know when he's coming round a bend or through the trees, and even when it's dark you know who it is. He's usually out quite late, because he spends all his money at the pictures. He has three sisters, and they and the mother are all working as maids or ayahs, and as they are quite indulgent to him (the only brother) he doesn't have to work too hard. His shoes are always torn, even though his clothes look new.

He has a reputation for being a waster, but he returned the few rupees he borrowed from me last month. I suppose a youth who is always singing and whistling on the roads gives everyone the impression that he has nothing to do from morn till night, unlike that jolly miller of Dee who worked *and* sang the whole day through. (I know one man who forbids his children from singing in the home.)

But back to the Whistler, he is really quite enterprising. The other day he asked me for one of my books, and as I knew he hadn't squandered too many years in school, I gave him an easy Hindi translation of one of my children's books. But it was the paper he valued, not the words. He flogged it to the bania's small son, who took it apart and converted the large pages into envelopes, which were then used for selling gram and peanuts. In India it doesn't take long for anything to be recycled. On the way home, I saw a couple of customers throwing their empty packets away, and these were promptly consumed by a stray cow. There went my beautiful story!

Is there a lesson to be learnt from this? Yes. Don't give away complimentaries.

It rained all night, and the morning is cool and fresh. Parrots are on the wing. I feel like tap-dancing like Gene Kelly, but you can't tap dance on a hillside, you'd break an ankle. Only the roads (and not all of them) are suitable for a song-and-dance act, and no doubt the Whistler will oblige before long. At forty, I must refrain from being too frisky and boyish. But I'll do a reel in the garden when no one is looking.

24 June

The first day of monsoon mist. And it's strange how all the birds fall silent as the mist comes climbing up the hill. Perhaps that's what makes the mist so melancholy; not only does it conceal the hills, it blankets them in silence too. Only an hour ago the trees were ringing with birdsong. And now the forest is deathly still, as though it were midnight.

Through the mist Bijju is calling to his sister. I can hear

him running about on the hillside but I cannot see him.

Feeling sorry for Sir E (or maybe for myself), I walked over to see him. The door was closed, so I looked in at the French window (nothing could be more *English* than a French window, and no Agatha Christie mystery would be complete without one), I saw him sleeping in his chair with his chin on his chest. There was no dagger sticking out of his back, only a bit of stuffing from his old coat. My footsteps on the gravel woke him, and he got up and opened the door for me. He said he felt a bit tipsy; had taken his usual peg, but thought the quality of whisky varied from bottle to bottle, and wished he could lay his hands on a bottle of Scotch or even Irish. He could only offer me an Uttar Pradesh brand. I said I'd given up drinking, and this pleased him because in truth he hates anyone drinking his whisky; said he might give it up himself, it 'cost too damn much'! I told him it would be unwise to give up drinking at this stage of his life. As he had reached the age of eighty-six on two pegs a day, he was obviously thriving on it. Giving it up now would only play havoc with the orderly working of his system. I'd given it up in order to help an alcoholic friend abstain, and also because I wanted to give up *something*, and strong drink seemed the easiest thing to do without.

A cicada starts up in the tree nearest my window seat. What has he been doing all these weeks, and why does he choose this particular moment and this particular evening to play the fiddle so loudly? The cicadas are late this year, the monsoon has been late. But soon the forest will be ringing with the sound of the cicadas—an orchestra constantly tuning up but never quite getting into tune—and the sound of the birds will be pushed into the background.

Outside the front door I found an elegant young praying mantis reclining on a leaf of the honeysuckle creeper. I say young because he hadn't grown to his full size, and was that very tender pale green which is the colour of a young mantis. They are light brown to begin with, like dry twigs, but as they grow older and the monsoon foliage becomes greener, they too change, and by mid-August they are dark green.

◆

As though to make up for lost time, the monsoon rains are now here with a vengeance. It has been pouring all day, and already the roof is leaking. But nothing dampens Prem's spirits. He is still singing love songs in the kitchen.

Kailash, whom I have known for a couple of weeks, asks me for twenty-five rupees.

'What do you need it for?' I ask.

'It's for my Sanskrit teacher,' he says. 'I have failed in Sanskrit but if I give the teacher twenty-five rupees he'll alter my marks. You see, I've passed in all the other subjects, but if I fail in Sanskrit I'll fail the entire exam and remain a pre-Inter student for another year.'

I took a little time to digest this information and ponder on the pitfalls of the examination system.

'He must be failing a lot of boys,' I said. 'Twenty-five rupees each! Are there many others?'

'Some. But he dare not fail the good ones. They can ask for a recheck. It's the borderline cases like me who give him a chance to make money.'

This placed me in a quandary. Should I yield to the evils of the examination system and provide the money for pass-marks? Or should I adopt a high moral stance and allow the boy to fail?

Whatever the evils of the exam system, they are not the fault of the student. And either way he isn't going to turn into a great Sanskrit scholar. So why be a hypocrite? I gave him the money.

Kailash slogs in his uncle's orchard all morning, gets a midday meal (no breakfast), and hasn't any shoes. And yet his uncle, a member of one of Garhwal's well-known upper-caste families, is a wealthy man.

Kailash tells me he will return to his village once he knows his result. According to him his uncle is such a miser that at mealtimes he pauses before each mouthful, wondering: 'Ought I to eat it? Or should I keep it for tomorrow?'

I am visited by another kind of student, a small girl from one of the private schools. Her mother has brought her to me for my autograph.

'She studies your book in Class six,' I was informed.

'And what book is that?' I asked the little girl.

'Tom Sawyer,' she replied promptly. So I signed for Mark Twain. When a small storeroom collapsed during the last heavy rains, I was forced to rescue a couple of old packing cases that had been left there for three or four years—since my arrival here, in fact. The contents were well soaked and most of it had to be thrown away—old manuscripts that had been obliterated, negatives that had got stuck together, gramophone records that had taken on strange shapes (dear 'Ink Spots', how will I ever listen to you again?*)... Unlike most writers, I have no compunction about throwing away work that hasn't quite come off, and I am sure there are a few critics who would prefer that I throw away the lot! Sentimental rubbish, no doubt. Well, we can't please everyone; and we can't preserve everything either. Time and the elements will take their toll.

But a couple of old diaries, kept in exercise books almost twenty years ago, had managed to survive the rain, and I put them out in the sun to dry, and then, almost unwillingly, started

*This was before the advent of audiotapes.

browsing through them. It was instructive, and sometimes a little disconcerting, to discover the sort of person I had been in my twenties. In some ways, no different from what I am today. In other ways, radically different. A diary is a useful tool for self-examination, particularly if both diary and diarist are still around after some years.

One particular entry caught my eye, and I reproduce it here without any alteration, because it represented my credo as a young writer, and it set me wondering if I had lived up to my own expectations. (Nobody else had any expectations of me!)

The entry was made on 19 January 1958, when I was living on my own in Dehradun:

> The things I do best are those things I do on my own, alone, of my own accord, without the advice or approval of others. Once I start doing what other people tell me to do, both my character and creativity take a dip. It is when I strike out on my own that I succeed best.
>
> There was a time when I was much younger and poorer than I am now. I had been over a year in Jersey, in the Channel Islands; I was unhappy, and the atmosphere in which I was writing was one of discouragement and disapproval. And that was why I wrote so well—because I was defiant! That was why I finished the only book I have finished so far. I had to prove to myself that I could do it.
>
> One night I was walking alone along the beach. There was a strong wind blowing, dashing the salt spray in my face, and the sea was crashing against the St Helier rocks. I told myself: I will go to London; I will take up a job; I will finish my book; I will find a publisher; I will save money and I will return to India, because I can be happier there than here.

> And that was just what I did.
> I had guts then.
> What's more, I had an end in view.
> The writing itself is not enough for me. Success and money are not enough. I had a little of both recently,* but they did not help me to do anything wonderful. I must have something to write for, just as I must have something to live for. And that's something I have yet to find.

There was more in that vein, but I give this excerpt as an example of a young man's determination to be a writer in what were then adverse circumstances. Thirty-five years later, I'm still trying.

27 June

The rains have heralded the arrival of some seasonal visitors—a leopard; and several thousand leeches.

Yesterday afternoon the leopard lifted a dog from near the servants' quarters below the school. In the evening it attacked one of Bijju's cows but fled at the approach of Bijju's mother, who came screaming imprecations.

As for the leeches, I shall soon get used to a little bloodletting every day. Bijju's mother sat down in the shrubbery to relieve herself, and later discovered two fat black leeches feeding on her fair round bottom. I told her she could use one of the spare bathrooms downstairs. But she prefers the wide open spaces.

Other new arrivals are the scarlet minivets (the females are yellow), flitting silently among the leaves like brilliant jewels. No

---

*When *The Room on the Roof* was published (1956).

matter how leafy the trees, these brightly coloured birds cannot conceal themselves, although, by remaining absolutely silent, they sometimes contrive to go unnoticed. Along come a pair of drongos, unnecessarily aggressive, chasing the minivets away.

A tree creeper moves rapidly up the trunk of the oak tree, snapping up insects all the way. Now that the rains are here, there is no dearth of food for the insectivorous birds.

In spite of there being water in several places, the whistling thrush still comes to my pool. He, at least, is a permanent resident.

Kailash has a round, cheerful face, only slightly marred by a swivel eye. His hair comes down over his forehead, hiding a deep scar. He is short, but quite compact and energetic. He chatters a good deal but in a general sort of way, and a response isn't obligatory.

It's quite possible that he will go away as soon as he gets his exam results. He's fed up with being the Cinderella of his uncle's house. He tells of how his miserly uncle went to see a rather permissive film, and was very shocked and wanted to walk out, but couldn't bear the thought of losing his ticket money; so he sat through the film with his eyes closed.

Sir E departed for Dehra with his large retinue of servants and their dependants, all of whom would have done justice to an eighteenth-century nabob. 'I am at the mercy of my servants,' he told me the other day.

But he had placed himself at their mercy long ago, by setting himself up as a country squire surrounded by 'faithful retainers'—all of whom received generous salaries but did little or no work. If he sold his white elephant of a farm, he'd be quite comfortable with one servant.

'I'll probably come up in September, after the rains,' he said. 'If I live that long… I'm just living from day to day.'

'So am I,' I told him. 'It's the best way to live.'

A couple of days passed before Kailash came to see me. I was beginning to wonder if he'd come again. Apparently the teacher had at first proved elusive; but the deed was done, and Kailash passed with the marks he needed. Ironically, his uncle was so impressed that he is now urging the boy to remain with him and complete the Intermediate exam.

'I must write a story about your uncle,' I remark.

'Don't give him a story,' says Kailash. 'A short note will do.'

Now that Prem is preoccupied with his wife, and the house is at the mercy of uninvited visitors, I stay out most of the time, and these days Kailash is my only companion. Yesterday we took Camel's Back Road, past the cemetery. He chatters away, and I can listen if I want to, or think of other things if I don't want to listen; apparently it makes no difference to him. He is a cheerful soul, with an infectious laugh. He walks with a slight swagger, or roll. He says he doesn't mind staying here now that he has me for a friend; that he can put up with two sour uncles as long as he knows I'm around. I suspect he's quite capable of pulling a fast one on his uncle; but all the same, I find myself liking him.

Moody. And when I'm moody I'm bad.

Prem says: 'It is easier to please God than it is to please you.'

'But God is easily pleased,' I respond. 'God makes absolutely no demands on us. We just imagine them.'

The eyes.

Prem's eyes have great gentleness in them.

His wife's eyes are round and mischievous and suggestive…

Suggestive enough to invite the attention of a mischievous or malignant spirit.

At about two in the morning I am awakened by Prem's shouts, muffled by rain. Shouting back that I am on my way, for it is obviously an emergency, I leap out of bed, grab an umbrella, dash outside and then down the stairs to his room. His wife is sobbing in bed. Whatever had possessed her has now gone away, and the crying is due more to Prem's ministrations—he exorcizes the ghost by thumping her on the head—than to the 'possession' itself. But there is no doubt that she is subject to hallucinatory or subconscious actions. It is not simply a hysterical fit. She walks in her sleep, moves restlessly from door to window, holds conversations with an invisible presence, and resists all efforts to bring her back to reality. When she comes out of the trance, she is quite normal.

This sort of thing is apparently quite common in the hills, where people believe it to be a ghost taking temporary possession of a human mind. It's happened to Prem's wife before, and it also happens to her brother, so it seems to run in families. It never happens to Prem, who deeply resents the interruption to his sleep.

I calm the girl and then make them bring their bedding upstairs. I give her a sleeping tablet and she is soon fast asleep.

During a lull in the rain, I hear a most hideous sound coming from the forest—a maniacal shrieking, followed by a mournful hooting. But Prem and his wife sleep through it all. The rain starts again, and the shrieking stops. Perhaps it's a hyena. Perhaps something else.

A morning of bright sunshine, and the whistling thrush welcomes it with a burst of song. Where do the birds shelter when it rains? How does that frail butterfly survive the battering of strong winds and heavy raindrops? How do the snakes manage in their flooded holes?

◆

I saw a bright green snake sunning itself on some rocks; no doubt waiting for its hole to dry out.

In my vagrant days, ten to fifteen years ago (long before the hippies made vagrancy a commonplace), I was a great frequenter of tea shops, those dingy little shacks with a table and three chairs, a grimy tea kettle, and a cracked gramophone. Tea shops haven't changed much, and once again I find myself lingering in them, sometimes in company with Kailash, who, although he doesn't eat much, drinks a lot of tea.

One can sit all day in a tea shop and watch the world go by. Amazing the number of people who actually do this! And not all of them unemployed. The tea shop near the clock tower is ideal for this purpose. It is a busy part of the bazaar but the tea shop, though small, is gloomy within, and one can loll about unseen, observing everyone who passes by a few feet away in the sunlit (or rain-spattered) street. The tea itself is indifferent, the buns are stale, the boiled eggs have been peppered too liberally. Kailash is unusually quiet; there is no one else in the shop. People who would stop me in the road pass by without glancing into the murky interior. This is the ideal place; not as noble as my window opening into the trees, but familiar, reminiscent of days gone by in Dehra, when cares sat lightly upon me simply because I did not care at all. And now perhaps I have begun to care too much.

I gave Bijju a cake. He licked all the icing off it, only then did he eat the rest.

◆

It was a dark windy corner in Landour bazaar, but I always found the old man there, hunched up over the charcoal fire on which he roasted his peanuts. He'd been there for as long as I could remember, and he could be seen at almost any hour of the day or night. Summer or winter, he stayed close to his fire.

He was probably quite tall, but we never saw him standing

up. One judged his height from his long, loose limbs. He was very thin, and the high cheekbones added to the tautness of his tightly stretched skin.

His peanuts were always fresh, crisp and hot. They were popular with the small boys who had a few paise to spend on their way to and from school, and with the patrons of the cinemas, many of whom made straight for the windy corner during intervals or when the show was over. On cold winter evenings, or misty monsoon days, there was always a demand for the old man's peanuts.

No one knew his name. No one had ever thought of asking him for it. One just took him for granted. He was as fixed a landmark as the clock tower or the old cherry tree that grew crookedly from the hillside. The tree was always being lopped; the clock often stopped. The peanut vendor seemed less perishable than the tree, more dependable than the clock.

He had no family, but in a way all the world was his family, because he was in continuous contact with people. And yet he was a remote sort of being; always polite, even to children, but never familiar. There is a distinction to be made between aloneness and loneliness. The peanut vendor was seldom alone; but he must have been lonely.

Summer nights he rolled himself up in a thin blanket and slept on the ground, beside the dying embers of his fire. During the winter, he waited until the last show was over, before retiring to the rickshaw-coolies' shed where there was some protection from the biting wind.

Did he enjoy being alive? I wonder now. He was not a joyful person; but then, neither was he miserable. I should think he was a genuine stoic, one of those who do not attach overmuch importance to themselves, who are emotionally uninvolved, content with their limitations, their dark corners.

I wanted to get to know the old man better, to sound him out on the immense questions involved in roasting peanuts all his life; but it's too late now. The last time I visited the bazaar the dark corner was deserted; the old man had vanished; the coolies had carried him down to the cremation ground.

'He died in his sleep,' said the tea-shop owner. 'He was very old.'

Very old. Sufficient reason to die.

But that corner is very empty, very dark, and whenever I pass it I am haunted by visions of the old peanut vendor, troubled by the questions I failed to ask; and I wonder if he was really as indifferent to life as he appeared to be.

◆

Prem brought his wife some of her favourite mangoes. This afternoon he took her into my room so that she could listen to the radio. They both fell asleep at opposite ends of the bed; are still asleep as I write this in the next room, at my window. If I curled up a little, I could fall asleep here on the window seat. Nothing would induce me to disturb those innocents; they look far too blissful in their slumbers.

◆

Kailash and I are caught in a storm and it's by far the worst storm of the year. To make matters worse, there is absolutely no shelter for a mile along the main road from the town. It was fierce, lashing rain, quite cold, whipping along on the wind from all angles. The road was soon a torrent of muddy water, as earth and stones came rushing down the hillsides. Our one umbrella was useless and was very nearly blown away. The cardboard carton in which we were carrying vegetables was soon reduced to pulp. We broke into a run, although we could hardly see our way. There were blinding flashes of lightning—is an umbrella a good or a bad conductor of electricity? Kailash sees humour in these situations and was in peals of laughter all the way home, even when we slid into a ditch.

He takes my hand and holds it between his hands. He is happy. He has got his self-confidence back, and can now deal with his uncles and Sanskrit teachers.

In the morning I work on a story. There is a dove cooing in the garden. Now it is very quiet, the only sound is the distant tapping of a woodpecker. The trees are muffled in ferns and creepers. It is mid-monsoon.

Kailash, his hair falling in an untidy mop across his forehead, drags me out of the house and over the wet green grass on the hillside. I protest that I do not like leeches, so we make for the high rocks. He laughs, talks, chuckles, and when he grins his large front teeth make him look like a 1940s' Mickey Rooney. When he looks sullen (this happens when he talks about his uncle), he looks Brando-ish. He has the gift of being able to convey his effervescence to me. Am I, at thirty-eight, too old to be gambolling about on the hill slopes like a young colt? (Am I, sobering thought, going to be a character of enforced youthfulness like the man on the boat in *Death in Venice?* Well, better that than the Gissing hero of *New Grub Street* who's old at forty.) If I am fit enough to gambol, then I must gambol. If I can still climb a tree, then I must climb trees, instead of just watching them from my window. I was in such high spirits yesterday that I kept playing the clown, and I haven't done this in years. To walk in the rain was fun, and to get wet was fun, and to fall down was fun, and to get hurt was fun.

'Will it last?' asks Kailash.

'This feeling of love between us?'

'*This* won't last. Not in this way. But if something *like* it lasts, we should be happy.'

◆

Prem is happy, laughing, giggling all the time. Sometimes it is a little annoying for me, because he is obviously unaware of what is happening around him—such as the fact that part of the roof blew away in the storm—but I am a good Taoist, I say nothing, I wait for the right moment! Besides, it's a crime to interfere with anyone's happiness.

Prem notices the roof is missing and scolds his wife for seeing too many pictures. 'She's seen ten pictures in two months. More than she'd seen in her whole life, before coming here.' She pulls a face. Says Prem: 'My grandfather will be here any day to take her home.'

'Then she can see pictures with your grandfather,' I venture. 'While we repair the roof.'

'I wouldn't go anywhere with that old man,' she says.

'Don't speak like that of my grandfather. Do you want a beating? Look at Binya'—we all look at Binya, who is perched very prettily on the wall—'she hasn't seen more than two pictures in her life!'

'I'll take her to the pictures,' I offer.

Binya gives me a radiant smile. She'd love to go to the pictures, but her mother won't allow it.

Prem relents and takes his wife to the pictures.

Binya's mother has a bad attack of hiccups. Serves her right, for stealing my walnuts and not letting me take Binya to the pictures.

In the evening I find Prem teaching his wife the alphabet, using the kitchen door as a blackboard. It is covered with chalk marks. Love is teaching your wife to read and write!

◆

These entries were made in 1973, twenty years ago.

The following year I did not keep a journal, but these are some of the things that happened:

Sir E had a stroke and, like a stranded whale, finally heaved his last breath. According to his wishes, he was cremated on his farm near Dehra.

To Prem and Chandra was born a son, Rakesh, who immediately stole my heart—and gave me many a sleepless night, for as a baby he cried lustily.

Kailash went into the army and disappeared from my life, as well as from his uncle's.

Bijju and Binya were to remain a part of the hillside for several years.

Ferns in Foliage

At the bottom of the hill there is a small rippling stream, its water almost hidden by the bright green, tangled growth along its course. It is only by its sound as it batters over the pebbles, that we become aware of it. Here we came across many plants that delight to grow in such places—wild strawberries, wood sorrel, orchids, violets and dandelions, and a nest of ferns.

The first thing one notices is a beautiful group of ferns growing almost to the water. This is the Lady Fern, whose broad fronds must be four to five feet high, a delicate plant, frail and almost transparent in the fineness of its foliage, and looking so tender that you would think the sun and wind would almost scorch or shrivel it up. But the abundant supply of flowing water keeps these ferns cool and fresh.

When the frosts of winter come, the fronds will crumple up into a heap of brown fragments. But their strength has by that time returned into the thick clump of roots to be stored and used for a still finer group of fronds next year.

In the moist parts of any forest there are sure to be several other kinds of ferns such as the Male Fern, with its strong, upright fronds looking like a large green shuttlecock three feet high. One of the commonest of Indian ferns is the Maidenhair which grows along the west coast and in the Himalayan foothills. During the monsoon, it can be found on almost every wall and rock—a delicate, tender fern, easily torn by the wind.

On the stump of a fallen tree grow the Prickly-toothed Buckler fern and the Broad Buckler fern, whose rootlets penetrate the soft, rotting wood to obtain their moisture. They are hardy, often remaining green all through the winter. The handsome Bracken fern often grows to a height of six or seven feet.

Then there is the lovely Hart's tongue fern, great clumps of which grow beside the forest paths. It has broad, green crinkled fronds and is quite unlike other ferns. If you look at the back of the fronds you will see from the little heaps of rust-coloured spore cases, that this is indeed a fern; all ferns grow their seeds in this way.

There are several hundred varieties of ferns. They are easily pressed and preserved. They may also be grown indoors in pots. But they are loveliest in the open, in cool, damp places, in the depths of the forest or by the side of a mountain stream.

The history of ferns goes back to the mists of antiquity. There was a time when ferns and plants like them filled the earth. It was a wet and dripping time. Flowers would have been of no use at all but spores could carry on their lives in the prevailing dampness. Some ferns grew as large as trees. The falling stems of these mighty tree ferns were floated together by mighty streams, carried away to the sea and buried under sand and mud. The remains of these plants being thus shut off from the air, could not rot but were slowly changed into coal. The impressions of leaves and stems of these ferns can be distinctively seen on many pieces of coal.

As the earth became drier, ferns retired to the damp, shady spots in which we now find them. They are a declining family but let us hope they will remain with us for some time, for a forest stream without ferns would be like a maiden whose loveliest tresses have been shorn.

The School Among the Pines

1

A leopard, lithe and sinewy, drank at the mountain stream, and then lay down on the grass to bask in the late February sunshine. Its tail twitched occasionally and the animal appeared to be sleeping. At the sound of distant voices it raised its head to listen, then stood up and leapt lightly over the boulders in the stream, disappearing among the trees on the opposite bank.

A minute or two later, three children came walking down the forest path. They were a girl and two boys, and they were singing in their local dialect an old song they had learnt from their grandparents.

'Five more miles to go!
We climb through rain and snow.
A river to cross…
A mountain to pass…
Now we've four more miles to go!'

Their school satchels looked new, their clothes had been washed and pressed. Their loud and cheerful singing startled a Spotted Forktail. The bird left its favourite rock in the stream and flew down the dark ravine.

'Well, we have only three more miles to go,' said the bigger boy, Prakash, who had been this way hundreds of times. 'But first we have to cross the stream.'

He was a sturdy twelve-year-old with eyes like raspberries and a mop of bushy hair that refused to settle down on his head. The girl and her younger brother were taking this path for the first time.

'I'm feeling tired, Bina,' said the little boy.

Bina smiled at him, and Prakash said, 'Don't worry, Sonu, you'll get used to the walk. There's plenty of time.' He glanced at the old watch he'd been given by his grandfather. It needed constant winding. 'We can rest here for five or six minutes.'

They sat down on a smooth boulder and watched the clear water of the shallow stream tumbling downhill. Bina examined the old watch on Prakash's wrist. The glass was badly scratched and she could barely make out the figures on the dial. 'Are you sure it still gives the right time?' she asked.

'Well, it loses five minutes every day, so I put it ten minutes forward at night. That means by morning it's quite accurate! Even our teacher, Mr Mani, asks me for the time. If he doesn't ask, I tell him! The clock in our classroom keeps stopping.'

They removed their shoes and let the cold mountain water run over their feet. Bina was the same age as Prakash. She had pink cheeks, soft brown eyes, and hair that was just beginning to lose its natural curls. Hers was a gentle face, but a determined little chin showed that she could be a strong person. Sonu, her younger brother, was ten. He was a thin boy who had been sickly as a child but was now beginning to fill out. Although he did not look very athletic, he could run like the wind.

Bina had been going to school in her own village of Koli, on the other side of the mountain. But it had been a Primary School, finishing at Class Five. Now, in order to study in the Sixth, she would have to walk several miles every day to Nauti, where there was a High School going up to the Eighth. It had been decided that Sonu would also shift to the new school, to give Bina company. Prakash, their neighbour in Koli, was already a pupil at the Nauti school. His mischievous nature, which sometimes got him into trouble, had resulted in his having to repeat a year.

But this didn't seem to bother him. 'What's the hurry?' he had told his indignant parents. 'You're not sending me to a foreign land when I finish school. And our cows aren't running away, are they?'

'You would prefer to look after the cows, wouldn't you?' asked Bina, as they got up to continue their walk.

'Oh, school's all right. Wait till you see old Mr Mani. He always gets our names mixed up, as well as the subjects he's supposed to be teaching. At our last lesson, instead of maths, he gave us a geography lesson!'

'More fun than maths,' said Bina.

'Yes, but there's a new teacher this year. She's very young, they say, just out of college. I wonder what she'll be like.'

Bina walked faster and Sonu had some trouble keeping up with them. She was excited about the new school and the prospect of different surroundings. She had seldom been outside her own village, with its small school and single ration shop. The day's routine never varied—helping her mother in the fields or with household tasks like fetching water from the spring or cutting grass and fodder for the cattle. Her father, who was a soldier, was away for nine months in the year and Sonu was still too small for the heavier tasks.

As they neared Nauti village, they were joined by other children coming from different directions. Even where there were no major roads, the mountains were full of little lanes and shortcuts. Like a game of snakes and ladders, these narrow paths zigzagged around the hills and villages, cutting through fields and crossing narrow ravines until they came together to form a fairly busy road along which mules, cattle and goats joined the throng.

Nauti was a fairly large village, and from here a broader but dustier road started for Tehri. There was a small bus, several trucks and (for part of the way) a road-roller. The road hadn't been completed because the heavy diesel roller couldn't take the steep climb to Nauti. It stood on the roadside halfway up the road from Tehri.

Prakash knew almost everyone in the area, and exchanged greetings and gossip with other children as well as with muleteers, bus drivers, milkmen and labourers working on the road. He loved telling everyone the time, even if they weren't interested.

'It's nine o'clock,' he would announce, glancing at his wrist. 'Isn't your bus leaving today?'

'Off with you!' the bus driver would respond, 'I'll leave when I'm ready.'

As the children approached Nauti, the small flat school buildings came into view on the outskirts of the village, fringed with a line of long-leaved pines. A small crowd had assembled on the playing field. Something unusual seemed to have happened. Prakash ran forward to see what it was all about. Bina and Sonu stood aside, waiting in a patch of sunlight near the boundary wall.

Prakash soon came running back to them. He was bubbling over with excitement.

'It's Mr Mani!' he gasped. 'He's disappeared! People are saying a leopard must have carried him off!'

2

Mr Mani wasn't really old. He was about fifty-five and was expected to retire soon. But for the children, adults over forty seemed ancient! And Mr Mani had always been a bit absent-minded, even as a young man.

He had gone out for his early morning walk, saying he'd be back by eight o'clock, in time to have his breakfast and be ready for class. He wasn't married, but his sister and her husband stayed with him. When it was past nine o'clock his sister presumed he'd stopped at a neighbour's house for breakfast (he loved tucking into other people's breakfast) and that he had gone on to school from there. But when the school bell rang at ten o'clock, and everyone but Mr Mani was present, questions were asked and guesses were made.

No one had seen him return from his walk and enquiries made in the village showed that he had not stopped at anyone's house. For Mr Mani to disappear was puzzling; for him to disappear without his breakfast was extraordinary.

Then a milkman returning from the next village said he had seen a leopard sitting on a rock on the outskirts of the pine forest. There had been talk of a cattle-killer in the valley, of leopards and other animals being displaced by the construction of a dam. But as yet no one had heard of a leopard attacking a man. Could Mr Mani have been its first victim? Someone found a strip of red cloth entangled in a blackberry bush and went running through the village showing it to everyone. Mr Mani had been known to wear red pyjamas. Surely, he had been seized and eaten! But where were his remains? And why had he been in his pyjamas?

Meanwhile, Bina and Sonu and the rest of the children had followed their teachers into the school playground. Feeling a little lost, Bina looked around for Prakash. She found herself facing a dark slender young woman wearing spectacles, who must have been in her early twenties—just a little too old to be another student. She had a kind, expressive face and she seemed a little concerned by all that had been happening.

Bina noticed that she had lovely hands; it was obvious that the new teacher hadn't milked cows or worked in the fields!

'You must be new here,' said the teacher, smiling at Bina. 'And is this your little brother?'

'Yes, we've come from Koli village. We were at school there.'

'It's a long walk from Koli. You didn't see any leopards, did you? Well, I'm new too. Are you in the Sixth class?'

'Sonu is in the Third. I'm in the Sixth.'

'Then I'm your new teacher. My name is Tania Ramola. Come along, let's see if we can settle down in our classroom.'

Mr Mani turned up at twelve o'clock, wondering what all the fuss was about. No, he snapped, he had not been attacked by a leopard; and yes, he had lost his pyjamas and would someone kindly return them to him?

'How did you lose your pyjamas, Sir?' asked Prakash.

'They were blown off the washing line!' snapped Mr Mani.

After much questioning, Mr Mani admitted that he had gone further than he had intended, and that he had lost his way coming back. He had been a bit upset because the new teacher, a slip of a girl, had been given charge of the Sixth, while he was still with the Fifth, along with that troublesome boy Prakash, who kept on reminding him of the time! The headmaster had explained that as Mr Mani was due to retire at the end of the year, the school did not wish to burden him with a senior class. But Mr Mani looked upon the whole thing as a plot to get rid of him. He glowered at Miss Ramola whenever he passed her. And when she smiled back at him, he looked the other way!

Mr Mani had been getting even more absent-minded of late—putting on his shoes without his socks, wearing his homespun waistcoat inside out, mixing up people's names, and of course, eating other people's lunches and dinners. His sister had made a special mutton broth (pai) for the postmaster, who was down with flu and had asked Mr Mani to take it over in a thermos. When the postmaster opened the thermos, he found only a few drops of broth at the bottom—Mr Mani had drunk the rest somewhere along the way.

When sometimes Mr Mani spoke of his coming retirement, it was to describe his plans for the small field he owned just behind the house. Right now, it was full of potatoes, which did not require much looking after; but he had plans for growing dahlias, roses, French beans, and other fruits and flowers.

The next time he visited Tehri, he promised himself, he would buy some dahlia bulbs and rose cuttings. The monsoon season would be a good time to put them down. And meanwhile, his potatoes were still flourishing.

3

Bina enjoyed her first day at the new school. She felt at ease with Miss Ramola, as did most of the boys and girls in her class. Tania Ramola had been to distant towns such as Delhi and Lucknow—places they had only read about—and it was said that she had a brother who was a pilot and flew planes all over the world. Perhaps he'd fly over Nauti someday!

Most of the children had, of course, seen planes flying overhead, but none of them had seen a ship, and only a few had been on a train. Tehri mountain was far from the railway and hundreds of miles from the sea. But they all knew about the big dam that was being built at Tehri, just forty miles away.

Bina, Sonu and Prakash had company for part of the way home, but gradually the other children went off in different directions. Once they had crossed the stream, they were on their own again.

It was a steep climb all the way back to their village. Prakash had a supply of peanuts which he shared with Bina and Sonu, and at a small spring they quenched their thirst.

When they were less than a mile from home, they met a postman who had finished his round of the villages in the area and was now returning to Nauti.

'Don't waste time along the way,' he told them. 'Try to get home before dark.'

'What's the hurry?' asked Prakash, glancing at his watch. 'It's only five o'clock.'

'There's a leopard around. I saw it this morning, not far from the stream. No one is sure how it got here. So don't take any chances. Get home early.'

'So there really is a leopard,' said Sonu.

They took his advice and walked faster, and Sonu forgot to complain about his aching feet.

They were home well before sunset.

There was a smell of cooking in the air and they were hungry.

'Cabbage and roti,' said Prakash gloomily. 'But I could eat anything today.' He stopped outside his small slate-roofed house, and Bina and Sonu waved him goodbye, then carried on across a couple of ploughed fields until they reached their small stone house.

'Stuffed tomatoes,' said Sonu, sniffing just outside the front door.

'And lemon pickle,' said Bina, who had helped cut, sun and salt the lemons a month previously.

Their mother was lighting the kitchen stove. They greeted her with great hugs and demands for an immediate dinner. She was a good cook who could make even the simplest of dishes taste delicious. Her favourite saying was, 'Home-made pai is better than chicken soup in Delhi,' and Bina and Sonu had to agree.

Electricity had yet to reach their village, and they took their meal by the light of a kerosene lamp. After the meal, Sonu settled down to do a little homework, while Bina stepped outside to look at the stars.

Across the fields, someone was playing a flute. 'It must be Prakash,' thought Bina. 'He always breaks off on the high notes.' But the flute music was simple and appealing, and she began singing softly to herself in the dark.

4

Mr Mani was having trouble with the porcupines. They had been getting into his garden at night and digging up and eating his potatoes. From his bedroom window—left open, now that the mild-April weather had arrived—he could listen to them enjoying the vegetables he had worked hard to grow. Scrunch, scrunch! *Katar, katar!* Their sharp teeth sliced through the largest and juiciest of potatoes. For Mr Mani, it was as though they were biting through his own flesh. And the sound of them digging industriously as they rooted up those healthy, leafy plants, made him tremble with rage and indignation. The unfairness of it all!

Yes, Mr Mani hated porcupines. He prayed for their destruction, their removal from the face of the earth. But, as his friends were quick to point out, 'Bhagwan protected porcupines too,' and in any case you could never see the creatures or catch them, they were completely nocturnal.

Mr Mani got out of bed every night, torch in one hand, a stout stick in the other, but as soon as he stepped into the garden, the crunching and digging stopped and he was greeted by the most infuriating of silences. He would grope around in the dark, swinging wildly with the stick, but not a single porcupine was to be seen or heard. As soon as he was back in bed—the sounds would start all over again. Scrunch, scrunch, *katar, katar*...

Mr Mani came to his class tired and dishevelled, with rings beneath his eyes and a permanent frown on his face. It took some time for his pupils to discover the reason for his misery, but when they did, they felt sorry for their teacher and took to discussing ways and means of saving his potatoes from the porcupines.

It was Prakash who came up with the idea of a moat or waterditch. 'Porcupines don't like water,' he said knowledgeably.

'How do you know?' asked one of his friends.

'Throw water on one and see how it runs! They don't like getting their quills wet.'

There was no one who could disprove Prakash's theory, and the class fell in with the idea of building a moat, especially as it meant getting most of the day off.

'Anything to make Mr Mani happy,' said the headmaster, and the rest of the school watched with envy as the pupils of Class Five, armed with spades and shovels collected from all parts of the village, took up their positions around Mr Mani's potato field and began digging a ditch.

By evening the moat was ready, but it was still dry and the porcupines got in again that night and had a great feast.

'At this rate,' said Mr Mani gloomily, 'there won't be any potatoes left to save.'

But next day Prakash and the other boys and girls managed to divert the water from a stream that flowed past the village. They had the satisfaction of watching it flow gently into the ditch. Everyone went home in a good mood. By nightfall, the ditch had overflowed, the potato field was flooded, and Mr Mani found himself trapped inside his house. But Prakash and his friends had won the day. The porcupines stayed away that night!

A month had passed, and wild violets, daisies and buttercups now sprinkled the hill slopes, and on her way to school Bina gathered enough to make a little posy. The bunch of flowers fitted easily into an old ink-well. Miss Ramola was delighted to find this little display in the middle of her desk.

'Who put these here?' she asked in surprise.

Bina kept quiet, and the rest of the class smiled secretively. After that, they took turns bringing flowers for the classroom.

On her long walks to school and home again, Bina became aware that April was the month of new leaves. The oak leaves were bright green above and silver beneath, and when they rippled in the breeze they were like clouds of silvery green. The path was strewn with old leaves, dry and crackly. Sonu loved kicking them around.

Clouds of white butterflies floated across the stream. Sonu was chasing a butterfly when he stumbled over something dark and repulsive. He went sprawling on the grass. When he got to his feet, he looked down at the remains of a small animal.

'Bina! Prakash! Come quickly!' he shouted.

It was part of a sheep, killed some days earlier by a much larger animal.

'Only a leopard could have done this,' said Prakash.

'Let's get away, then,' said Sonu. 'It might still be around!'

'No, there's nothing left to eat. The leopard will be hunting elsewhere by now. Perhaps it's moved on to the next valley.'

'Still, I'm frightened,' said Sonu. 'There might be more leopards!'

Bina took him by the hand. 'Leopards don't attack humans!' she said.

'They will, if they get a taste for people!' insisted Prakash.

'Well, this one hasn't attacked any people as yet,' said Bina, although she couldn't be sure. Hadn't there been rumours of a leopard attacking some workers near the dam? But she did not want Sonu to feel afraid, so she did not mention the story. All she said was, 'It has probably come here because of all the activity near the dam.'

All the same, they hurried home. And for a few days, whenever they reached the stream, they crossed over very quickly, unwilling to linger too long at that lovely spot.

5

A few days later, a school party was on its way to Tehri to see the new dam that was being built.

Miss Ramola had arranged to take her class, and Mr Mani, not wishing to be left out, insisted on taking his class as well. That meant there were about fifty boys and girls taking part in the outing. The little bus could only take thirty. A friendly truck driver agreed to take some children if they were prepared to sit on sacks of potatoes. And Prakash persuaded the owner of the diesel-roller to turn it round and head it back to Tehri—with him and a couple of friends up on the driving seat.

Prakash's small group set off at sunrise, as they had to walk some distance in order to reach the stranded road-roller. The bus left at 9 a.m. with Miss Ramola and her class, and Mr Mani and some of his pupils. The truck was to follow later.

It was Bina's first visit to a large town and her first bus ride.

The sharp curves along the winding, downhill road made several children feel sick. The bus driver seemed to be in a tearing hurry. He took them along at rolling, rollicking speed, which made Bina feel quite giddy. She rested her head on her arms and refused to look out of the window. Hairpin bends and cliff edges, pine forests and snow-capped peaks, all swept past her, but she felt too ill to want to look at anything. It was just as well—those sudden drops, hundreds of feet to the valley below, were quite frightening. Bina began to wish that she hadn't come—or that she had joined Prakash on the road-roller instead!

Miss Ramola and Mr Mani didn't seem to notice the lurching and groaning of the old bus. They had made this journey many times. They were busy arguing about the advantages and disadvantages of large dams—an argument that was to continue on and off for much of the day; sometimes in Hindi, sometimes in English, sometimes in the local dialect!

Meanwhile, Prakash and his friends had reached the roller. The driver hadn't turned up, but they managed to reverse it and get it going in the direction of Tehri. They were soon overtaken by both the bus and the truck but kept moving along at a steady chug. Prakash spotted Bina at the window of the bus and waved cheerfully. She responded feebly.

Bina felt better when the road levelled out near Tehri. As they crossed an old bridge over the wide river, they were startled by a loud bang which made the bus shudder. A cloud of dust rose above the town.

'They're blasting the mountain,' said Miss Ramola.

'End of a mountain,' said Mr Mani mournfully.

While they were drinking cups of tea at the bus stop, waiting for the potato truck and the road-roller, Miss Ramola and Mr Mani continued their argument about the dam. Miss Ramola maintained that it would bring electric power and water for irrigation to large areas of the country, including the surrounding area. Mr Mani declared that it was a menace, as it was situated in an earthquake zone. There would be a terrible disaster if the dam burst! Bina found it all very confusing. And what about the animals in the area, she wondered, what would happen to them?

The argument was becoming quite heated when the potato truck arrived. There was no sign of the road-roller, so it was decided that Mr Mani should wait for Prakash and his friends while Miss Ramola's group went ahead.

Some eight or nine miles before Tehri, the road-roller had broken down, and Prakash and his friends were forced to walk. They had not gone far, however, when a mule train came along—five or six mules that had been delivering sacks of grain in Nauti. A boy rode on the first mule, but the others had no loads.

'Can you give us a ride to Tehri?' called Prakash.

'Make yourselves comfortable,' said the boy.

There were no saddles, only gunny sacks strapped on to the mules with rope. They had a rough but jolly ride down to the Tehri bus stop. None of them had ever ridden mules; but they had saved at least an hour on the road.

Looking around the bus stop for the rest of the party, they could find no one from their school. And Mr Mani, who should have been waiting for them, had vanished.

6

Tania Ramola and her group had taken the steep road to the hill above Tehri. Half-an-hour's climbing brought them to a little plateau which overlooked the town, the river and the dam-site.

The earthworks for the dam were only just coming up, but a wide tunnel had been bored through the mountain to divert the river into another channel. Down below, the old town was still spread out across the valley and from a distance it looked quite charming and picturesque.

'Will the whole town be swallowed up by the waters of the dam?' asked Bina.

'Yes, all of it,' said Miss Ramola. 'The clock tower and the old palace. The long bazaar, and the temples, the schools and the jail, and hundreds of houses, for many miles up the valley.

All those people will have to go—thousands of them! Of course, they'll be resettled elsewhere.'

'But the town's been here for hundreds of years,' said Bina. 'They were quite happy without the dam, weren't they?'

'I suppose they were. But the dam isn't just for them—it's for the millions who live further downstream, across the plains.'

'And it doesn't matter what happens to this place?'

'The local people will be given new homes, somewhere else.' Miss Ramola found herself on the defensive and decided to change the subject. 'Everyone must be hungry. It's time we had our lunch.'

Bina kept quiet. She didn't think the local people would want to go away. And it was a good thing, she mused, that there was only a small stream and not a big river running past her village. To be uprooted like this—a town and hundreds of villages—and put down somewhere on the hot, dusty plains—seemed to her unbearable.

'Well, I'm glad I don't live in Tehri,' she said.

She did not know it, but all the animals and most of the birds had already left the area. The leopard had been among them.

They walked through the colourful, crowded bazaar, where fruit-sellers did business beside silversmiths, and pavement vendors sold everything from umbrellas to glass bangles. Sparrows attacked sacks of grain, monkeys made off with bananas, and stray cows and dogs rummaged in refuse bins, but nobody took any notice. Music blared from radios. Buses blew their horns. Sonu bought a whistle to add to the general din, but Miss Ramola told him to put it away. Bina had kept ten rupees aside, and now she used it to buy a cotton head-scarf for her mother.

As they were about to enter a small restaurant for a meal, they were joined by Prakash and his companions; but of Mr Mani there was still no sign.

'He must have met one of his relatives,' said Prakash. 'He has relatives everywhere.'

After a simple meal of rice and lentils, they walked the length of the bazaar without seeing Mr Mani. At last, when they were about to give up the search, they saw him emerge from a by-lane, a large sack slung over his shoulder.

'Sir, where have you been?' asked Prakash. 'We have been looking for you everywhere.'

On Mr Mani's face was a look of triumph.

'Help me with this bag,' he said breathlessly.

'You've bought more potatoes, sir,' said Prakash.

'Not potatoes, boy. Dahlia bulbs!'

7

It was dark by the time they were all back in Nauti. Mr Mani had refused to be separated from his sack of dahlia bulbs, and had been forced to sit in the back of the truck with Prakash and most of the boys.

Bina did not feel so ill on the return journey. Going uphill was definitely better than going downhill! But by the time the bus reached Nauti it was too late for most of the children to walk back to the more distant villages. The boys were put up in different homes, while the girls were given beds in the school veranda.

The night was warm and still. Large moths fluttered around the single bulb that lit the veranda. Counting moths, Sonu soon fell asleep. But Bina stayed awake for some time, listening to the sounds of the night. A nightjar went *tonk-tonk* in the bushes, and somewhere in the forest an owl hooted softly. The sharp call of a barking deer travelled up the valley, from the direction of the stream. Jackals kept howling. It seemed that there were more of them than ever before.

Bina was not the only one to hear the barking deer. The leopard, stretched full length on a rocky ledge, heard it too. The leopard raised its head and then got up slowly. The deer was its natural prey. But there weren't many left, and that was why the leopard, robbed of its forest by the dam, had taken to attacking dogs and cattle near the villages.

As the cry of the barking deer sounded nearer, the leopard left its lookout point and moved swiftly through the shadows towards the stream.

8

In early June the hills were dry and dusty, and forest fires broke out, destroying shrubs and trees, killing birds and small animals. The resin in the pines made these trees burn more fiercely, and the wind would take sparks from the trees and carry them into the dry grass and leaves, so that new fires would spring up before the old ones had died out. Fortunately, Bina's village was not in the pine belt; the fires did not reach it. But Nauti was surrounded by a fire that raged for three days, and the children had to stay away from school.

And then, towards the end of June, the monsoon rains arrived and there was an end to forest fires. The monsoon lasts three months and the lower Himalayas would be drenched in rain, mist and cloud for the next three months.

The first rain arrived while Bina, Prakash and Sonu were returning home from school. Those first few drops on the dusty path made them cry out with excitement. Then the rain grew heavier and a wonderful aroma rose from the earth.

'The best smell in the world!' exclaimed Bina.

Everything suddenly came to life. The grass, the crops, the

trees, the birds. Even the leaves of the trees glistened and looked new.

That first wet weekend, Bina and Sonu helped their mother plant beans, maize and cucumbers. Sometimes, when the rain was very heavy, they had to run indoors. Otherwise they worked in the rain, the soft mud clinging to their bare legs.

Prakash now owned a black dog with one ear up and one ear down. The dog ran around getting in everyone's way, barking at cows, goats, hens and humans, without frightening any of them. Prakash said it was a very clever dog, but no one else seemed to think so. Prakash also said it would protect the village from the leopard, but others said the dog would be the first to be taken—he'd run straight into the jaws of Mr Spots!

In Nauti, Tania Ramola was trying to find a dry spot in the quarters she'd been given. It was an old building and the roof was leaking in several places. Mugs and buckets were scattered about the floor in order to catch the drip.

Mr Mani had dug up all his potatoes and presented them to the friends and neighbours who had given him lunches and dinners. He was having the time of his life, planting dahlia bulbs all over his garden.

'I'll have a field of many-coloured dahlias!' he announced. 'Just wait till the end of August!'

'Watch out for those porcupines,' warned his sister. 'They eat dahlia bulbs too!'

Mr Mani made an inspection tour of his moat, no longer in flood, and found everything in good order. Prakash had done his job well.

Now, when the children crossed the stream, they found that the water-level had risen by about a foot. Small cascades had turned into waterfalls. Ferns had sprung up on the banks. Frogs chanted.

Prakash and his dog dashed across the stream. Bina and Sonu followed more cautiously. The current was much stronger now and the water was almost up to their knees. Once they had crossed the stream, they hurried along the path, anxious not to be caught in a sudden downpour.

By the time they reached school, each of them had two or three leeches clinging to their legs. They had to use salt to remove them. The leeches were the most troublesome part of the rainy season. Even the leopard did not like them. It could not lie in the long grass without getting leeches on its paws and face.

One day, when Bina, Prakash and Sonu were about to cross the stream they heard a low rumble, which grew louder every second. Looking up at the opposite hill, they saw several trees shudder, tilt outwards and begin to fall. Earth and rocks bulged out from the mountain, then came crashing down into the ravine.

'Landslide!' shouted Sonu.

'It's carried away the path,' said Bina. 'Don't go any further.'

There was a tremendous roar as more rocks, trees and bushes fell away and crashed down the hillside.

Prakash's dog, who had gone ahead, came running back, tail between his legs.

They remained rooted to the spot until the rocks had stopped falling and the dust had settled. Birds circled the area, calling wildly. A frightened barking deer ran past them.

'We can't go to school now,' said Prakash. 'There's no way around.'

They turned and trudged home through the gathering mist.

In Koli, Prakash's parents had heard the roar of the landslide. They were setting out in search of the children when they saw them emerge from the mist, waving cheerfully.

9

They had to miss school for another three days, and Bina was afraid they might not be able to take their final exams. Although Prakash was not really troubled at the thought of missing exams, he did not like feeling helpless just because their path had been swept away. So he explored the hillside until he found a goat-track going around the mountain. It joined up with another path near Nauti. This made their walk longer by a mile, but Bina did not mind. It was much cooler now that the rains were in full swing.

The only trouble with the new route was that it passed close to the leopard's lair. The animal had made this area its own since being forced to leave the dam area.

One day Prakash's dog ran ahead of them, barking furiously. Then he ran back, whimpering.

'He's always running away from something,' observed Sonu. But a minute later he understood the reason for the dog's fear.

They rounded a bend and Sonu saw the leopard standing in their way. They were struck dumb—too terrified to run. It was a strong, sinewy creature. A low growl rose from its throat. It seemed ready to spring.

They stood perfectly still, afraid to move or say a word. And the leopard must have been equally surprised. It stared at them for a few seconds, then bounded across the path and into the oak forest.

Sonu was shaking. Bina could hear her heart hammering. Prakash could only stammer: 'Did you see the way he sprang? Wasn't he beautiful?'

He forgot to look at his watch for the rest of the day.

A few days later Sonu stopped and pointed to a large outcrop of rock on the next hill.

The leopard stood far above them, outlined against the sky. It looked strong, majestic. Standing beside it were two young cubs.

'Look at those little ones!' exclaimed Sonu.

'So it's a female, not a male,' said Prakash.

'That's why she was killing so often,' said Bina. 'She had to feed her cubs too.'

They remained still for several minutes, gazing up at the leopard and her cubs. The leopard family took no notice of them.

'She knows we are here,' said Prakash, 'but she doesn't care. She knows we won't harm them.'

'We are cubs too!' said Sonu.

'Yes,' said Bina. 'And there's still plenty of space for all of us. Even when the dam is ready there will still be room for leopards and humans.'

10

The school exams were over. The rains were nearly over too. The landslide had been cleared, and Bina, Prakash and Sonu were once again crossing the stream.

There was a chill in the air, for it was the end of September.

Prakash had learnt to play the flute quite well, and he played on the way to school and then again on the way home. As a result he did not look at his watch so often.

One morning they found a small crowd in front of Mr Mani's house.

'What could have happened?' wondered Bina. 'I hope he hasn't got lost again.'

'Maybe he's sick,' said Sonu.

'Maybe it's the porcupines,' said Prakash.

But it was none of these things.

Mr Mani's first dahlia was in bloom, and half the village

had turned out to look at it! It was a huge red double dahlia, so heavy that it had to be supported with sticks. No one had ever seen such a magnificent flower!

Mr Mani was a happy man. And his mood only improved over the coming week, as more and more dahlias flowered—crimson, yellow, purple, mauve, white—button dahlias, pompom dahlias, spotted dahlias, striped dahlias… Mr Mani had them all! A dahlia even turned up on Tania Romola's desk—he got on quite well with her now—and another brightened up the headmaster's study.

A week later, on their way home—it was almost the last day of the school term—Bina, Prakash and Sonu talked about what they might do when they grew up.

'I think I'll become a teacher,' said Bina. 'I'll teach children about animals and birds, and trees and flowers.'

'Better than maths!' said Prakash.

'I'll be a pilot,' said Sonu. 'I want to fly a plane like Miss Ramola's brother.'

'And what about you, Prakash?' asked Bina.

Prakash just smiled and said, 'Maybe I'll be a flute-player,' and he put the flute to he lips and played a sweet melody.

'Well, the world needs flute-players too,' said Bina, as they fell into step beside him.

The leopard had been stalking a barking deer. She paused when she heard the flute and the voices of the children. Her own young ones were growing quickly, but the girl and the two boys did not look much older.

They had started singing their favourite song again.

Five more miles to go!
We climb through rain and snow,
A river to cross…

A mountain to pass…
Now we've four more miles to go!

The leopard waited until they had passed, before returning to the trail of the barking deer.

Gentle Shade by Day

Those who have spent time in non-air-conditioned parts of India will remember with gratitude those gracious trees that provide shade and shelter during the summer months—the banyan, peepul, mango, neem and others. Coastal dwellers are not so fortunate for there is not much shade to be had from a palm tree unless you keep moving in its long but insubstantial shadow.

I am not surprised that the sages of old were given to sitting beneath the peepul tree. They might have had various religious reasons for calling it sacred but I am sure there was a good practical reason as well. Few trees provide a cooler shade than it does. Even on the stillest of days, the peepul leaves are forever twirling and with thousands of leaves spinning like tops, there is quite a breeze for anyone sitting below.

However, there are warnings about peepul trees—'Gentle shade by day and terror by night!' During the night, the tree is said to be alive with various spirits, most of them inimical to man. One is advised not to sleep beneath it, for this is construed by a ghost as an invitation to jump down your throat and take possession of you, or at the very least, ruin your digestion.

It is also said to be unlucky to sleep beneath a tamarind, but I have often reclined in the pleasant shade of this noble tree and have come to no harm. A famous tamarind stands over the tomb of Tansen, the great musician and singer of Akbar's court at Gwalior. Its leaves, though bitter, are eaten by singers to improve their voices.

A mango grove is a wonderful place for an afternoon siesta. But if the mangoes are ripening, there is usually a great deal of activity going on with parrots, crows, monkeys and small boys, all attempting to evade the watchman who uses an empty kerosene tin as a drum to try and frighten them away. So it's not the ideal place for a nap then, but the shade under a mango grove is dark, deep and very soothing.

The banyan tree with its aerial roots represents the matted hair of Lord Shiva. There is always shade and space beneath a venerable old banyan. It is still a popular community centre in our Indian villages but is becoming a rarity in cities simply because it covers so large an area. And if you cut its aerial roots, the tree topples over. Other handsome trees related to the banyan are the pilkhan and the chilkhan, large spreading evergreens, both quite noticeable on some of New Delhi's wider avenues.

The neem is a tall tree, but its numerous branches give it a shady head. One of my greatest pleasures is to walk beneath an avenue of neem trees after a shower of rain. As the fallen berries are crushed underfoot, they give out a sharp heady fragrance, which I find exhilarating. Apart from its medicinal uses, the tree is connected in legends with the Sun God, as in the story of neem-barak. 'The Sun in a Neem Tree', who invited to dinner a Bairagi tribal, whose rules forbade him to eat anything except by daylight. When dinner was delayed after sundown, Suraj Narayan, the Sun God, obligingly descended from a neem tree and continued shining till dinner was over.

On this pleasant note I end this tribute, only adding that shade-giving trees symbolize the harmony between man and nature and that our ancestors in their devotion to trees and reverence for them, clearly showed that they knew what was good for them.

Under the Deodars

The names of trees often find their way into the titles of books and stories. Kipling's earliest stories were published in India under the title *Under the Deodars*—for it was under the deodars of Shimla that all the scandals, intrigues, romances and hauntings took place!

As you ascend the Himalayan foothills, the trees of the plains give way to the trees of the mountains, and at seven thousand feet you will be welcomed by the deodars (*Cedrus Deodara*), singly or in large numbers, for these great trees are indigenous to the Himalayas. In the presence of deodars, the air is purer, more bracing. They will give you a sense of renewal.

Deodar, comes from 'devdar', Sanskrit for 'Tree of God'. And indeed no tree could be nobler, growing to a great height and living for two or three hundred years, sometimes longer. Some of the oldest and most magnificent specimens are found in the premises of temples, where they are protected. These great trees are, at their most luxuriant, around eight thousand feet.

A similar tree is the cedar of Lebanon, which grows on the mountains of Lebanon and Syria. Some are reputed to be about two thousand years old with a girth of some forty feet. Legend has it that it provided the timber used by King Solomon for building his temple.

Mr V.P. Mehta tells me that at the Forest Research Institute in Dehradun, a cross section of an old deodar shows seven hundred distinct annual growth rings. The tree was born some time during the reign of Alauddin Khilji in the twelfth century, and lived through the Mughal period and the great part of the British rule in India.

If only trees could talk, what great historians they would be!

The Coconut Tree

The beginnings of most cultivated plants are a mystery, and few have received as much attention from scientists and botanists as the familiar coconut palm.

Though it cannot be proved that the coconut first originated in India, there is no doubt that this tree has been with us since earliest times. Mention is made of it in several of the Puranas, which are the oldest books after the Vedas. There is also mention of it in the Ramayana and the Mahabharata as well as in ancient Tamil literature. In some Hindu ceremonies, worship is offered to Varuna, the god presiding over the water and the oceans. This god is represented by a pot of water with a coconut placed at the mouth. The offering of an unbroken coconut to the sea probably comes from the idea that the coconut came from the seas. And there is a Ceylonese legend that says that it was brought to India from Nagaloka, a blissful region beyond the seas.

The Papuans of New Guinea take pride in calling themselves the Coconut People. They hate the non-Papuans of their island who, they say, are not true Coconuts. They have a fantastic legend regarding the origin of the coconut. Even before the creation of man, their god killed another god, Somoali by name, who later became the god of the bushmen and the nomads. He placed the head of his victim on the bank of the Wamagao River, and after six nights, when he returned to see the head of his enemy, he found leaves sprouting from it. He then planted the sprouting head in the earth and from it grew the first coconut.

Most botanists seem to think that the original home of the coconut is not far from India, probably 'somewhere in the lands now under the sea, which existed in the western parts of the Indian Ocean'. All are agreed that its home is somewhere between Zanzibar and New Guinea. The seafaring Polynesians and wandering Malays probably carried it eastwards and westwards. It was probably the adventurous Polynesian mariners who first planted it in the New World.

The Malay seafarers, the once-maritime Tamils and the ancient mariners of the Bengal coast have probably been responsible for a much wider distribution of the coconut into the lands of the Indian Ocean. Ocean currents and monsoon drifts have also played a part in its spread.

So old is the plant in India that from early times the Arabs have called it the Indian Nut. Marco Polo called it by the same name. For Hindus it is the Kalpaka Vriksha, or Tree of Heaven.

Apart from the refreshing qualities of the flesh and water of the coconut fruit, this tree has many uses. In Goa, brooms are made from the leaf ribs, while in Kerala the fermented sap is known as palm wine or toddy. The sugar from the sap gives us jaggery, the fibre from the outer rind provides coir fibre, the dry fleshy kernel provides copra and the oil extracted from the dry copra gives us coconut oil or coconut butter.

Several other palms are well-known in India—the tall, slim betel-nut palm; the shaggy wild date palm; and the palmyra palm, on whose strong leaves the ancient scriptures were written.

Music in the Trees

In India, the monsoon is the season when our insect orchestra is at its best. It is true that the shrill music of the cicada is heard throughout the hot weather; but theirs is a prelude to the great concert that comes into full play once the rainy season begins. When the monsoon with its magic touch brings life and greenness to rock and earth and tree, the whole air seems to come alive with the music of insects. Grasshoppers shrill in the bushes, crickets chirp from under stones, and in the water-laden fields there are hundreds of minor artists providing a medley of sounds.

Amongst our more vocal and better-known insect musicians are those that dwell in trees, the cicadas and the crickets. As musicians, the cicadas are in a class by themselves. Most of the species in India are forest dwellers, but there are some who inhabit the open country in the plains. All through the hot weather their chorus rings through the jungle, while a shower of rain, far from damping their spirits, only rouses them to a deafening, combined effort. The ancient Greeks knew the cicada well. They appreciated his music so much that they kept him captive in a cage to sing. Only the males were chosen, for the females, like most insect musicians, were completely dumb. This moved one of the Greek poets to exclaim, 'Happy are the cicadas, for they have voiceless wives.'

The cicada's sound-producing organs are amongst the most remarkable in the animal kingdom. The underside of his body carries a pair of flaps, each of which covers an oval membrane, which looks like the head of a drum. These are set into motion by a great pair of muscles attached to them from within the body, and the sound is produced by their vibration. The whole abdomen, which is practically hollow, helps to increase or diminish the sound.

Simple, isn't it? To be truthful, I find it extremely complicated, and am able to describe the process only by consulting the notes of S.H. Prater, one-time curator of the Bombay Natural History Society.

Let it be added that the female carries these structures in a modified form, but as she has no muscles to bring them into play, she is unable to use them. This is why she must remain silent while her spouse shrieks away. I would change the line from that Greek poet (Xenarchos, I think) and say instead: 'Pity the female cicadas, for they have singing husbands!'

The object of the cicadas' mirthful music is a mystery. It may attract the opposite sex, or it may be just a diversion of the male. Or perhaps he sings because he is happy.

The tree crickets are a band of willing artists who commence their performance as soon as it is dusk. Their sounds are familiar, but the crickets are seldom seen. If one of them enters the house and treats us to a solo, the sound is so surprisingly loud that we can hardly believe it is being produced by so small a creature.

The common Indian tree cricket is a delicate pale-green little creature with hazy, transparent green wings. In full song he holds his wings outspread over his back. They vibrate so rapidly that they are but a blurred outline. A tap on the bush or leaf on which he sits will put an immediate stop to his performance. His music ceases, and he lowers his wings and folds them flat on his back. The grasshopper makes his music by rubbing his legs against his forewing.

I won't go into detail over how the cricket produces its music, except to say that its louder notes are produced by a rapid vibration of the wings, the right wing usually working over the left, and the edge of one acting on the file of the other to produce a shrill, long-sustained note.

One of the best-known crickets is a large black fellow who lives underground and rarely comes out by day, except when the rains flood him out of his burrow. But when night falls, he sits on his doorstep and pours out his soul in a strident song. This cricket's name is as impressive as his sound—*Brachytrypes portentosus.*

The mole cricket is a genius by itself. Mole crickets are tillers of the soil. They use their powerful forelimbs for shovelling up the earth and their hard heads for butting into it. Notwithstanding its earthy occupations, the mole cricket is sometimes moved to creating music. But as he repeats his note—a solemn deep-toned chirp, about a hundred times a minute—the performance can be monotonous.

In India, the cone-headed katydids are probably the most notable performers. Katydids are trim, slender grasshopper-like insects, much in evidence in the fresh green grass of the monsoon. In the fields, the loud, shrill notes of the males may be heard both by day and by night. Sometimes one of them comes into a house and treats its occupants to a sudden outburst of high-pitched fiddling. His song rises in pitch as the performer warms to his work. In a room it can be quite deafening, and the sound is always difficult to locate—it seems to come from everywhere.

Finally we come to the tree crickets, a band of willing artistes who commence their performance at dusk. Their sounds are familiar, but it is difficult to see the musicians. Presumably the males sing in order to attract their more silent females. The music advertises the presence of the male; just as in other creatures, it is the colour or smell that does the job. And if music be the food of love, play on, cicada!

Why are grasshoppers and crickets such persistent little singers? Do they really sing to charm and attract the females, or is their song the voice of mirth? A curious habit has been noticed among certain tree crickets, which may offer a clue to the mystery. Sometimes, as a male sings, a female steals up to him from behind. The male ceases his music. He sits quite still with his wings uplifted. The female noses about his back and soon discovers the object of her search—a deep cavity situated just behind the base of his wings. This cavity contains a clear liquid which she eagerly laps up. Well, even the human male seeks to please his sweetheart with the offer of chocolates.

It is supposed that in this instance, the lady is attracted rather by the sweets the male has to offer than by his music. But the music advertises his whereabouts. She hears his sound and knows that he has a sweet nectar to offer her and comes after it. If the artful luring of the male sometimes results in mating, we see the real reason for the male possessing his musical instruments, and understand his urge to play them so continuously. After all, the luring of the female with music and sweets is even practised by human beings. It may not always succeed in its purpose. Sometimes, as with the crickets, the female accepts the gifts so generously offered—and then takes her leave!

When the Chestnuts Fall

When the horse-chestnut comes into new leaf, we know that spring has come to the hills. And by the end of April these handsome trees are festooned with candelabra of lovely pink blossom. Then, during the rains, the chestnuts begin to form. By October they have split their green jackets, and shiny brown chestnuts are falling to the grounds.

Why 'horse-chestnuts'? Well, these beautiful chestnuts are not really edible, except perhaps for horses. Even the monkeys disdain them. Being destructive by nature, the rhesus monkeys will bite into the chestnut and then spit them out; they will destroy as many as they possibly can, just because they are not to their taste!

As schoolboys we collected whole chestnuts and used them to play a game called 'conkers'. You attached your chestnut to a length of string and used it to strike your opponents' chestnut in an effort to shatter it. I remember having a very strong, sturdy chestnut, which resisted all the blows it received. Such simple games are no more. Technology has robbed children of their innocence.

But I still collect chestnuts when I can find them. Plant a chestnut whole, and in the coming spring you will have the pleasure of seeing a young tree sprung up.

Growing up with Trees

Dehradun was a good place for trees, and Grandfather's house was surrounded by several kinds—peepul, neem, mango, jackfruit and papaya. There was also an ancient banyan tree. I grew up amongst these trees, and some of them planted by Grandfather grew with me.

There were two types of trees that were of special interest to a boy—trees that were good for climbing, and trees that provided fruit.

The jackfruit tree was both these things. The fruit itself—the largest in the world—grew only on the trunk and main branches. I did not care much for the fruit, although cooked as a vegetable it made a good curry. But the tree was large and leafy and easy to climb. It was a very dark tree and if I hid in it, I could not be easily seen from below. In a hole in the tree trunk I kept various banned items—a catapult, some lurid comics, and a large stock of chewing-gum. Perhaps they are still there, because I forgot to collect them when we finally went away.

The banyan tree grew behind the house. Its spreading branches, which hung to the ground and took root again, formed a number of twisting passageways and gave me endless pleasure. The tree was older than the house, older than my grandparents, as old as Dehra. I could hide myself in its branches, behind thick green leaves, and spy on the world below. I could read in it, too, propped up against the bole of the tree, with *Treasure Island* or the *Jungle Books* or comics like *Wizard* or *Hotspur* which, unlike the forbidden Superman and others like him, were full of clean-cut schoolboy heroes.

The banyan tree was a world in itself, populated with small beasts and large insects. While the leaves were still pink and tender, they would be visited by the delicate map butterfly, who committed her eggs to their care. The 'honey' on the leaves—an edible smear—also attracted the little striped squirrels, who soon grew used to my presence and became quite bold. Red-headed parakeets swarmed about the tree early in the morning.

But the banyan really came to life during the monsoon, when the branches were thick with scarlet figs. These berries were not fit for human consumption, but the many birds that gathered in the tree—gossipy rosy pastors, quarrelsome mynas, cheerful bulbuls and coppersmiths, and sometimes a raucous bullying crow—feasted on them. And when night fell, and the birds were resting, the dark flying foxes flapped heavily about the tree, chewing and munching as they clambered over the branches.

Among nocturnal visitors to the jackfruit and banyan trees was the Brainfever bird, whose real name is the Hawk-Cuckoo. 'Brainfever, brainfever!' it seems to call, and this shrill, nagging cry will keep the soundest of sleepers awake on a hot summer night.

The British called it the Brainfever bird, but there are other names for it. The Mahrattas called it 'Paos-ala' which means 'Rain is coming!' Perhaps Grandfather's interpretation of its call was the best. According to him, when the bird was tuning up for its main concert, it seemed to say: 'Oh dear, oh dear! How very hot it's getting! we feel it...WE FEEL IT...WE FEEL IT!'

Yes, the banyan tree was a noisy place during the rains. If the Brainfever bird made music by night, the crickets and cicadas orchestrated during the day. As musicians, the cicadas were in a class by themselves. All through the hot weather their chorus rang through the garden, while a shower of rain, far from damping their spirits, only roused them to a greater vocal effort.

The tree crickets were a band of willing artistes who commenced their performance at almost any time of the day, but preferably in the evenings. Delicate pale green creatures with transparent green wings, they were hard to find amongst the lush monsoon foliage; but once located, a tap on the leaf or bush on which they sat would put an immediate end to the performance.

At the height of the monsoon, the banyan tree was like an orchestra pit with the musicians constantly turning up. Birds, insects and squirrels expressed their joy at the end of the hot weather and the cool quenching relief of the rains.

A flute in my hands, I would try adding my shrill piping to theirs. But they thought poorly of my musical ability, for whenever I played on the flute, the birds and insects would subside into a pained and puzzled silence.

A Special Tree

One day, when Rakesh was six, he walked home from the Mussoorie bazaar eating cherries. They were a little sweet, a little sour; small, bright red cherries, which had come all the way from the Kashmir Valley.

Here in the Himalayan foothills where Rakesh lived, there were not many fruit trees. The soil was stony, and the dry cold winds stunted the growth of most plants. But on the more sheltered slopes there were forests of oak and deodar.

Rakesh lived with his grandfather on the outskirts of Mussoorie, just where the forest began. His father and mother lived in a small village fifty miles away, where they grew maize and rice and barley in narrow terraced fields on the lower slopes of the mountain. But there were no schools in the village, and Rakesh's parents were keen that he should go to school. As soon as he was of school-going age, they sent him to stay with his grandfather in Mussoorie. He had a little cottage outside the town.

Rakesh was on his way home from school when he bought the cherries. He paid fifty paise for the bunch. It took him about half an hour to walk home, and by the time he reached the cottage there were only three cherries left.

'Have a cherry, Grandfather,' he said, as soon as he saw his grandfather in the garden.

Grandfather took one cherry and Rakesh promptly ate the other two. He kept the last seed in his mouth for some time, rolling it round and round on his tongue until all the tang had gone. Then he placed the seed on the palm of his hand and studied it.

'Are cherry seeds lucky?' asked Rakesh.

'Of course.'

'Then I'll keep it.'

'Nothing is lucky if you put it away. If you want luck, you must put it to some use.'

'What can I do with a seed?'

'Plant it.'

So Rakesh found a small space and began to dig up a flowerbed.

'Hey, not there,' said Grandfather, 'I've sown mustard in that bed. Plant it in that shady corner, where it won't be disturbed.'

Rakesh went to a corner of the garden where the earth was soft and yielding. He did not have to dig. He pressed the seed into the soil with his thumb and it went right in.

Then he had his lunch, and ran off to play cricket with his friends, and forgot all about the cherry seed.

When it was winter in the hills, a cold wind blew down from the snows and went *whoo-whoo-whoo* in the deodar trees, and the garden was dry and bare. In the evenings Grandfather and Rakesh sat over a charcoal fire, and Grandfather told Rakesh stories—stories about people who turned into animals, and ghosts who lived in trees, and beans that jumped and stones that wept—and in turn Rakesh would read to him from the newspaper, Grandfather's eyesight being rather weak. Rakesh found the newspaper very dull—especially after the stories—but Grandfather wanted all the news...

They knew it was spring when the wild duck flew north again, to Siberia. Early in the morning, when he got up to chop wood and light a fire, Rakesh saw the V-shaped formation streaming northward, the calls of the birds carrying clearly through the thin mountain air.

One morning in the garden he bent to pick up what he thought was a small twig and found to his surprise that it was well rooted. He stared at it for a moment, then ran to fetch Grandfather, calling, 'Dada, come and look, the cherry tree has come up!'

'What cherry tree?' asked Grandfather, who had forgotten about it.

'The seed we planted last year—look, it's come up!'

Rakesh went down on his haunches, while Grandfather bent almost double and peered down at the tiny tree. It was about four inches high.

'Yes, it's a cherry tree,' said Grandfather. 'You should water it now and then.'

Rakesh ran indoors and came back with a bucket of water.

'Don't drown it!' said Grandfather.

Rakesh gave it a sprinkling and circled it with pebbles.

'What are the pebbles for?' asked Grandfather.

'For privacy,' said Rakesh.

He looked at the tree every morning but it did not seem to be growing very fast, so he stopped looking at it except quickly, out of the corner of his eye. And, after a week or two, when he allowed himself to look at it properly, he found that it had grown—at least an inch!

That year the monsoon rains came early and Rakesh plodded to and from school in raincoat and chappals. Ferns sprang from the trunks of trees, strange-looking lilies came up in the long grass, and even when it wasn't raining the trees dripped and mist came curling up the valley. The cherry tree grew quickly in this season.

It was about two feet high when a goat entered the garden and ate all the leaves. Only the main stem and two thin branches remained.

'Never mind,' said Grandfather, seeing that Rakesh was upset. 'It will grow again, cherry trees are tough.'

Towards the end of the rainy season new leaves appeared on the tree. Then a woman cutting grass scrambled down the hillside, her scythe swishing through the heavy monsoon foliage. She did not try to avoid the tree: one sweep, and the cherry tree was cut in two.

When Grandfather saw what had happened, he went after the woman and scolded her; but the damage could not be repaired.

'Maybe it will die now,' said Rakesh.

'Maybe,' said Grandfather.

But the cherry tree had no intention of dying.

By the time summer came round again, it had sent out several new shoots with tender green leaves. Rakesh had grown taller too. He was eight now, a sturdy boy with curly black hair and deep black eyes. 'Blackberry eyes,' Grandfather called them.

That monsoon Rakesh went home to his village, to help his father and mother with the planting and ploughing and sowing. He was thinner but stronger when he came back to Grandfather's house at the end of the rains to find that the cherry tree had grown another foot. It was now up to his chest.

Even when there was rain, Rakesh would sometimes water the tree. He wanted it to know that he was there.

One day he found a bright green praying-mantis perched on a branch, peering at him with bulging eyes. Rakesh let it remain there; it was the cherry tree's first visitor.

The next visitor was a hairy caterpillar, who started making a meal of the leaves. Rakesh removed it quickly and dropped it on a heap of dry leaves.

'Come back when you're a butterfly,' he said.

Winter came early. The cherry tree bent low with the weight of snow. Field mice sought shelter in the roof of the cottage.

The road from the valley was blocked, and for several days there was no newspaper, and this made Grandfather quite grumpy. His stories began to have unhappy endings.

In February it was Rakesh's birthday. He was nine—and the tree was four, but almost as tall as Rakesh.

One morning, when the sun came out, Grandfather came into the garden to 'let some warmth get into my bones,' as he put it. He stopped in front of the cherry tree, stared at it for a few moments, and then called out, 'Rakesh! Come and look! Come quickly before it falls!'

Rakesh and Grandfather gazed at the tree as though it had performed a miracle. There was a pale pink blossom at the end of a branch.

The following year there were more blossoms. And suddenly the tree was taller than Rakesh, even though it was less than half his age. And then it was taller than Grandfather, who was older than some of the oak trees.

But Rakesh had grown too. He could run and jump and climb trees as well as most boys, and he read a lot of books, although he still liked listening to Grandfather's tales.

In the cherry tree, bees came to feed on the nectar in the blossoms, and tiny birds pecked at the blossoms and broke them off. But the tree kept blossoming right through the spring, and there were always more blossoms than birds.

That summer there were small cherries on the tree. Rakesh tasted one and spat it out.

'It's too sour,' he said.

'They'll be better next year,' said Grandfather.

But the birds liked them—especially the bigger birds, such as the bulbuls and scarlet minivets—and they flitted in and out of the foliage, feasting on the cherries.

On a warm sunny afternoon, when even the bees looked

sleepy, Rakesh was looking for Grandfather without finding him in any of his favourite places around the house. Then he looked out of the bedroom window and saw Grandfather reclining on a cane chair under the cherry tree.

'There's just the right amount of shade here,' said Grandfather. 'And I like looking at the leaves.'

'They're pretty leaves,' said Rakesh. 'And they are always ready to dance if there's a breeze.'

After Grandfather had come indoors, Rakesh went into the garden and lay down on the grass beneath the tree. He gazed up through the leaves at the great blue sky; and turning on his side, he could see the mountains striding away into the clouds. He was still lying beneath the tree when the evening shadows crept across the garden. Grandfather came back and sat down beside Rakesh, and they waited in silence until the stars came out and the nightjar began to call. In the forest below, the crickets and cicadas began tuning up; and suddenly the trees were full of the sound of insects.

'There are so many trees in the forest,' said Rakesh. 'What's so special about this tree? Why do we like it so much?'

'We planted it ourselves,' said Grandfather. 'That's why it's special.'

'Just one small seed,' said Rakesh, and he touched the smooth bark of the tree that he had grown. He ran his hand along the trunk of the tree and put his finger to the tip of a leaf. 'I wonder,' he whispered. 'Is this what it feels to be God?'

The Coral Tree

The night had been hot, the rain frequent, and I had been sleeping on the verandah instead of in the house. I was in my twenties, had begun to earn a living and felt I had certain responsibilities.

In a short time, a tonga would take me to the railway station, and from there a train would take me to Bombay, and then a ship would take me to England. There would be work, interviews, a job, a different kind of life, so many things that this small bungalow of my grandfather would be remembered fitfully, in rare moments of reflection.

When I awoke on the veranda, I saw a grey morning, smelt the rain on the red earth and remembered that I had to go away. A girl was standing on the veranda porch, looking at me very seriously. When I saw her, I sat up in bed with a start.

She was a small dark girl, her eyes big and black, her pigtails tied up in a bright red ribbon, and she was fresh and clean like the rain and the red earth.

She stood looking at me and was very serious.

'Hullo,' I said, smiling and trying to put her at ease. But the girl was business-like and acknowledged my greeting with a brief nod.

'Can I do anything for you?' I asked, stretching my limbs. 'Do you stay nearby?'

With great assurance she said, 'Yes, but I can stay on my own.'

'You're like me,' I said, and for a while, forgot about being an old man of twenty. 'I like to be on my own but I'm going away today.'

'Oh,' she said, a little breathlessly.

'Would you care to go to England?'

'I want to go everywhere,' she said. 'To America and Africa and Japan and Honolulu.'

'Maybe you will,' I said. 'I'm going everywhere, and no one can stop me… But what is it you want, what did you come for?'

'I want some flowers but I can't reach them.' She waved her hand towards the garden, 'That tree, see?'

The coral tree stood in front of the house surrounded by pools of water and broken, fallen blossoms. The branches of the tree were thick with scarlet, pea-shaped flowers.

'All right, just let me get ready.'

The tree was easy to climb and I made myself comfortable on one of the lower branches, smiling down at the serious upturned face of the girl.

'I'll throw them down to you,' I said.

I bent a branch but the wood was young and green and I had to twist it several times before it snapped.

'I'm not sure I ought to do this,' I said as I dropped the flowering branch to the girl.

'Don't worry,' she said.

I felt a sudden nostalgic longing for childhood and an urge to remain behind in my grandfather's house with its tangled memories and ghosts of yesteryear. But I was the only one left and what could I do except climb tamarind and jackfruit trees?

'Have you many friends?' I asked.

'Oh yes.'

'And who is the best?'

'The cook. He lets me stay in the kitchen which is more interesting than the house. And I like to watch him cooking. And he gives me things to eat and tells me stories...'

'And who is your second best friend?'

She inclined her head to one side and thought very hard.

'I'll make you second best,' she said.

I sprinkled coral blossoms on her head. 'That's very kind of you. I'm happy to be second best.'

A tonga bell sounded at the gate and I looked out from the tree and said, 'It's come for me. I have to go now.'

I climbed down.

'Will you help me with my suitcases?' I asked, as we walked together towards the veranda. 'There's no one here to help me. I am the last to go. Not because I want to go but because I have to.'

I sat down on the cot and packed a few last things in my suitcase. All the doors of the house were locked. On my way to the station, I would leave the keys with the caretaker. I had already given instructions to the agent to try and sell the house. There was nothing more to be done. We walked in silence to the waiting tonga, thinking and wondering about each other. The girl stood at the side of the path, on the damp earth, looking at me.

'Thank you,' I said, 'I hope I shall see you again.'

'I'll see you in London,' she said. 'Or America or Japan, I want to go everywhere.'

'I'm sure you will,' I said. 'And perhaps I'll come back and we'll meet again in this garden. That would be nice, wouldn't it?'

She nodded and smiled. We knew it was an important moment. The tonga driver spoke to his pony and the carriage set off down the gravel path, rattling a little. The girl and I waved to each other. In the girl's hand was a spring of coral blossom. As she waved, the blossoms fell apart and danced lightly in the breeze.

'Goodbye!' I called.

'Goodbye!' called the girl.

The ribbon had come loose from her pigtail and lay on the ground with the coral blossoms.

And she was fresh and clean like the rain and the red earth.

Death of the Trees

The peace and quiet of the Maplewood hillside disappeared forever one winter. The powers-that-be decided to build another new road into the mountains and the PWD saw fit to take it right past the cottage, about six feet from the window that overlooked the forest.

In my journal I wrote—Already they have felled most of the trees. The walnut was one of the first to go. A tree I had lived with for over ten years, watching it grow as I had watched Prem's small son Rakesh grow up, looking forward to its new leaf-buds, the broad green leaves or summer turning to spears of gold in September when the walnuts were ripe and ready to fall. I knew this tree better than the others. It was just below the window where a buttress for the road was going up.

Another tree I will miss is the young deodar, the only one growing in this stretch of the woods. Some years back it was stunted from lack of sunlight. The oaks covered it with their shaggy branches, so I cut away some of the overhanging ones and after that the deodar grew much faster. It was just coming into its own this year—now cut down in its prime like my young brother on the road to Delhi last month. Both victims of the roads—the tree killed by the PWD, my brother by a truck.

Twenty oaks have been felled just in this small stretch near the cottage. By the time this bypass reaches Jabai khet, about six miles from here, over a thousand oaks will have been slaughtered, besides many other fine trees—maples, deodars and pines—most of them unnecessarily as they grew some fifty or sixty yards from the roadside.

The trouble is, hardly anyone (with the exception of the contractor who buys the felled trees) really believes that trees and shrubs are necessary. They get in the way so much, don't they? According to my milkman, the only useful tree is the one that can be picked clean of its leaves for fodder! And a young man remarked to me, 'You should come to Pauri. The view is terrific, there's not a tree in the way!'

Well he can stay here now and enjoy the view of the ravaged hillside. But as the oaks have gone, the milkman will have to look further afield for his fodder.

Rakesh calls the maples butterfly trees because when the winged seeds fall, they flutter like butterflies in the breeze. No maples now. No bright red leaves to flame against the sky. No birds! That is to say, no birds near the house. No longer will it be possible for me to open the window and watch the scarlet minivets flitting through the dark green foliage of the oaks… the long-tailed magpies gliding through the trees, the barbet calling insistently from his perch on the top of the deodar. Forest birds, all of them, they will now be in search of some other stretch of surviving forest. The only visitors will be the crows who have learnt to live with and off humans and seem to multiply along with roads, houses and people. And even when all the people have gone, the crows will still be there.

Other things to look forward to—trucks thundering past in the night, perhaps a tea and pakora shop around the corner. The grinding of gears, the music of motor horns. Will the whistling thrush be heard above them? The explosions that continually shatter the silence of the mountains as thousand-year-old rocks are dynamited have frightened away all but the most intrepid of birds and animals. Even the bold langurs haven't shown their faces for over a fortnight.

Somehow, I don't think we shall wait for the tea shop to arrive. There must be some other quiet corner, possibly on the next mountain where new roads have yet to come into being. No doubt this is a negative attitude and if I had any sense I'd open my own tea shop. To retreat is to be a loser. But the trees are losers too and when they fall, they do so with a certain dignity.

Never mind. Men come and go, the mountains remain.

Wild Fruit

It was a long walk to school. Down the hill, through the rhododendron trees, across a small stream, around a bare, brown hill, and then through the narrow little bazaar, past fruit stalls piled high with oranges, guavas, bananas, and apples.

The boy's gaze often lingered on those heaps of golden oranges—oranges grown in the plains, now challenging the pale winter sunshine in the hills. His nose twitched at the sharp smell of melons in summer; his fingers would sometimes touch for a moment the soft down on the skin of a peach. But these were forbidden fruit. The boy hadn't the money for them.

He took one meal at seven in the morning when he left home; another at seven in the evening when he returned from school. There were times—especially when he was at school, and his teacher droned on and on, lecturing on honesty, courage, duty, and self-sacrifice—when he felt very hungry; but on the way to school, or on the way home, there was nearly always the prospect of some wild fruit.

The boy's name was Vijay, and he belonged to a village near Mussoorie. His parents tilled a few narrow terraces on the hill slopes. They grew potatoes, onions, barley, maize; barely enough to feed themselves. When greens were scarce, they boiled the tops of the stinging-nettle and made them into a dish resembling spinach.

Vijay's parents realized the importance of sending him to school, and it didn't cost them much, except for the books. But it was all of four miles to the town, and a long walk makes a boy hungry.

But there was nearly always the wild fruit. The purple berries of the thorny bilberry bushes, ripening in May and June. Wild strawberries, growing in shady places like spots of blood on the deep green monsoon grass. Small, sour cherries, and tough medlars. Vijay's strong teeth and probing tongue extracted whatever tang or sweetness lay hidden in them. And in March there were the rhododendron flowers.

His mother made them into jam. But Vijay liked them as they were. He placed the petals on his tongue and chewed them till the sweet juice trickled down his throat. But in November, there was no wild fruit. Only acorns on the oak trees, and they were bitter, fit only for the monkeys.

He walked confidently through the bazaar, strong in the legs. He looked a healthy boy, until you came up close and saw the patches on his skin and the dullness in his eyes.

He passed the fruit stalls, wondering who ate all that fruit, and what happened to the fruit that went bad; he passed the sweet shop, where hot, newly-fried *jelabies* lay protected like twisted orange jewels in a glass case, and where a fat, oily man raised a knife and plunged it deep into a thick slab of rich amber-coloured *halwa*.

The saliva built up in Vijay's mouth; there was a dull ache in his stomach. But his eyes gave away nothing of the sharp pangs he felt.

And now, a confectioner's shop. Glass jars filled with chocolates, peppermints, toffees—sweets he didn't know the names of, English sweets—wrapped up in bits of coloured paper.

A boy had just bought a bag of sweets. He had one in his mouth. He was a well-dressed boy; coins jingled in his pocket. The sweet moved from one cheek to the other. He bit deep into it, and Vijay heard the crunch and looked up. The boy smiled at Vijay, but moved away.

They met again, further along the road. Once again the boy smiled, even looked as though he was about to offer Vijay a sweet; but this time, Vijay shyly looked away. He did not want it to appear that he had noticed the sweets, or that he hungered for one.

But he kept meeting the boy, who always managed to reappear at some corner, sucking a sweet, moving it about in his mouth, letting it show between his wet lips—a sticky green thing, temptingly, lusciously beautiful.

The bag of sweets was nearly empty.

Reluctantly, Vijay decided that he must overtake the boy, forget all about the sweets, and hurry home. Otherwise, he would be tempted to grab the bag and run!

And then, he saw the boy leave the bag on a bench, look at him once, and smile—smile shyly and invitingly—before moving away.

Was the bag empty? Vijay wondered with mounting excitement. It couldn't be, or it would have blown away almost immediately. Obviously, there were still a few sweets in it. The boy had disappeared. He had gone for his tea, and Vijay could have the rest of the sweets.

Vijay took the bag and jammed it into a pocket of his shirt. Then he hurried homewards. It was getting late, and he wanted to be home before dark.

As soon as he was out of the town, he opened the bag and shook the sweets out. Their red wrappers glowed like rubies in the palm of his hand.

Carefully, he undid a wrapper.

There was no sweet inside, only a smooth, round stone.

Vijay found stones in all the wrappers. In his mind's eye,

Vijay saw the smiling face of the boy in the bazaar: a boy who smiled sweetly but exchanged stones for sweets.

Forcing back angry tears, Vijay flung the stones down the hillside. Then he shouldered his bag of books and began the long walk home.

There were patches of snow on the ground. The grass was a dirty brown, the bushes were bare.

There is no wild fruit in November.

The Trees Are My Brothers

It's good to know that my old friend the jackfruit is finally coming into its own. Apparently it is now much in demand in the West, a fashionable substitute for meat, being used as filling for burgers, sandwiches, pies etc., with one enthusiast even calling it 'mutton hanging from a tree'.

Here in India we have always appreciated a good jackfruit curry, or even better, a jackfruit pickle. I'm a pickle friend myself, and among the twenty different pickles on my sideboard there is always a jar of jackfruit piddle; that's why I call it an old friend. But I had no idea it tasted like mutton. The seed and the pulp have their own individual flavor. As it grows on a tree we call it a fruit, but we cook it as though it were a vegetable. And it, to some, tastes like mutton, then perhaps some meat-eaters will become vegetarians. On the other hand, some vegetarians might not care for its meaty flavour!

When I was a boy, we had an old jackfruit tree growing beside the side verandah. I spent a lot of time in the trees surrounding my grandmother's bungalow, and this one was easy to climb. The others included several guava and litchi trees, lemons and grapefruits, and of course a couple of mango trees—but these last were difficult to climb.

'Why do you spend so much time in the trees?' complained my grandmother. 'Why not do something useful for a change?'

'The trees are my brothers,' I would say, 'I like to play with them.'

And I still think of them as my brothers, although I can no longer climb trees or play in them. But I still think of them as human beings possessed of individuality and charm. Just as no two humans are exactly alike (unless they happen to be twins), so no two trees are the same. Like humans they grow from seed. They develop branches as arms and leaves like flowing hair. We give birth to children, they give birth to fruits and flowers. We shelter our young, they shelter the small creatures of the forest.

However, unlike us they spring from the soul, from the land—that very land that gives us food and pasture and protection; the land that we so casually take for granted, preferring to build upon it rather than grow upon it. Where will our cattle graze when the last green spaces have gone?

'No problem,' says a young friend. 'We can always import our milk.'

The other day I came across an old book that had been on my shelf for many years. *Farmer's Glory* by A.G. Street, written several decades ago. In his epilogue he writes:

> It is perhaps nothing to boast about, but there is little doubt that the present prosperity of British farming is mainly due to one man, who is now dead. His name was Adolf Hitler. There is no disputing that it was the fear of famine during the early 1940s which taught the British nation that despite all man's cleverness and inventions, when real danger comes an island people must turn for succour to the only permanent asset they possess, the land of their own country. It has never, and will never, let them down; always provided they realize and obey this eternal truth—that to make the land serve man, man must first be content to serve the land.

Surely it is this love of the land and willingness to serve it that is at the heart of true patriotism. The patriotic songs and speeches that we hear from time to time are fine for stirring up the emotions, but it is really the connect between ourselves and the '*do bigha zameen*' on which we grow our fruit and grain that emboldens us to protect it.

I think I am correct in saying that most of our jawans, the young men who join the solid ranks of the Indian Army, come from rural backgrounds; some from the hills, some from the vast plains and hinterland of our country. They know the value of the land. They have grown up in villages and have worked with their families in the rice fields, or sugarcane plantations, or mango-groves, or wheat or corn or mustard or fields of an infinite variety of crops. More than city folk, they know the value of the land—its true worth in terms of either prosperity or poverty. And so they are ready to defend it, to fight for it against all corners. The best soldiers come from the soil that they and their forefathers have tilled.

So let us protect the land—not just from the intruder or the enemy, but also from those who would turn the field or the forest into one more concrete jungle.

Of course there are those who prefer concrete jungles. Like my young friend who wants to live in a Smart City and never mind the cities that are no longer smart. My advice to him (unheeded of course) is to go back to his roots, create a smart little village, and plant jackfruit trees!

Sounds I Like to Hear

All night the rain has been drumming on the corrugated tin roof. There has been no storm, no thunder, just the steady swish of a tropical downpour. It helps one to lie awake; at the same time, it doesn't keep one from sleeping.

It is a good sound to read by the rain outside, the quiet within—and, although tin roofs are given to springing unaccountable leaks, there is in general a feeling of being untouched by, and yet in touch with, the rain.

Gentle rain on a tin roof is one of my favourite sounds. And early in the morning, when the rain has stopped, there are other sounds I like to hear—a crow shaking the raindrops from his feathers and cawing rather disconsolately; babblers and bulbuls bustling in and out of bushes and long grass in search of worms and insects; the sweet, ascending trill of the Himalayan whistling-thrush; dogs rushing through damp undergrowth.

A cherry tree, bowed down by the heavy rain, suddenly rights itself, flinging pellets of water in my face.

Some of the best sounds are made by water. The water of a mountain stream, always in a hurry, bubbling over rocks and chattering, 'I'm late, I'm late!' like the White Rabbit, tumbling over itself in its anxiety to reach the bottom of the hill, the sound of the sea, especially when it is far away—or when you hear it by putting a sea shell to your ear. The sound made by dry and thirsty earth, as it sucks at a sprinkling of water. Or the sound of a child drinking thirstily the water running down his chin and throat.

Water gushing out of the pans of an old well outside a village while a camel moves silently round the well. Bullock-cart wheels creaking over rough country roads. The clip-clop of a pony carriage, and the tinkle of its bell, and the singsong call of its driver...

Bells in the hills. A schoolbell ringing, and children's voices drifting through an open window. A temple-bell, heard faintly from across the valley. Heavy silver ankle-bells on the feet of sturdy hill women. Sheep bells heard high up on the mountainside.

Do falling petals make a sound? Just the tiniest and softest of sounds, like the drift of falling snow. Of course big flowers, like dahlias, drop their petals with a very definite flop. These are showoffs, like the hawk-moth who comes flapping into the rooms at night instead of emulating the butterfly dipping lazily on the afternoon breeze.

One must return to the birds for favourite sounds, and the birds of the plains differ from the birds of the hills. On a cold winter morning in the plains of northern India, if you walk some way into the jungle you will hear the familiar call of the black partridge: *Bhagwan teri giedrat* it seems to cry, which means: 'Oh God! Great is thy might.'

The cry rises from the bushes in all directions; but an hour later not a bird is to be seen or heard and the jungle is so very still that the silence seems to shout at you.

There are sounds that come from a distance, beautiful because they are far away, voices on the wind—they 'walketh upon the wings of the wind'. The cries of fishermen out on the river. Drums beating rhythmically in a distant village. The croaking of frogs from the rainwater pond behind the house. I mean frogs at a distance. A frog croaking beneath one's window is as welcome as a motor horn.

But some people like motor horns. I know a taxi-driver who never misses an opportunity to use his horn. It was made to his own specifications, and it gives out a resonant bugle-call. He never tires of using it. Cyclists and pedestrians always scatter at his approach. Other cars veer off the road. He is proud of his horn. He loves its strident sound, which only goes to show that some men's sounds are other men's noises!

Homely sounds, though we don't often think about them, are the ones we miss most when they are gone. A kettle on the boil. A door that creaks on its hinges. Old sofa springs. Familiar voices lighting up the dark. Ducks quacking in the rain.

And so we return to the rain, with which my favourite sounds began.

I have sat out in the open at night, after a shower of rain when the whole air is murmuring and tinkling with the voices of crickets and grasshoppers and little frogs. There is one melodious sound, a sweet repeated trill, which I have never been able to trace to its source. Perhaps it is a little tree frog. Or it may be a small green cricket. I shall never know.

I am not sure that I really want to know. In an age when a scientific and rational explanation has been given for almost everything we see and touch and hear, it is good to be left with one small mystery, a mystery sweet and satisfying and entirely my own.

Listen!

Listen to the night wind in the trees,
Listen to the summer grass singing;
Listen to the time that's tripping by,

And the dawn dew falling.
Listen to the moon as it climbs the sky,
Listen to the pebbles humming;
Listen to the mist in the trembling leaves,
And the silence calling.

The Crooked Tree

You must pass your exams and go to college, but do not feel that if you fail, you will be able to do nothing.

My room in Shahganj was very small. I had paced about in it so often that I knew its exact measurements: twelve feet by ten. The string of my cot needed tightening. The dip in the middle was so pronounced that I invariably woke up in the morning with a backache; but I was hopeless at tightening charpoy strings.

Under the cot was my tin trunk. Its contents ranged from old, rejected manuscripts to clothes and letters and photographs. I had resolved that one day, when I had made some money with a book, I would throw the trunk and everything else out of the window, and leave Shahganj forever. But until then I was a prisoner. The rent was nominal, the window had a view of the bus stop and rickshaw stand, and I had nowhere else to go.

I did not live entirely alone. Sometimes a beggar spent the night on the balcony; and, during cold or wet weather, the boys from the tea shop, who normally slept on the pavement, crowded into the room.

Usually I woke early in the mornings, as sleep was fitful, uneasy, crowded with dreams. I knew it was five o'clock when I heard the first upcountry bus leaving its shed. I would then get up and take a walk in the fields beyond the railroad tracks.

One morning, while I was walking in the fields, I noticed someone lying across the pathway, his head and shoulders hidden by the stalks of young sugar cane. When I came near, I saw he was a boy of about sixteen. His body was twitching convulsively, his face was very white, except where a little blood had trickled down his chin. His legs kept moving and his hands fluttered restlessly, helplessly.

'What's the matter with you?' I asked, kneeling down beside him.

But he was still unconscious and could not answer me.

I ran down the footpath to a well and, dipping the end of my shirt in a shallow trough of water, ran back and sponged the boy's face. The twitching ceased and, though he still breathed heavily, his hands became still and his face calm. He opened his eyes and stared at me without any immediate comprehension.

'You have bitten your tongue,' I said, wiping the blood from his mouth. 'Don't worry. I'll stay with you until you feel better.'

He sat up now and said, 'I'm all right, thank you.'

'What happened?' I asked, sitting down beside him.

'Oh, nothing much. It often happens, I don't know why. But I cannot control it.'

'Have you seen a doctor?'

'I went to the hospital in the beginning. They gave me some pills, which I had to take every day. But the pills made me so tired and sleepy that I couldn't work properly. So I stopped taking them. Now this happens once or twice a month. But what does it matter? I'm all right when it's over, and I don't feel anything while it is happening.'

He got to his feet, dusting his clothes and smiling at me. He was slim, long-limbed and bony. There was a little fluff on his cheeks and the promise of a moustache.

'Where do you live?' I asked. 'I'll walk back with you.'

'I don't live anywhere,' he said. 'Sometimes I sleep in the temple, sometimes in the gurdwara. In summer months I sleep in the municipal gardens.'

'Well, then let me come with you as far as the gardens.'

He told me that his name was Kamal, that he studied at the Shahganj High School, and that he hoped to pass his examinations in a few months' time. He was studying hard and, if he passed with a good division, he hoped to attend a college. If he failed, there was only the prospect of continuing to live in the municipal gardens…

He carried with him a small tray of merchandise, supported by straps that went round his shoulders. In it were combs and buttons and cheap toys and little vials of perfume. All day he walked about Shahganj, selling odds and ends to people in the bazaar or at their houses. He made, on an average, two rupees a day, which was enough for his food and his school fees.

He told me all this while we walked back to the bus stand. I returned to my room, to try and write something, while Kamal went on to the bazaar to try and sell his wares.

There was nothing very unusual about Kamal's being an orphan and a refugee. During the communal holocaust of 1947, thousands of homes had been broken up, and women and children had been killed. What was unusual in Kamal was his sensitivity, a quality I thought rare in a Punjabi youth who had grown up in the Frontier Provinces during a period of hate and violence. And it was not so much his positive attitude to life that appealed to me (most people in Shahganj were completely resigned to their lot) as his gentleness, his quiet voice and the smile that flickered across his face regardless of whether he was sad or happy. In the morning, when I opened my door, I found Kamal asleep at the top of the steps. His tray lay a few feet away. I shook him gently, and he woke at once.

'Have you been sleeping here all night?' I asked. 'Why didn't you come inside?'

'It was very late,' he said. 'I didn't want to disturb you.'

'Someone could have stolen your things while you slept.'

'Oh, I sleep quite lightly. Besides, I have nothing of special value. But I came to ask you something.'

'Do you need any money?'

'No. I want you to take your meal with me tonight.'

'But where? You don't have a place of your own. It will be too expensive in a restaurant.'

'In your room,' said Kamal. 'I will bring the food and cook it here. You have a stove?'

'I think so,' I said. 'I will have to look for it.'

'I will come at seven,' said Kamal, strapping on his tray. 'Don't worry. I know how to cook!'

He ran down the steps and made for the bazaar. I began to look for the oil stove, found it at the bottom of my tin trunk, and then discovered I hadn't any pots or pans or dishes. Finally, I borrowed these from Deep Chand, the barber.

Kamal brought a chicken for our dinner. This was a costly luxury in Shahganj, to be taken only two or three times a year. He had bought the bird for three rupees, which was cheap, considering it was not too skinny. While Kamal set about roasting it, I went down to the bazaar and procured a bottle of beer on credit, and this served as an appetizer.

'We are having an expensive meal,' I observed. 'Three rupees for the chicken and three rupees for the beer. But I wish we could do it more often.'

'We should do it at least once a month,' said Kamal. 'It should be possible if we work hard.'

'You know how to work. You work from morning to night.'

'But you are a writer, Rusty. That is different. You have to wait for a mood.'

'Oh, I'm not a genius that I can afford the luxury of moods. No, I'm just lazy, that's all.'

'Perhaps you are writing the wrong things.'

'I know I am. But I don't know how I can write anything else.'

'Have you tried?'

'Yes, but there is no money in it. I wish I could make a living in some other way. Even if I repaired cycles, I would make more money.'

'Then why not repair cycles?'

'No, I will not repair cycles. I would rather be a bad writer than a good repairer of cycles. But let us not think of work. There is time enough for work. I want to know more about you.'

Kamal did not know if his parents were alive or dead. He had lost them, literally, when he was six. It happened at the Amritsar railroad station, where trains coming across the border disgorged thousands of refugees, or pulled into the station half empty, drenched with blood and littered with corpses.

Kamal and his parents were lucky to escape the massacre. Had they travelled on an earlier train (they had tried desperately to get into one), they might well have been killed; but circumstances favoured them then, only to trick them later.

Kamal was clinging to his mother's sari, while she remained close to her husband, who was elbowing his way through the frightened, bewildered throng of refugees. Glancing over his shoulder at a woman who lay on the ground, wailing and beating her breasts, Kamal collided with a burly Sikh and lost his grip on his mother's sari.

The Sikh had a long curved sword at his waist; and Kamal stared up at him in awe and fascination—at his long hair, which had fallen loose, and his wild black beard, and the bloodstains on his white shirt. The Sikh pushed him out of the way and when Kamal looked around for his mother, she was not to be seen. She was hidden from him by a mass of restless bodies, pushed in different directions. He could hear her calling, 'Kamal, where are you, Kamal?' He tried to force his way through the crowd, in the direction of the voice, but he was carried the other way…

At night, when the platform was empty, he was still searching for his mother. Eventually, some soldiers took him away. They looked for his parents, but without success, and finally, they sent Kamal to a refugee camp. From there he went to an orphanage. But when he was eight, and felt himself a man, he ran away.

He worked for some time as a helper in a tea shop; but, when he started getting epileptic fits, the shopkeeper asked him to leave, and he found himself on the streets, begging for a living. He begged for a year, moving from one town to another, and ended up finally at Shahganj. By then he was twelve and too old to beg; but he had saved some money, and with it he bought a small stock of combs, buttons, cheap perfumes and bangles; and, converting himself into a mobile shop, went from door to door, selling his wares.

Shahganj was a small town, and there was no house which Kamal hadn't visited. Everyone recognized him, and there were some who offered him food and drink; the children knew him well, because he played a small flute whenever he made his rounds, and they followed him to listen to the flute.

I began to look forward to Kamal's presence. He dispelled some of my own loneliness. I found I could work better, knowing that I did not have to work alone. And Kamal came to me, perhaps because I was the first person to have taken a personal interest in his life, and because I saw nothing frightening in his sickness. Most people in Shahganj thought epilepsy was infectious; some considered it a form of divine punishment for sins committed in a former life. Except for children, those who knew of his condition generally gave him a wide berth.

At sixteen, a boy grows like young wheat, springing up so fast that he is unaware of what is taking place within him. His mind quickens, his gestures become more confident. Hair sprouts like young grass on his face and chest, and his muscles begin to mature. Never again will he experience so much change and growth in so short a time. He is full of currents and countercurrents.

Kamal combined the bloom of youth with the beauty of the short-lived. It made me sad even to look at his pale, slim body. It hurt me to look into his eyes. Life and death were always struggling in their depths.

'Should I go to Delhi and take up a job?' I asked.

'Why not? You are always talking about it.'

'Why don't you come, too? Perhaps they can stop your fits.'

'We will need money for that. When I have passed my examinations, I will come.'

'Then I will wait,' I said. I was twenty-two, and there was world enough and time for everything.

We decided to save a little money from his small earnings and my occasional payments. We would need money to go to Delhi, money to live there until we could earn a living. We put away twenty rupees one week, but lost it the next when we lent it to a friend who owned a cycle rickshaw. But this gave us the occasional use of his cycle rickshaw, and early one morning, with Kamal sitting on the crossbar, I rode out of Shahganj.

After cycling for about two miles, we got down and pushed the cycle off the road, taking a path through a paddy field and then through a field of young maize, until in the distance we saw a tree, a crooked tree, growing beside an old well.

I do not know the name of that tree. I had never seen one like it before. It had a crooked trunk and crooked branches, and was clothed in thick, broad, crooked leaves, like the leaves on which food is served in the bazaar.

In the trunk of the tree there was a hole, and when we set the bicycle down with a crash, a pair of green parrots flew out, and went dipping and swerving across the fields. There was grass around the well, cropped short by grazing cattle.

We sat in the shade of the crooked tree, and Kamal untied the red cloth in which he had brought our food. When we had eaten, we stretched ourselves out on the grass. I closed my eyes and became aware of a score of different sensations. I heard a cricket singing in the tree, the cooing of pigeons from the walls of the old well, the quiet breathing of Kamal, the parrots returning to the tree, the distant hum of an airplane. I smelled the grass and the old bricks round the well and the promise of rain. I felt Kamal's fingers against my arm, and the sun creeping over my cheek. And when I opened my eyes, there were clouds on the horizon, and Kamal was asleep, his arm thrown across his face to keep out the glare.

I went to the well, and putting my shoulders to the ancient handle, turned the wheel, moving it around while cool, clean water gushed out over the stones and along the channel to the fields. The discovery that I could water a field, that I had the power to make things grow, gave me a thrill of satisfaction; it was like writing a story that had the ring of truth. I drank from one of the trays; the water was sweet with age.

Kamal was sitting up, looking at the sky.

'It's going to rain,' he said.

We began cycling homeward; but we were still some way out of Shahganj when it began to rain. A lashing wind swept the rain across our faces, but we exulted in it, and sang at the top of our voices until we reached the Shahganj bus stop.

Across the railroad tracks and the dry riverbed, fields of maize stretched away, until there came a dry region of thorn bushes and lantana scrub, where the earth was cut into jagged cracks, like a jigsaw puzzle. Dotting the landscape were old, abandoned brick kilns. When it rained heavily, the hollows filled up with water.

Kamal and I came to one of these hollows to bathe and swim. There was an island in the middle of it, and on this small mound lay the ruins of a hut where a nightwatchman had once lived, looking after the brick kilns. We would swim out to the island, which was only a few yards from the banks of the hollow. There was a grassy patch in front of the hut, and early in the mornings, before it got too hot, we would wrestle on the grass.

Though I was heavier than Kamal, my chest as sound as a new drum, he had strong, wiry arms and legs, and would often pinion me around the waist with his bony knees. Now, while we wrestled on the new monsoon grass, I felt his body go tense. He stiffened, his legs jerked against my body, and a shudder passed through him. I knew that he had a fit coming on, but I was unable to extricate myself from his arms.

He gripped me more tightly as the fit took possession of him. Instead of struggling, I lay still, tried to absorb some of his anguish, tried to draw some of his agitation to myself. I had a strange fancy that by identifying myself with his convulsions, I might alleviate them.

I pressed against Kamal, and whispered soothingly into his ear; and then, when I noticed his mouth working, I thrust my fingers between his teeth to prevent him from biting his tongue. But so violent was the convulsion that his teeth bit into the flesh of my palm and ground against my knuckles.

I shouted with the pain and tried to jerk my hand away, but it was impossible to loosen the grip of his jaws. So I closed my eyes and counted—counted till seven—until consciousness returned to him and his muscles relaxed.

My hand was shaking and covered with blood. I bound it in my handkerchief and kept it hidden from Kamal.

We walked back to the room without talking much. Kamal looked depressed and weak. I kept my hand beneath my shirt, and Kamal was too dejected to notice anything. It was only at night, when he returned from his classes, that he noticed the cuts, and I told him I had slipped in the road, cutting my hand on some broken glass.

Rain upon Shahganj. And, until the rain stops, Shahganj is fresh and clean and alive. The children run out of their houses, glorying in their nakedness. The gutters choke, and the narrow street becomes a torrent of water, coursing merrily down to the bus stop. It swirls over the trees and the roofs of the town, and the parched earth soaks it up, exuding a fragrance that comes only once in a year, the fragrance of quenched earth, that most exhilarating of smells.

The rain swept in through the door and soaked the cot. When I had succeeded in closing the door, I found the roof leaking, the water trickling down the walls and forming new pictures on the cracking plaster. The door flew open again, and there was Kamal standing on the threshold, shaking himself like a wet dog. Coming in, he stripped and dried himself, and then sat shivering on the bed while I made frantic efforts to close the door again.

'You need some tea,' I said.

He nodded, forgetting to smile for once, and I knew his mind was elsewhere, in one of a hundred possible places from his dreams.

'One day I will write a book,' I said, as we drank strong tea in the fast-fading twilight. 'A real book, about real people. Perhaps it will be about you and me and Shahganj. And then we will run away from Shahganj, fly on the wings of Garuda, and all our troubles will be over and fresh troubles will begin. Why should we mind difficulties, as long as they are new difficulties?'

'First I must pass my exams,' said Kamal. 'Otherwise, I can do nothing, go nowhere.'

'Don't take exams too seriously. I know that in India they are the passport to any kind of job, and that you cannot become a clerk unless you have a degree. But do not forget that you are studying for the sake of acquiring knowledge, and not for the sake of becoming a clerk. You don't want to become a clerk or a bus conductor, do you? You must pass your exams and go to college, but do not feel that if you fail, you will be able to do nothing. Why, you can start making your own buttons instead of selling other people's!'

'You are right,' said Kamal. 'But why not be an educated button manufacturer?'

'Why not, indeed? That's just what I mean. And, while you are studying for your exams, I will be writing my book. I will start tonight! It is an auspicious night, the beginning of the monsoon.'

The light did not come on. A tree must have fallen across the wires. I lit a candle and placed it on the windowsill and, while the candle spluttered in the steamy air, Kamal opened his books and, with one hand on a book and the other hand playing with his toes—this attitude helped him to concentrate—he devoted his attention to algebra.

I took an ink bottle down from a shelf and, finding it empty, added a little rainwater to the crusted contents. Then I sat down beside Kamal and began to write; but the pen was useless and made blotches all over the paper, and I had no idea what I should write about, though I was full of writing just then. So I began to look at Kamal instead; at his eyes, hidden in shadow, and his hands, quiet in the candlelight; and I followed his breathing and the slight movement of his lips as he read softly to himself.

And, instead of starting my book, I sat and watched Kamal.

Sometimes Kamal played the flute at night, while I was lying awake; and, even when I was asleep, the flute would play in my dreams. Sometimes he brought it to the crooked tree, and played it for the benefit of the birds; but the parrots only made harsh noises and flew away.

Once, when Kamal was playing his flute to a group of children, he had a fit. The flute fell from his hands, and he began to roll about in the dust on the roadside. The children were frightened and ran away. But the next time they heard Kamal play his flute, they came to listen as usual.

That Kamal was gaining in strength I knew from the way he was able to pin me down whenever we wrestled on the grass near the old brick kilns. It was no longer necessary for me to yield deliberately to him. And, though his fits still recurred from time to time—as we knew they would continue to do—he was not so depressed afterwards. The anxiety and the death had gone from his eyes.

His examinations were nearing, and he was working hard. (I had yet to begin the first chapter of my book.) Because of the necessity of selling two or three rupees' worth of articles every day, he did not get much time for studying; but he stuck to his books until past midnight, and it was seldom that I heard his flute.

He put aside his tray of odds and ends during the examinations, and walked to the examination centre instead. And after two weeks, when it was all over, he took up his tray and began his rounds again. In a burst of creativity, I wrote three pages of my novel.

On the morning the results of the examination were due, I rose early, before Kamal, and went down to the news agency. It was five o'clock and the newspapers had just arrived. I went through the columns relating to Shahganj, but I couldn't find Kamal's roll number on the list of successful candidates. I had the number written down on a slip of paper, and I looked at it again to make sure that I had compared it correctly with the others; then I went through the newspaper once more.

When I returned to the room, Kamal was sitting on the doorstep. I didn't have to tell him he had failed. He knew by the look on my face. I sat down beside him, and we said nothing for some time.

'Never mind,' said Kamal, eventually. 'I will pass next year.'

I realized that I was more depressed than he was, and that he was trying to console me.

'If only you'd had more time,' I said.

'I have plenty of time now. Another year. And you will have time in which to finish your book; then we can both go away. Another year of Shahganj won't be so bad. As long as I have your friendship, almost everything else can be tolerated, even my sickness.'

And then, turning to me with an expression of intense happiness, he said, 'Yesterday I was sad, and tomorrow I may be sad again, but today I know that I am happy. I want to live on and on. I feel that life isn't long enough to satisfy me.'

He stood up, the tray hanging from his shoulders.

'What would you like to buy?' he said. 'I have everything you need.'

At the bottom of the steps he turned and smiled at me, and I knew then that I had written my story.

My Father's Trees in Dehra

Our trees still grow in Dehra. This is one part of the world where trees are a match for man. An old peepul may be cut down to make way for a new building; two peepul trees will sprout from the walls of the building. In Dehra the air is moist, the soil hospitable to seeds and probing roots. The valley of Dehra Dun lies between the first range of the Himalayas and the smaller but older Siwalik range. Dehra is an old town, but it was not in the reign of Rajput princes or Mughal kings that it really grew and flourished; it acquired a certain size and importancc with the coming of British and Anglo-Indian settlers. The English have an affinity with trees, and in the rolling hills of Dehra they discovered a retreat which, in spite of snakes and mosquitoes, reminded them, just a little bit, of England's green and pleasant land.

The mountains to the north are austere and inhospitable; the plains to the south are flat, dry and dusty. But Dehra is green. I look out of the train window at daybreak to see the sal and shisham trees sweep by majestically, while trailing vines and great clumps of bamboo give the forest a darkness and density which add to its mystery. There are still a few tigers in these forests; only a few, and perhaps they will survive, to stalk the spotted deer and drink at forest pools.

I grew up in Dehra. My grandfather built a bungalow on the outskirts of the town at the turn of the century. The house was sold a few years after independence. No one knows me now in Dehra, for it is over twenty years since I left the place, and my boyhood friends are scattered and lost. And although the India of Kim is no more, and the Grand Trunk Road is now a procession of trucks instead of a slow-moving caravan of horses and camels, India is still a country in which people are easily lost and quickly forgotten.

From the station I can take either a taxi or a snappy little scooter rickshaw (Dehra had neither before 1950), but, because I am on an unashamedly sentimental pilgrimage, I take a tonga, drawn by a lean, listless pony, and driven by a tubercular old Muslim in a shabby green waistcoat. Only two or three tongas stand outside the station. There were always twenty or thirty here in the 1940s when I came home from boarding school to be met at the station by my grandfather; but the days of the tonga are nearly over, and in many ways this is a good thing, because most tonga ponies are overworked and underfed. Its wheels squeaking from lack of oil and its seat slipping out from under me, the tonga drags me through the bazaars of Dehra. A couple of miles at this slow, funereal pace makes me impatient to use my own legs, and I dismiss the tonga when we get to the small Dilaram Bazaar.

It is a good place from which to start walking.

The Dilaram Bazaar has not changed very much. The shops are run by a new generation of bakers, barbers and banias, but professions have not changed. The cobblers belong to the lower castes, the bakers are Muslims, the tailors are Sikhs. Boys still fly kites from the flat rooftops, and women wash clothes on the canal steps. The canal comes down from Rajpur and goes underground here, to emerge about a mile away.

I have to walk only a furlong to reach my grandfather's house. The road is lined with eucalyptus, jacaranda and laburnum trees.

In the compounds there are small groves of mangoes, litchis and papayas. The poinsettia thrusts its scarlet leaves over garden walls. Every veranda has its bougainvillaea creeper, every garden its bed of marigolds. Potted palms, those symbols of Victorian snobbery, are popular with Indian housewives. There are a few houses, but most of the bungalows were built by 'old India hands' on their retirement from the army, the police or the railways. Most of the present owners are Indian businessmen or government officials.

I am standing outside my grandfather's house. The wall has been raised, and the wicket gate has disappeared; I cannot get a clear view of the house and garden. The nameplate identifies the owner as Major General Saigal; the house has had more than one owner since my grandparents sold it in 1949.

On the other side of the road there is an orchard of litchi trees. This is not the season for fruit, and there is no one looking after the garden. By taking a little path that goes through the orchard, I reach higher ground and gain a better view of our old house.

Grandfather built the house with granite rocks taken from the foothills. It shows no sign of age. The lawn has disappeared; but the big jackfruit tree, giving shade to the side veranda, is still there. In this tree I spent my afternoons, absorbed in my Magnets, Champions and Hotspurs, while sticky mango juice trickled down my chin. (One could not eat the jackfruit unless it was cooked into a vegetable curry.) There was a hole in the bole of the tree in which I kept my pocketknife, top, catapult and any badges or buttons that could be saved from my father's RAF tunics when he came home on leave. There was also an Iron Cross, a relic of the First World War, given to me by my grandfather. I have managed to keep the Iron Cross; but what did I do with my top and catapult? Memory fails me. Possibly they are still in the hole in the jackfruit tree; I must have forgotten to collect them when we went away after my father's death. I am seized by a whimsical urge to walk in at the gate, climb into the branches of the jackfruit tree, and recover my lost possessions. What would the present owner, the major general (retired), have to say if I politely asked permission to look for a catapult left behind more than twenty years ago?

An old man is coming down the path through the litchi trees. He is not a major general but a poor street vendor. He carries a small tin trunk on his head, and walks very slowly. When he sees me he stops and asks me if I will buy something. I can think of nothing I need, but the old man looks so tired, so very old, that I am afraid he will collapse if he moves any further along the path without resting. So I ask him to show me his wares. He cannot get the box off his head by himself, but together we manage to set it down in the shade, and the old man insists on spreading its entire contents on the grass; bangles, combs, shoelaces, safety pins, cheap stationery, buttons, pomades, elastic and scores of other household necessities.

When I refuse buttons because there is no one to sew them on for me, he piles me with safety pins. I say no; but as he moves from one article to another, his querulous, persuasive voice slowly wears down my resistance, and I end up by buying envelopes, a letter pad (pink roses on bright blue paper), a one-rupee fountain pen guaranteed to leak and several yards of elastic. I have no idea what I will do with the elastic, but the old man convinces me that I cannot live without it.

Exhausted by the effort of selling me a lot of things I obviously do not want, he closes his eyes and leans back against the trunk of a litchi tree. For a moment I feel rather nervous. Is he going to die sitting here beside me? He sinks to his haunches and puts his chin on his hands. He only wants to talk.

'I am very tired, huzoor,' he says. 'Please do not mind if I sit here for a while.'

'Rest for as long as you like,' I say. 'That's a heavy load you've been carrying.'

He comes to life at the chance of a conversation and says, 'When I was a young man, it was nothing. I could carry my box up from Rajpur to Mussoorie by the bridle path—seven steep miles! But now I find it difficult to cover the distance from the station to the Dilaram Bazaar.'

'Naturally. You are quite old.'

'I am seventy, sahib.'

'You look very fit for your age.' I say this to please him; he looks frail and brittle. 'Isn't there someone to help you?' I ask.

'I had a servant boy last month, but he stole my earnings and ran off to Delhi. I wish my son were alive—he would not have permitted me to work like a mule for a living—but he was killed in the riots in '47.'

'Have you no other relatives?'

'I have outlived them all. That is the curse of a healthy life. Your friends, your loved ones, all go before you, and at the end you are left alone. But I must go too, before long. The road to the bazaar seems to grow longer every day. The stones are harder. The sun is hotter in the summer, and the wind much colder in the winter. Even some of the trees that were there in my youth have grown old and have died. I have outlived the trees.'

He has outlived the trees. He is like an old tree himself, gnarled and twisted. I have the feeling that if he falls asleep in the orchard, he will strike root here, sending out crooked branches. I can imagine a small bent tree wearing a black waistcoat; a living scarecrow.

He closes his eyes again, but goes on talking.

'The English memsahibs would buy great quantities of

elastic. Today it is ribbons and bangles for the girls, and combs for the boys. But I do not make much money. Not because I cannot walk very far. How many houses do I reach in a day? Ten, fifteen. But twenty years ago I could visit more than fifty houses. *That* makes a difference.'

'Have you always been here?'

'Most of my life, huzoor. I was here before they built the motor road to Mussoorie. I was here when the sahibs had their own carriages and ponies and the memsahibs their own rickshaws. I was here before there were any cinemas. I was here when the Prince of Wales came to Dehra Dun… Oh, I have been here a long time, huzoor. I was here when that house was built,' he says pointing with his chin towards my grandfather's house. 'Fifty, sixty years ago it must have been. I cannot remember exactly. What is ten years when you have lived seventy? But it was a tall, red-bearded sahib who built that house. He kept many creatures as pets. A kachwa (turtle) was one of them. And there was a python, which crawled into my box one day and gave me a terrible fright. The sahib used to keep it hanging from his shoulders, like a garland. His wife, the burra mem, always bought a lot from me—lots of elastic. And there were sons, one a teacher, another in the Air Force, and there were always children in the house. Beautiful children. But they went away many years ago. Everyone has gone away.'

I do not tell him that I am one of the 'beautiful children'. I doubt if he will believe me. His memories are of another age, another place, and for him there are no strong bridges into the present.

'But others have come,' I say.

'True, and that is as it should be. That is not my complaint. My complaint—should God be listening—is that I have been left behind.'

He gets slowly to his feet and stands over his shabby tin box, gazing down at it with a mixture of disdain and affection. I help him to lift and balance it on the flattened cloth on his head. He does not have the energy to turn and make a salutation of any kind; but, setting his sights on the distant hills, he walks down the path with steps that are shaky and slow but still wonderfully straight.

I wonder how much longer he will live. Perhaps a year or two, perhaps a week, perhaps an hour. It will be an end of living, but it will not be death. He is too old for death; he can only sleep; he can only fall gently, like an old, crumpled brown leaf.

I leave the orchard. The bend in the road hides my grandfather's house. I reach the canal again. It emerges from under a small culvert, where ferns and maidenhair grow in the shade. The water, coming from a stream in the foothills, rushes along with a familiar sound; it does not lose its momentum until the canal has left the gently sloping streets of the town.

There are new buildings on this road, but the small police station is housed in the same old lime-washed bungalow. A couple of off-duty policemen, partly uniformed but with their pyjamas on, stroll hand in hand on the grass verge. Holding hands (with persons of the same sex of course) is common practice in northern India, and denotes no special relationship.

I cannot forget this little police station. Nothing very exciting ever happened in its vicinity until, in 1947, communal riots broke out in Dehra. Then, bodies were regularly fished out of the canal and dumped on a growing pile in the station compound. I was only a boy, but when I looked over the wall at that pile of corpses, there was no one who paid any attention to me. They were too busy to send me away. At the same time they knew that I was perfectly safe; while Hindus and Muslims were at each other's throats, a white boy could walk the streets in safety. No one was any longer interested in the Europeans.

The people of Dehra are not violent by nature, and the town has no history of communal discord. But when refugees from the partitioned Punjab poured into Dehra in their thousands, the atmosphere became charged with tension. These refugees, many of them Sikhs, had lost their homes and livelihoods; many had seen their loved ones butchered. They were in a fierce and vengeful frame of mind. The calm, sleepy atmosphere of Dehra was shattered during two months of looting and murder. Those Muslims who could get away, fled. The poorer members of the community remained in a refugee camp until the holocaust was over; then they returned to their former occupations, frightened and deeply mistrustful. The old boxman was one of them.

I cross the canal and take the road that will lead me to the riverbed. This was one of my father's favourite walks. He, too, was a walking man. Often, when he was home on leave, he would say, 'Ruskin, let's go for a walk,' and we would slip off together and walk down to the riverbed or into the sugar-cane fields or across the railway lines and into the jungle.

On one of these walks (this was before Independence), I remember him saying, 'After the war is over, we'll be going to England. Would you like that?'

'I don't know,' I said. 'Can't we stay in India?'

'It won't be ours any more.'

'Has it always been ours?' I asked.

'For a long time,' he said, 'over two hundred years. But we have to give it back now.'

'Give it back to whom?' I asked. I was only nine.

'To the Indians,' said my father.

The only Indians I had known till then were my ayah and the cook and the gardener and their children, and I could not imagine them wanting to be rid of us. The only other Indian who came to the house was Dr Ghose, and it was frequently said of him that he was more English than the English. I could understand my father better when he said, 'After the war, there'll be a job for me in England. There'll be nothing for me here.'

The war had at first been a distant event; but somehow it kept coming closer. My aunt, who lived in London with her two children, was killed with them during an air-raid; then my father's younger brother died of dysentery on the long walk out from Burma. Both these tragic events depressed my father. Never in good health (he had been prone to attacks of malaria), he looked more worn and wasted every time he came home. His personal life was far from being happy, as he and my mother had separated, she to marry again. I think he looked forward a great deal to the days he spent with me; far more than I could have realized at the time. I was someone to come back to; someone for whom things could be planned; someone who could learn from him.

Dehra suited him. He was always happy when he was among trees, and this happiness communicated itself to me. I felt like drawing close to him. I remember sitting beside him on the veranda steps when I noticed the tendril of a creeping vine that was trailing near my feet. As we sat there, doing nothing in particular—in the best gardens, time has no meaning—I found that the tendril was moving almost imperceptibly away from me and towards my father. Twenty minutes later it had crossed the veranda steps and was touching his feet. This, in India, is the sweetest of salutations.

There is probably a scientific explanation for the plant's behaviour—something to do with the light and warmth on the veranda steps—but I like to think that its movements were motivated simply by an affection for my father. Sometimes, when I sat alone beneath a tree, I felt a little lonely or lost. As soon as my father rejoined me, the atmosphere lightened, the tree itself became more friendly.

Most of the fruit trees round the house were planted by Father; but he was not content with planting trees in the garden. On rainy days we would walk beyond the riverbed, armed with cuttings and saplings, and then we would amble through the jungle, planting flowering shrubs between the sal and shisham trees.

'But no one ever comes here,' I protested the first time. 'Who is going to see them?'

'Some day,' he said, '*someone* may come this way... If people keep cutting trees, instead of planting them, there'll soon be no forests left at all, and the world will be just one vast desert.'

The prospect of a world without trees became a sort of nightmare for me (and one reason why I shall never want to live on a treeless moon), and I assisted my father in his tree planting with great enthusiasm.

'One day the trees will move again,' he said. 'They've been standing still for thousands of years. There was a time when they could walk about like people, but someone cast a spell on them and rooted them to one place. But they're always trying to move—see how they reach out with their arms!'

We found an island, a small rocky island in the middle of a dry riverbed. It was one of those riverbeds, so common in the foothills, which are completely dry in the summer but flooded during the monsoon rains. The rains had just begun, and the stream could still be crossed on foot, when we set out with a number of tamarind, laburnum and coral-tree saplings and cuttings. We spent the day planting them on the island, then ate our lunch there, in the shelter of a wild plum.

My father went away soon after that tree planting. Three months later, in Calcutta, he died.

I was sent to boarding school. My grandparents sold the house and left Dehra. After school, I went to England. The years passed, my grandparents died, and when I returned to India I was the only member of the family in the country.

And now I am in Dehra again, on the road to the riverbed. The houses with their trim gardens are soon behind me, and I am walking through fields of flowering mustard, which make a carpet of yellow blossom stretching away towards the jungle and the foothills.

The riverbed is dry at this time of the year. A herd of skinny cattle graze on the short brown grass at the edge of the jungle. The sal trees have been thinned out. Could our trees have survived? Will our island be there, or has some flash flood during a heavy monsoon washed it away completely?

As I look across the dry water-course, my eye is caught by the spectacular red plumes of the coral blossom. In contrast with the dry, rocky riverbed, the little island is a green oasis. I walk across to the trees and notice that a number of parrots have come to live in them. A koel challenges me with a rising *who-are-you, who-are-you...*

But the trees seem to know me. They whisper among themselves and beckon me nearer. And looking around, I find that other trees and wild plants and grasses have sprung up under the protection of the trees we planted.

They have multiplied. They are moving. In this small forgotten corner of the world, my father's dreams are coming true, and the trees are moving again.

Granny's Tree-Climbing

Granny was a genius. You'd like to know why?
Because she could climb trees. Spreading or high,
She'd be up their branches in a trice. And mind you,
When last she climbed a tree she was sixty-two.

Ever since childhood, she'd had this gift
For being happier in a tree than in a lift;
And though, as time went by, she would be told
That climbing trees should stop when one grew old—
And that growing old should be gone about gracefully—
She'd laugh and say, 'Well, I'll grow old disgracefully!
I can do it better.' And we had to agree;
For in all the garden there wasn't a tree
She hadn't been up at one time or another—
(Having learned to climb from a loving brother
When she was six)—but it was feared by all
That one day she'd suffer a terrible fall.

The outcome was different—while we were in town
She climbed a tree and couldn't come down!
She remained on her perch until we came home,
We fetched her a ladder, and she came down alone.

As she looked a bit shaken, we sent for out doc,
Who said, 'She is fine—just a bit of a shock.'

He took Granny's temperature. 'Some fever,' he said;
'I strongly recommend a quiet week in bed.'

We sighed with relief and tucked her up well—
Poor Granny! It was just like a season in hell:
Confined to her bedroom, while every breeze
Murmured of summer and dancing leaves...
But she held her peace till she felt stronger,
Then sat up and said, 'I'll lie here no longer!'
She called for my father and told him undaunted
That a house in a tree-top was what she now wanted.
My Dad knew his duty. He said, 'That's all right—
'You'll have what you want—I shall start work tonight.'

With my expert assistance, he soon finished the chore,

Made her a tree-house with windows and a door.
So Granny moved up; and now, everyday,
I go to her room with glasses and a tray.
She sits there in state and drinks cocktails with me,
Upholding her right to reside in a tree.

[Written for Grandmothers' Rights Everywhere]

The Rhododendrons

We cannot leave the hills without first having a glimpse of the rhododendrons in flower. But for this you will have to visit a hill-station towards the end of March, when it is still winter in the Himalayan foothills.

When, as a boy, I went to a boarding school in Shimla, the little narrow-gauge train would come huffing and puffing up the steep incline towards Summerhill, and we would look out of the windows to admire the scarlet blossoms of the rhododendrons. For eight years of boarding school life we would be brought up the mountains by a little steam-engine, and always the rhododendrons were there to welcome us. Sometimes there was snow on the ground, and the fallen petals would stand out against the snow—scarlet against white.

Dalhousie is especially blessed with rhododendrons; at least it was, when I was last there, fifty years ago! So are the northern slopes of Mussoorie. The hill people call the flower 'baras'; it makes a good wine, if the juice is fermented by a good winemaker.

When Gautam was small, he was having some difficulty with the word 'rhododendron', so to amuse him, I played on the word:

'One rode a horse,' I said, 'and the other rhododendron!'

'Can you ride on a rhododendron?' he asked, not to be fooled.

'Maybe not,' I said, 'but you can make jam with it.'

That aroused his interest, and we got his mother to make us rhododendron jam. It went down quite well; but you'll have to ask his mother for the recipe.

As you go further up in the Himalayas, you will find other varieties of the rhododendron—smaller trees with flowers coming in white, yellow, purple, and other shades. These sturdy trees, sometimes forming small forests, can be found up to eight thousand feet in Himachal, Kumaon, Garhwal, and Kashmir. Others are found at elevations of ten thousand to fourteen thousand feet in the Sutlej valley, while the rare white Rhododendron Falconeri makes its home at a similar altitude in Kashmir.

Now grown as an ornamental tree or shrub in Europe, the rhododendrons are truly at home in the Himalayas.

But why such a long name, Gautam wants to know.

Well it came from the Greek (via Latin) into English: *rhodon* meaning rose + *dendron*, meaning tree. So let's simply call it the Rose Tree!

Visitors from the Forest

When mist fills the Himalayan valleys, and heavy monsoon rain sweeps across the hills, it is natural for wild creatures to seek shelter. And sometimes my cottage in the forest is the most convenient refuge.

There is no doubt I make things easier for all concerned by leaving most of my windows open. I like plenty of fresh air indoors, and if a few birds, beasts and insects come in too, they're welcome, provided they don't make too much of a nuisance of themselves.

I must confess, I did lose patience with a bamboo beetle who blundered in the other night and fell into the water jug. I rescued him and pushed him out of the window. A few seconds later he came whirring in again, and with unerring accuracy landed with a plop in the same jug. I fished him out once more and offered him the freedom of the night. But attracted no doubt by the light and warmth of my small sitting room, he came buzzing back, circling the room like a helicopter looking for a place to land. Quickly I covered the water jug. He landed in a bowl of wild dahlias, and I allowed him to remain there, comfortably curled up in the hollow of a flower.

Sometimes during the day, a bird visits me—a deep blue whistling thrush, hopping about on long, dainty legs, too nervous to sing. She perches on the windowsill, looking out at the rain. She does not permit any familiarity. But if I sit quietly in my chair she will sit quietly on my windowsill, glancing quickly at me now and then to make sure I am keeping my distance. When the rain stops, she glides away, and it is only then, confident in her freedom, that she bursts into full-throated song, her broken but haunting melody echoing down the ravine.

A squirrel comes sometimes, when his home in the oak tree gets waterlogged. Apparently he is a bachelor; anyway, he lives alone. He knows me well, this squirrel, and is bold enough to climb on to the dining table looking for titbits which he always finds because I leave them there deliberately. Had I met him when he was a youngster, he would have learnt to eat from my hand; but I have only been here for a few months. I like it this way. I am not looking for pets; these are simply guests.

Last week, as I was sitting down at my desk to write a long-deferred article, I was startled to see an emerald-green praying mantis sitting on my writing pad. He peered at me with his protuberant glass-bead eyes, and I stared down at him through my glasses. When I gave him a prod, he moved off in a leisurely way. Later, I found him examining the binding of *Leaves of Grass;* perhaps he had found a succulent bookworm. He disappeared for a couple of days, and then I found him on my dressing table, preening himself before the mirror.

Out in the garden, I spotted another mantis, perched on the jasmine bush. Its arms were raised like a boxer's. Perhaps they are a pair, I thought, and went indoors, fetched my mantis and placed him on the jasmine bush opposite his fellow insect. He did not like what he saw—no comparison with his own image!—and made off in a hurry.

My most interesting visitor comes at night, when the lights are still burning—a tiny bat who prefers to fly in through the open door, and will use the window only if there is no alternative. His object is to snap up the moths who cluster round the lamps.

All the bats I have seen fly fairly high, keeping near the ceiling; but this particular bat flies in low like a dive bomber, zooming in and out of chair legs and under tables. Once he passed straight between my legs. Has his radar gone wrong, I wondered, or is he just plain mad?

I went to my shelves of natural history and looked up bats, but could find no explanation for this erratic behaviour. As a last resort, I turned to an ancient volume, Sterndale's *Indian Mammalia* (Calcutta, 1884), and in it, to my delight, found what I was looking for: 'A bat found near Mussoorie by Captain Hutton, on the southern range of hills at one thousand eight hundred metres; head and body about three centimetres, skims close to the ground, instead of flying high as bats generally do. Habitat, Jharipani, north-west Himalayas.' Apparently, the bat was rare even in 1884.

Perhaps I have come across one of the few surviving members of the species. Jharipani is only three kilometres from where I live. I am happy that this bat survives in my small corner of the woods, and I undertake to celebrate it in prose and verse. Once, I found it suspended upside down from the railing at the foot of my bed. I decided to leave it there. For a writer alone in the woods, even an eccentric bat is welcome company.

A Week in the Jungle

Grandfather never hunted wild animals, he couldn't understand the pleasure some people obtained from killing the creatures of our forests. Birds and animals, he felt, had as much right to live as humans. We could kill them for food, he said, because even animals killed for food; but not for pleasure.

At the age of twelve I did not have the same high principles as Grandfather. Nevertheless, I disliked shooting. I found it boring.

Uncle Henry and some of his sporting friends once took me on a shikar expedition into the Terai jungles in the Shivalik range. The prospect of a week in the jungle, as camp-follower to several adults with guns, filled me with dismay. I knew that long, weary hours would be spent tramping behind these tall, professional-looking huntsmen who spoke in terms of bagging this tiger or that wild elephant, when all they ever got, if they were lucky, was a wild hare or a partridge. Tigers and excitement, it seemed, came only to Jim Corbett.

This particular expedition proved to be no different from others. There were four men with guns and at the end of the week all that they had shot were two miserable, underweight wildfowl. But I managed, on our second day in the jungle, to be left behind in the rest house. And, in the course of a morning's exploration of the old bungalow, I discovered a shelf of books half-hidden in a corner of the back veranda.

Who had left them there? A literary forest officer? A memsahib who had been bored by her husband's campfire boasting? Or someone who had no interest in the 'manly' sport of slaughtering wild animals and had brought his library along to pass the time? He must have left it behind for others like him.

Or possibly the poor fellow had gone into the jungle one day, as a gesture to his more bloodthirsty companions, and been trampled by an elephant, or gored by a wild boar, or (more likely) accidentally shot by one of the shikaris—and his sorrowing friends had taken his remains away and left his books behind.

Anyway, there they were—a shelf of some thirty volumes, in different shapes, sizes, and colours. I wiped the thick dust off the covers and examined the titles. As my reading tastes had not yet formed, I was willing to try anything. The bookshelf was varied in its contents—and my own interests have since remained fairly universal.

On that second day in the forest rest house, I discovered P. G. Wodehouse and read his *Love Among the Chickens*, an early Ukridge story and still one of my favourites. By the time the perspiring hunters came home in the evening, with their spent cartridges and impressive excuses, I had made a start with M. R. James's *Ghost Stories of an Antiquary*. This kept me awake most of the night, until the oil in the kerosene lamp was exhausted.

Next morning, fresh and optimistic again, the shikaris set out for a different area, where they hoped to get a tiger. They had employed a party of villagers to beat the jungle, and all day I could hear the tom-toms throbbing in the distance. This did not prevent me from finishing M.R. James, or discovering a little book called *A Naturalist on the Prowl* by 'E.H.A'. It described the tremendous fun and interest to be had from studying the wildlife in one's own back garden—the grasshoppers, beetles, ants, butterflies and praying mantises, all living such fascinating lives just outside (and sometimes inside) our bedroom windows.

Before I had finished the book, I was looking for spiders in the corners of the old bungalow and stalking grasshoppers in the long grass of the compound. My concentration was disturbed only once, when I looked up and saw a spotted deer crossing the open space in front of the house. The deer disappeared among the sal trees and I returned to the veranda and my book.

Dusk had fallen when I heard the party returning from the hunt. The hunters were talking loudly and seemed excited. Perhaps they had got their tiger. I put down my book and came out of the house to meet them.

'Did you get the tiger?' I asked excitedly.

'No, laddie,' said Uncle Henry. 'I think we'll get it tomorrow. You should have been with us—we saw a spotted deer!'

There were three days left and I knew I would never get through the entire bookshelf. This I did not intend doing, as not all the authors on the shelf appealed to me. I chose at random *The Wind in the Willows*, *The Jungle Book*, and *David Copperfield*.

On the day I made the literary acquaintance of Mowgli, the wolf-boy, the shikaris shot the two wildfowl already mentioned. As the party had from the first intended living off the jungle, only some tinned foods had been brought along; but two lean birds were insufficient for a party of five, and once again the meal consisted mostly of corned meat and mustard.

Next day, while the grown-ups were looking for their tiger and I was learning wisdom from the Water Rat, Toad, and other river people of *The Wind in the Willows*, an event took place which disturbed my reading for a little while.

I had noticed, on the previous day, that a number of stray mongrels—belonging to watchmen, villagers and forest-guards—always hung about the house, waiting for scraps of food to be thrown away. It was ten o'clock in the morning (a time when wild animals seldom come into the open), when I heard a sudden yelp in the clearing. Looking up, I saw a full-grown panther making off into the jungle with one of the dogs held in its mouth. The panther had either been driven towards the house by the beaters, or had watched the party leave the bungalow and decided to help itself to a meal.

There was no one else about at the time. Since the dog was obviously dead within seconds of being seized, and the panther had disappeared, I saw no point in raising an alarm but returned to my book.

It was getting late when the shikaris returned. They were dirty, sweaty and, as usual, disappointed. This time their excuses held a note of defiance. They took their corned meat in silence. Next day, we were to return to 'civilization', and none of the hunters had anything to show for a week in the jungles of India.

'No game left in these jungles,' said the leading member of the party, famed for once having shot two man-eating tigers and a basking crocodile in rapid succession.

'It's the weather,' said another. 'No rain at all this winter.'

'Don't know what the country's coming to,' grumbled the third.

'I saw a panther this morning,' I said modestly.

In fact, I was altogether too modest. I might just as well have said, 'I saw a donkey this morning,' for all the impression I made.

'Did you really?' said the leading hunter. He glanced at the book lying beside me. 'Young Master Copperfield says he saw a panther!'

The others were only faintly amused. They did not have the energy to laugh.

'Too imaginative for his age,' said one of them. 'Comes from reading so much, I suppose.'

'If you were to get out of the house and into the jungle a little,' said Uncle Henry reproachfully, 'you might really see a panther.'

'Don't know what young fellows are coming to these days...'

'Why didn't you grab it, man, and take it to Grandfather?' And everyone laughed.

I went to bed early and left them to their tales of the 'good old days' when rhinos, cheetahs, and possibly even the legendary phoenix were still available for slaughter.

I came home with a poor reputation. My uncle's friends thought I was both a sissy and a liar. And Uncle Henry, poor man, seemed to think I was responsible for the failure of the entire expedition. He did not take me with him again. But Grandfather, when I told him all about the hunt, doubled up with laughter and said he wished he had been with us, if only to see the faces of Uncle Henry and his friends. As a measure of his delight, he bought me a copy of *David Copperfield*, for I had not been able to finish the one in the forest rest house. I finally got through it in the banyan tree, in the company of several squirrels and a very noisy cicada.

The Prospect of Flowers

Fern Hill, The Oaks, Hunter's Lodge, The Parsonage, The Pines, Dumbarnie, MacKinnon's Hall and Windermere. These are the names of some of the old houses that still stand on the outskirts of one of the smaller Indian hill stations. Most of them have fallen into decay and ruin. They are very old, of course—built over a hundred years ago by Britishers who sought relief from the searing heat of the plains. Today's visitors to the hill stations prefer to live near the markets and cinemas and many of the old houses, set amidst oak and maple and deodar, are inhabited by wild cats, bandicoots, owls, goats, and the occasional charcoal burner or mule driver.

But amongst these neglected mansions stands a neat, whitewashed cottage called Mulberry Lodge. And in it, up to a short time ago, lived an elderly English spinster named Miss Mackenzie.

In years Miss Mackenzie was more than 'elderly', being well over eighty. But no one would have guessed it. She was clean, sprightly, and wore old-fashioned but well-preserved dresses. Once a week, she walked the two miles to town to buy butter and jam and soap and sometimes a small bottle of eau de cologne.

She had lived in the hill station since she had been a girl in her teens, and that had been before the First World War. Though she had never married, she had experienced a few love affairs and was far from being the typical frustrated spinster of fiction. Her parents had been dead thirty years; her brother and sister were also dead. She had no relatives in India, and she lived on a small pension of forty rupees a month and the gift parcels that were sent out to her from New Zealand by a friend of her youth.

Like other lonely old people, she kept a pet, a large black cat with bright yellow eyes. In her small garden she grew dahlias, chrysanthemums, gladioli and a few rare orchids. She knew a great deal about plants, and about wild flowers, trees, birds and insects. She had never made a serious study of these things, but having lived with them for so many years, had developed an intimacy with all that grew and flourished around her.

She had few visitors. Occasionally the padre from the local church called on her, and once a month the postman came with a letter from New Zealand or her pension papers. The milkman called every second day with a litre of milk for the lady and her cat. And sometimes she received a couple of eggs free, for the egg seller remembered a time when Miss Mackenzie, in her earlier prosperity bought eggs from him in large quantities. He was a sentimental man. He remembered her as a ravishing beauty in her twenties when he had gazed at her in round-eyed, nine-year-old wonder and consternation.

Now it was September and the rains were nearly over and Miss Mackenzie's chrysanthemums were coming into their own. She hoped the coming winter wouldn't be too severe because she found it increasingly difficult to bear the cold.

One day, as she was pottering about in her garden, she saw a schoolboy plucking wild flowers on the slope about the cottage.

'Who's that?' she called. 'What are you up to, young man?'

The boy was alarmed and tried to dash up the hillside, but he slipped on pine needles and came slithering down the slope into Miss Mackenzie's nasturtium bed.

When he found there was no escape, he gave a bright disarming smile and said, 'Good morning, miss.'

He belonged to the local English-medium school, and wore a bright red blazer and a red and black striped tie. Like most polite Indian schoolboys, he called every woman 'miss'.

'Good morning,' said Miss Mackenzie severely. 'Would you mind moving out of my flower bed?'

The boy stepped gingerly over the nasturtiums and looked up at Miss Mackenzie with dimpled cheeks and appealing eyes. It was impossible to be angry with him.

'You're trespassing,' said Miss Mackenzie.

'Yes, miss.'

'And you ought to be in school at this hour.'

'Yes, miss.'

'Then what are you doing here?'

'Picking flowers, miss.' And he held up a bunch of ferns and wild flowers.

'Oh,' Miss Mackenzie was disarmed. It was a long time since she had seen a boy taking an interest in flowers, and, what was more, playing truant from school in order to gather them.

'Do you like flowers?' she asked.

'Yes, miss. I'm going to be a botan—a botantist?'

'You mean a botanist.'

'Yes, miss.'

'Well, that's unusual. Most boys at your age want to be pilots or soldiers or perhaps engineers. But you want to be a botanist. Well, well. There's still hope for the world, I see. And do you know the names of these flowers?'

'This is a bukhilo flower,' he said, showing her a small golden flower. 'That's a Pahari name. It means puja or prayer. The flower is offered during prayers. But I don't know what this is...'

He held out a pale pink flower with a soft, heart-shaped leaf.

'It's a wild begonia,' said Miss Mackenzie. 'And that purple stuff is salvia, but it isn't wild. It's a plant that escaped from my garden. Don't you have any books on flowers?'

'No, miss.'

'All right, come in and I'll show you a book.'

She led the boy into a small front room, which was crowded with furniture and books and vases and jam jars and offered him a chair. He sat awkwardly on its edge. The black cat immediately leapt on to his knees, and settled down on them, purring loudly.

'What's your name?' asked Miss Mackenzie, as she rummaged among her books.

'Anil, miss.'

'And where do you live?'

'When school closes, I go to Delhi. My father has a business.'

'Oh, and what's that?'

'Bulbs, miss.'

'Flower bulbs?'

'No, electric bulbs.'

'Electric bulbs! You might send me a few, when you get home. Mine are always fusing, and they're so expensive, like everything else these days. Ah, here we are!' She pulled a heavy volume down from the shelf and laid it on the table. '*Flora Himaliensis,* published in 1892, and probably the only copy in India. This is a very valuable book, Anil. No other naturalist has recorded so many wild Himalayan flowers. And let me tell you this; there are many flowers and plants which are still unknown to the fancy botanists who spend all their time with microscopes instead of in the mountains. But perhaps, *you'll* do something about that, one day.'

'Yes, miss.'

They went through the book together, and Miss Mackenzie

pointed out many flowers that grew in and around the hill station, while the boy made notes of their names and seasons. She lit a stove, and put the kettle on for tea. And then the old English lady and the small Indian boy sat side by side over cups of hot sweet tea, absorbed in a book of wild flowers.

'May I come again?' asked Anil, when finally he rose to go.

'If you like,' said Miss Mackenzie. 'But not during school hours. You mustn't miss your classes.'

After that, Anil visited Miss Mackenzie about once a week, and nearly always brought a wildflower for her to identify. She found herself looking forward to the boy's visits—and sometimes, when more than a week passed and he didn't come, she was disappointed and lonely and would grumble at the black cat.

Anil reminded her of her brother, when the latter had been a boy. There was no physical resemblance. Andrew had been fair-haired and blue-eyed. But it was Anil's eagerness, his alert, bright look and the way he stood—legs apart, hands on hips, a picture of confidence—that reminded her of the boy who had shared her own youth in these same hills.

And why did Anil come to see her so often?

Partly because she knew about wild flowers, and he really did want to become a botanist. And partly because she smelt of freshly baked bread, and that was a smell his own grandmother had possessed. And partly because she was lonely and sometimes a boy of twelve can sense loneliness better than an adult. And partly because he was a little different from other children.

By the middle of October, when there was only a fortnight left for the school to close, the first snow had fallen on the distant mountains. One peak stood high above the rest, a white pinnacle against the azure-blue sky. When the sun set, this peak turned from orange to gold to pink to red.

'How high is that mountain?' asked Anil.

'It must be over twelve thousand feet,' said Miss Mackenzie. 'About thirty miles from here, as the crow flies. I always wanted to go there, but there was no proper road. At that height, there'll be flowers that you don't get here—the blue gentian and the purple columbine, the anemone and the edelweiss.'

'I'll go there one day,' said Anil.

'I'm sure you will, if you really want to.'

The day before his school closed, Anil came to say goodbye to Miss Mackenzie.

'I don't suppose you'll be able to find many wild flowers in Delhi,' she said. 'But have a good holiday.'

'Thank you, miss.'

As he was about to leave, Miss Mackenzie, on an impulse, thrust the *Flora Himaliensis* into his hands.

'You keep it,' she said. 'It's a present for you.'

'But I'll be back next year, and I'll be able to look at it then. It's so valuable.'

'I know it's valuable and that's why I've given it to you. Otherwise it will only fall into the hands of the junk dealers.'

'But, miss…'

'Don't argue. Besides, I may not be here next year.'

'Are you going away?'

'I'm not sure. I may go to England.'

She had no intention of going to England; she had not seen the country since she was a child, and she knew she would not fit in with the life of post-war Britain. Her home was in these hills, among the oaks and maples and deodars. It was lonely, but at her age it would be lonely anywhere.

The boy tucked the book under his arm, straightened his tie, stood stiffly to attention, and said, 'Goodbye, Miss Mackenzie.'

It was the first time he had spoken her name.

Winter set in early, and strong winds brought rain and

sleet, and soon there were no flowers in the garden or on the hillside. The cat stayed indoors, curled up at the foot of Miss Mackenzie's bed.

Miss Mackenzie wrapped herself up in all her old shawls and mufflers, but still she felt the cold. Her fingers grew so stiff that she took almost an hour to open a can of baked beans. And then it snowed and for several days the milkman did not come. The postman arrived with her pension papers, but she felt too tired to take them up to town to the bank.

She spent most of the time in bed. It was the warmest place. She kept a hot-water bottle at her back, and the cat kept her feet warm. She lay in bed, dreaming of the spring and summer months. In three months' time the primroses would be out and with the coming of spring the boy would return.

One night the hot-water bottle burst and the bedding was soaked through. As there was no sun for several days, the blanket remained damp. Miss Mackenzie caught a chill and had to keep to her cold, uncomfortable bed. She knew she had a fever but there was no thermometer with which to take her temperature. She had difficulty in breathing.

A strong wind sprang up one night, and the window flew open and kept banging all night. Miss Mackenzie was too weak to get up and close it, and the wind swept the rain and sleet into the room. The cat crept into the bed and snuggled close to its mistress's warm body. But towards morning that body had lost its warmth and the cat left the bed and started scratching about on the floor.

As a shaft of sunlight streamed through the open window, the milkman arrived. He poured some milk into the cat's saucer on the doorstep and the cat leapt down from the windowsill and made for the milk.

The milkman called a greeting to Miss Mackenzie, but

received no answer. Her window was open and he had always known her to be up before sunrise. So he put his head in at the window and called again. But Miss Mackenzie did not answer. She had gone away to the mountain where the blue gentian and purple columbine grew.

Wild Flowers Near a Mountain Stream

Below my house is a forest of oak and maple and Himalayan rhododendron. A path twists its way down through the trees, over an open ridge where red sorrel grows wild, and then steeply down through a tangle of thorn bushes, vines and rangal bamboo. At the bottom of the hill the path leads on to a grassy verge, surrounded by wild rose. A stream runs close by the verge, tumbling over smooth pebbles, over rocks worn yellow with age, on its way to the plains and the little Song River and finally to the sacred Ganges.

When I first discovered the stream it was April and the wild roses were flowering, small white blossoms lying in clusters. There were primroses on the hill slopes, and an occasional late-flowering rhododendron provided a splash of red against the dark green of the hill.

The St John's Wort was flowering profusely on small shrubs.

Many legends have grown around this flower of pure dazzling sunshine which takes its family name—Hypericaceae—from the great Titan god Hyperion, who was the father of the Greek God of the sun, Apollo.

Is a friend of yours insane? Then get him to drink the sap from the leaves and stalks of the St John's Wort. He will be well again.

Are you hurt? If your wounds do not heal, take the juice and put it on the wound; and if the bleeding will not stop, take more juice.

Is your father bald? Then he must rise early one morning and bathe his head with the dew from St John's Wort, and his hair will grow again.

Do you live on the Isle of Man? Then beware! Tread not on the St John's Wort after sunset, lest a fairy horseman arise and carry you off. He will land you anywhere.

These are all English or Irish superstitions, but the St John's Wort is as profuse in the lower ranges of the Himalayas as it is anywhere in Europe.

A spotted forktail, a bird of the Himalayan streams, was much in evidence during those early visits. It moved nimbly over the boulders with a fairy tread, and continually wagged its tail.

In May and June, when the hills are always brown and dry, it remained cool and green near the stream, where ferns and maidenhair and long grasses continued to thrive. Downstream I found a cave with water dripping from the roof, the water spangled gold and silver in the shafts of sunlight that pushed through the slits in the cave roof. Few people came there. Sometimes a milkman or a coal-burner would cross the stream on his way to a village; but the nearby hill station's summer visitors had not discovered this haven of wild and green things.

The monkeys—langurs, with white and silver-grey fur, black faces and long swishing tails—had discovered the place, but they kept to the trees and sunlit slopes. They grew quite accustomed to my presence, and carried on with their work and play as though I did not exist. The young ones scuffled and wrestled like boys, while their parents attended to each other's toilets, stretching themselves out on the grass, beautiful animals with slim waists and long sinewy legs, and tails full of character.

They were clean and polite, much nicer than the red monkeys of the plains.

During the rains the stream became a rushing torrent, bushes and small trees were swept away, and the friendly murmur of the water became a threatening boom. I did not visit the spot very often. There were leeches in the long grass, and they would fasten themselves on to my legs and feast on my blood. But it was always worthwhile tramping through the forest to feast my eyes on the foliage that sprang up in tropical profusion—soft, spongy moss; great stag ferns on the trunks of trees; mysterious and sometimes evil-looking orchids; the climbing convolvulus opening its purple secrets to the morning sun; and the wood sorrel, or oxalis—so named because of the oxalic acid derived from its roots—with its clover-like leaflets, which fold down like umbrellas at the first sign of rain.

And then, after a November hailstorm, it was winter, and one could not lie on the frostbitten grass. The sound of the stream was the same, but I missed the birds.

It snowed—the snow lay heavy on the branches of the oak trees and piled up in the culverts—and the grass and the ferns and wild flowers were pressed to sleep beneath a cold white blanket; but the stream flowed on, pushing its way through and under the whiteness, towards another river, towards another spring.

The Message of the Flowers

Apple Blossom	It's Spring, and apple blossom time Stands for temptation, Give in to it!
Bluebells	Stand for constancy and calm. For troubled souls they act as balm Ring out the old, ring in the new!
Carnation	Ah, a woman's love comes with this flower. Cherish the moment!
Chrysanthemum	When red, it's love. When white, it's youth. When bronze, it has the ring of truth.
Cornflower	How delicate you are!
Daisy	The power of innocence.
Daffodils	You purify the air. You're chivalry, gratitude and care.
Eglantine	Sweet brier-rose, the flower of poets. Keats called you rain-scented, dew-sweet.
Forget-me-not	Your name says it all. And I'll remember to remember.
Geranium	Especially the scarlet kind, They say scarlet is a sign of folly. In that case, you're my folly.
Honeysuckle	Who can resist your sweet fragrance? I want to be near you.

Ivy	You are friendship, fellowship and fidelity. You stand for permanence.
Jasmine	Flower of perfection, You stand high in my affection.
Lemon Blossom	What made me think of you today? You stir up memories of love and play.
Magnolia	Champa, Queen of the garden You bring good fortune.
Nasturtium	How can I forget you, humble friend? You gladden my heart to winter's end.
Oleander	Red or white You're the poet's delight.
Poppy	You're my scarlet lady— Extravagant, effervescent, evanescent!
Quercus	Q had me in a quandary Until I looked out of my window And saw my old friend the oak tree staring hard at me!
Roses	Of roses there are many kinds— The moss, the musk, the Eglantine; Roses speak of faithfulness, The red rose of voluptuousness.
Snapdragon	Your sweet scent fills the air and draws me to you; I'd follow you anywhere.
Tulips fame	I was offered a tulip, they said it stood for I'll settle for the Thorn-Apple, if to you it's just the same.
Urtica	The common nettle: You ignore it at your peril!
Violet	Modest and sweet— I look for you in quiet corners.

Wallflower	Wallflower bright against my wall, You are the sturdiest flower of all!
Xerophyte	You thought you'd fool me, Mr X I looked you up, I must confess In the desert you exist Where other plants like you persist...
Yellow Iris	You speak of passion—love's dream ends.
Zinnia	You bring me thoughts of absent friends.

The Friendly Oaks

When I remember the oak trees below the old cottage in the hills, I see again the long-tailed blue magpies fluttering from tree to tree; a woodpecker tapping away at the bark; brightly coloured minivets standing out against its dark foliage; and a band of langurs crashing through the branches in search of acorns. The oaks were always hospitable to birds, beasts and insects.

This is the Banj oak, growing from five thousand feet to seven thousand feet in the western Himalayas. Higher up, other species of oak take over, dominating the most northern slopes facing the snows.

Oaks like each other's company, but each one has a certain individuality—its branches growing as they please, avoiding symmetry, taking on shapes that often give the tree an untidy look, as though it could do with a little discipline. But that of course, is its charm.

Our Himalayan oaks are a little different from the famous oaks of England and Europe. The mighty oak is England's noblest tree. The Romans made the crown of oak leaves (which symbolizes bravery) their principal award, and it could only be given to a citizen who had slain an enemy, won a battle or saved the life of a fellow citizen. The Celts worshipped the oak, regarding it as the symbol of their most prized virtue, hospitality.

Even the moss grows more readily on the trunks of an old oak tree.

White Clouds, Green Mountains

Towards the end of September, those few monsoon clouds that still linger over the Himalayas are no longer burdened with rain and are able to assume unusual shapes and patterns, chasing each other across the sky and disappearing in spectacular sunset formations.

I have always found this to be the best time of the year in the hills. The sun-drenched hillsides are still an emerald green; the air is crisp, but winter's bite is still a month or two away; and for those who still like to take to the open road on foot, there are springs, streams and waterfalls tumbling over rocks that remain dry for most of the year. The lizard that basked on a sun-baked slab of granite last May is missing, but in his place the spotted forktail trips daintily among the boulders in a stream; and the strident sound of the cicadas is gradually replaced by the gentler trilling of the crickets and grasshoppers.

Cicadas, as you probably know, make their music with their legs, which are moved like the bows of violins against their bodies. It's rather like an orchestra tuning up but never quite getting on with the overture or symphony. Aunt Ruby, who is a little deaf, can nevertheless hear the cicadas when they are at their loudest. She lives not far from a large boarding-school, and one day when I remarked that I could hear the school choir or choral group singing, she nodded and remarked: 'Yes, dear. They do it with their legs, don't they?'

Come to think of it, that school choir does sound a bit squeaky.

Now, more than at any other time of the year, the wildflowers come into their own.

The hillside is covered with a sward of flowers and ferns. Sprays of wild ginger, tangles of clematis, flat clusters of yarrow and lady's mantle. The datura grows everywhere with its graceful white balls and prickly fruits. And the wild woodbine provides the stems from which the village boys make their flutes.

Aroids are plentiful and attract attention by their resemblance to snakes with protruding tongues—hence the popular name, cobra lily. This serpent's tongue is a perfect landing-stage for flies etc., who, crawling over the male flowers in their eager search for the liquor that lies at the base of the spike (a liquor that is most appealing to their depraved appetites), succeed in fertilizing the female flowers as they proceed. We see that it is not only humans who become addicted to alcohol. Bears have been known to get drunk on the juice of rhododendron flowers, while bumble bees can be out-and-out dipsomaniacs.

One of the more spectacular cobra lilies, which rejoices in the name *Sauromotum Guttatum*—ask your nearest botanist what that means!—bears a solitary leaf and purple spathe. When the seeds form, it withdraws the spike underground; and when the rains are over and the soil is not too damp, it sends it up again covered with scarlet berries. In the opinion of the hill folk, the appearance of the red spike is more to be relied on as a forecast of the end of the monsoon than any meteorological expertise. Up here on the ranges that fall between the Jumna and the Bhagirathi (known as the Rawain), we can be perfectly sure of fine weather a fortnight after the fiery spike appears.

But it is the commelina, more than any other Himalayan flower, that takes my breath away. The secret is in its colour—a pure pristine blue that seems to reflect the deepest blue of the sky. Towards the end of the rains it appears as if from nowhere, graces the hillside for the space of about two weeks, and disappears again until the following monsoon.

When I see the first commelina, I stand dumb before it and the world stands still while I worship. So absorbed do I become in its delicate beauty that I begin to doubt the reality of everything else in the world.

But only for a moment. The blare of a truck's horn reminds me that I am still lingering on the main road leading out of the hill station. A cloud of dust and blasts of diesel fumes are further indications that reality takes many different forms, assailing all my senses at once! Even my commelina seems to shrink from the onslaught. But as it is still there, I take heart and leave the highway for a lesser road.

Soon I have left the clutter of the town behind. What did Aunt Ruby say the other day? 'Stand still for five minutes, and they will build a hotel on top of you.'

Wasn't it Lot's wife who was turned into a pillar of salt when she looked back at the doomed city that had been her home? I have an uneasy feeling that I will be turned into a pillar of cement if I look back, so I plod on along the road to Devsari, a kindly village in the valley. It will be some time before 'developers' and big money boys get here, for no one will go to live where there is no driveway!

A tea shop beckons. How would one manage in the hills without these wayside tea shops? Miniature inns, they provide food, shelter and even lodging to dozens at a time.

I tackle some buns that have a pre-Independence look about them. They are rock-hard, to match the environment, but I manage to swallow some of the jagged pieces with the hot sweet tea, which is good.

Mountains in My Blood

It was while I was living in England, in the jostle and drizzle of London, that I remembered the Himalayas at their most vivid. I had grown up amongst those great blue and brown mountains; they had nourished my blood; and though I was separated from them by thousands of miles of ocean, plains and desert, I could not rid them from my system. It is always the same with mountains. Once you have lived with them for any length of time, you belong to them.

And so, in London in March, the fog became a mountain mist, and the boom of traffic became the boom of the Ganges emerging from the foothills.

I remembered a little mountain path which led my restless feet into a cool, sweet forest of oak and rhododendron, and then on to the windswept crest of a naked hilltop. The hill was called Clouds End. It commanded a view of the plains on one side, and of the snow peaks on the other. Little silver rivers twisted across the valley below, where the rice-fields formed a patchwork of emerald green. And on the hill itself, the wind made a hoo-hoo-hoo in the branches of the tall deodars where it found itself trapped. During the rains, cloud enveloped the valley but left the hill alone, an island in the sky.

On a spur of the hill stood the ruins of an old brewery. The roof had long since disappeared, and the rain had beaten the stone floors smooth and yellow. Some enterprising

Englishman had spent a lifetime here, making beer for his thirsty compatriots in the plains. Now, moss and ferns and maidenhair grew from the walls. In a hollow beneath a flight of worn stone steps, a wild cat had made its home. It was a beautiful grey creature, black-striped, with pale green eyes. Sometimes it watched me from the steps or the wall, but it never came near.

No one lived on the hill, except occasionally a coal-burner in a temporary grass-thatched hut. But villagers used the path, grazing their sheep and cattle on the grassy slopes. Each cow or sheep had a bell suspended from its neck, to let the shepherd boy know of its whereabouts. The boy could then lie in the sun and eat wild strawberries without fear of losing his animals.

I remembered some of the shepherd boys and girls. There was a boy who played a flute. Its rough, sweet and straightforward notes travelled clearly across the mountain air. He would greet me with a nod of his head, without taking the flute from his lips. There was a girl who was nearly always cutting grass for fodder. She wore heavy bangles on her feet, and long silver earrings. She did not speak much either, but she always had a wide grin on her face when she met me on the path. She used to sing to herself, or to the sheep, to the grass, or to the sickle in her hand. These things I remembered—these, and the smell of pine needles, the silver of oak leaves and the red of maple, the call of the Himalayan cuckoo, and the mist, like a wet face-cloth, pressing against the hills. Odd, how some little incident, some snatch of conversation, comes back to one again and again, in the most unlikely places. Standing in the aisle of a crowded tube train on a Monday morning, my nose tucked into the back page of someone else's newspaper, I suddenly had a vision of a bear making off with a ripe pumpkin.

A bear and a pumpkin—and there, between Goodge Street and Tottenham Court Road stations, all the smells and sounds of the Himalayas came rushing back to me.

The Gentle Nights Befriend Me

Here in Landour, India, on the first range of the Himalayas, I have grown accustomed to the night's brightness—moonlight, starlight, lamplight, firelight! Even fireflies and glow-worms light up the darkness.

Over the years, the night has become my friend. On the one hand, it gives me privacy; on the other, it provides me with limitless freedom.

Not many people relish the dark. Some even sleep with their lights burning all night. They feel safer with the lights on. Safer from the phantoms conjured up by their imaginations.

And yet, I have always felt safer by night, provided I do not deliberately wander about on cliff-tops or roads where danger may lurk. It's true that burglars and other lawbreakers often work by night. They are not into communing with the stars. Nor are late-night revelers, who are usually to be found in brightly lit places and so are easily avoided.

I feel safer by night, yes, but then I have the advantage of living in the mountains, in a region where crime is comparatively rare. I know that if I were living in a big city in some other part of the world, I would think twice about walking home at midnight, no matter how pleasing the night sky.

Walking home at midnight in Landour can be quite eventful, but in a different way. One is conscious all the time of the silent life in the surrounding trees and bushes. I have smelled a leopard without seeing it. I have seen jackals on the prowl. I have watched foxes dance in the moonlight. I have seen flying squirrels flit from one treetop to another. I have observed pine martens on their nocturnal journeys, and listened to the calls of nightjars, owls and other birds who live by night.

Not all on the same night, of course. That would be too many riches at once. Some night walks are uneventful. But usually there is something to see or hear or sense. Like those foxes dancing in the moonlight.

Who else, apart from foxes, flying squirrels and night-loving writers, are at home in the dark?

The nightjars, for one. They aren't much to look at, although their large, lustrous eyes gleam uncannily in the light of a lamp. But their sounds are distinctive. The breeding call of the Indian nightjar resembles the sound of a stone skimming over the surface of a frozen pond; it can be heard for a considerable distance.

Another nightjar species utters a loud grating call which, when close at hand, sounds exactly like a whiplash cutting the air. Horsfield's nightjar (with which I am more familiar) makes a noise similar to that made by striking a plank with a hammer.

I must not forget the owls, those most celebrated of night birds, much maligned by those who fear the night.

Most owls have very pleasant calls. The little jungle owlet has a note that is both mellow and musical. One misguided writer has likened its call to a motorcycle starting up, but this is libel. If only motorcycles sounded like the jungle owl, the world would be a more peaceful place in which to live and sleep.

The little Scops owl speaks only in monosyllables, occasionally saying 'wow' softly, but with great deliberation. He will continue to say 'wow' at intervals of about a minute for hours throughout the night.

Probably the most familiar of Indian owls is the spotted

owlet—a noisy bird that pours forth a volley of chuckles and squeaks in the early evening and at intervals all night. Toward sunset, I watch the owlets emerge from their holes, one after another. Before they come out, they stick out their queer little round heads with staring eyes. After emerging, they usually sit very quietly for a time as though only half awake. Then, all of a sudden, they begin to chuckle, finally breaking into a torrent of chattering. Having apparently 'psyched' themselves into the right frame of mind, they spread their short, rounded wings and sail off for the night's hunting.

I wend my way homeward. 'Night with her train of stars' is enticing. The English poet W.E. Henley found her so. But he also wrote of 'her great gift of sleep', and it is this gift that I am about to accept with gratitude and humility. For it is also good to be up and dancing in the morning dew.

In Search of a Winter Garden

If someone were to ask me to choose between writing an essay on the Taj Mahal or on the last rose of summer, I'd take the rose—even if it was down to its last petal. Beautiful, cold, white marble leaves me—well, just a little cold.

Roses are warm and fragrant, and almost every flower I know, wild or cultivated, has its own unique quality, whether it be subtle fragrance or arresting colour or loveliness of design. Unfortunately, winter has come to the Himalayas, and the hillsides are now brown and dry, the only colour being that of the red sorrel growing from the limestone rocks. Even my small garden looks rather forlorn, with the year's last dark-eyed nasturtium looking every bit like the Lone Ranger surveying the surrounding wilderness from his saddle. The marigolds have dried in the sun, and tomorrow I will gather the seed. The beanstalk that grew rampant during the monsoon is now down to a few yellow leaves and empty bean pods.

'This won't do,' I told myself the other day. 'I must have flowers!'

Prem, who had been down to the valley town of Dehra the previous week, had made me even more restless, because he had spoken of masses of sweet peas in full bloom in the garden of one of the town's public schools. Down in the plains, winter is the best time for gardens, and I remembered my grandmother's house in Dehra, with its long rows of hollyhocks, neatly staked sweet peas, and beds ablaze with red salvia and antirrhinum. Neither Grandmother nor the house are there anymore, but surely there are other beautiful gardens, I mused, and maybe I could visit the school where Prem had seen the sweet peas. It was a long time since I had enjoyed their delicate fragrance.

So I took the bus down the hill, and throughout the two-hour journey I dozed and dreamt of gardens—cottage gardens in the English countryside, tropical gardens in Florida, Mughal Gardens in Kashmir, the Hanging Gardens of Babylon! What had they really been like, I wondered.

And then we were in Dehra, and I got down from the bus and walked down the dusty, busy road to the school Prem had told me about.

It was encircled by a high wall, and, tiptoeing, I could see playing fields and extensive school buildings and, in the far distance, a dollop of colour that *may* have been a garden. Prem's eyesight was obviously better than mine!

I made my way to a wrought-iron gate that would have done justice to a medieval fortress, and found it chained and locked. On the other side stood a tough-looking guard, with a rifle.

'May I enter?' I asked.

'Sorry, sir. Today is holiday. No school today.'

'I don't want to attend classes. I want to see sweet peas.'

'Kitchen is on the other side of the ground.'

'Not green peas. Sweet peas. I'm looking for the garden.'

'I am guard here.'

'Garden.'

'No garden, only guard.'

I tried telling him that I was an old boy of the school and that I was visiting the town after a long interval. This was true up to a point, because I had once been admitted to this very school, and after one day's attendance had insisted on going back to my old school. The guard was unimpressed. And perhaps it was poetic justice that the gates were barred to me now.

Disconsolate, I strolled down the main road, past a garage, a cinema, and a row of eating houses and tea shops. Behind the shops there seemed to be a park of sorts, but you couldn't see much of it from the road because of the buildings, the press of people, and the passing trucks and buses. But I found the entrance, unbarred this time, and struggled through patches of overgrown shrubbery until, like Alice after finding the golden key to the little door in the wall, I looked upon a lovely little garden.

There were no sweet peas, and the small fountain was dry. But around it, filling a large circular bed, were masses of bright yellow California poppies.

They stood out like sunshine after rain, and my heart leapt as Wordsworth's must have, when he saw his daffodils. I found myself oblivious to the sounds of the bazaar and the road, just as the people outside seemed oblivious to this little garden. It was as though it had been waiting here all this time, waiting for me to come by and discover it.

I am fortunate. Something like this is always happening to me. As Grandmother often said, 'When one door closes, another door opens.' And while one gate had been closed upon the sweet peas, another had opened on California poppies.

Dust on the Mountain

I

Winter came and went, without so much as a drizzle. The hillside was brown all summer and the fields were bare. The old plough that was dragged over the hard ground by Bisnu's lean oxen made hardly any impression. Still, Bisnu kept his seeds ready for sowing. A good monsoon, and there would be plenty of maize and rice to see the family through the next winter.

Summer went its scorching way, and a few clouds gathered on the south-western horizon.

'The monsoon is coming,' announced Bisnu.

His sister Puja was at the small stream, washing clothes. 'If it doesn't come soon, the stream will dry up,' she said. 'See, it's only a trickle this year. Remember when there were so many different flowers growing here on the banks of the stream? This year there isn't one.'

'The winter was dry. It did not even snow,' said Bisnu.

'I cannot remember another winter when there was no snow,' said his mother. 'The year your father died, there was so much snow the villagers could not light his funeral pyre for hours. And now there are fires everywhere.' She pointed to the next mountain, half-hidden by the smoke from a forest fire. At night they sat outside their small house, watching the fire spread.

A red line stretched right across the mountain. Thousands of Himalayan trees were perishing in the flames. Oaks, deodars, maples, pines; trees that had taken hundreds of years to grow. And now a fire started carelessly by some campers had been carried up the mountain with the help of the dry grass and strong breeze.

There was no one to put it out. It would take days to die down by itself.

'If the monsoon arrives tomorrow, the fire will go out,' said Bisnu, ever the optimist. He was only twelve, but he was the man in the house; he had to see that there was enough food for the family and for the oxen, for the big black dog and the hens.

There were clouds the next day but they brought only a drizzle. 'It's just the beginning,' said Bisnu, as he placed a bucket of muddy water on the steps.

'It usually starts with a heavy downpour,' said his mother. But there were to be no downpours that year. Clouds gathered on the horizon but they were white and puffy and soon disappeared.

True monsoon clouds would have been dark and heavy with moisture. There were other signs—or lack of them—that warned of a long, dry summer. The birds were silent, or simply absent. The Himalayan barbet, who usually heralded the approach of the monsoon with strident calls from the top of a spruce tree, hadn't been seen or heard. And the cicadas, who played a deafening overture in the oaks at the first hint of rain, seemed to be missing altogether.

Puja's apricot tree usually gave them a basket full of fruit every summer. This year it produced barely a handful of apricots, lacking juice and flavour. The tree looked ready to die, its leaves curled up in despair. Fortunately, there was a store of walnuts, and a bin full of wheat grain and another of rice stored from the previous year, so they would not be entirely without food; but it looked as though there would be no fresh fruit or vegetables. And there would be nothing to store away for the following winter.

Money would be needed to buy supplies in Tehri, some thirty miles distant. And there was no money to be earned in the village.

'I will go to Mussoorie and find work,' announced Bisnu.

'But Mussoorie is a two-day journey by bus,' said his mother. 'There is no one there who can help you. And you may not get any work.'

'In Mussoorie there is plenty of work during the summer. Rich people come up from the plains for their holidays. It is full of hotels and shops and places where they can spend their money.'

'But they won't spend any money on you.'

'There is money to be made there. And if not, I will come home. I can walk back over the Nag Tibba mountain. It will take only two-and-a-half days and I will save the bus fare!'

'Don't go, Bhai,' pleaded Puja.

'There will be no one to prepare your food—you will only get sick.'

But Bisnu had made up his mind so he put a few belongings in a cloth shoulder bag, while his mother prised several rupee coins out of a cache in the wall of their living room. Puja prepared a special breakfast of parathas and an egg scrambled with onions, the hen having laid just one for the occasion. Bisnu put some of the parathas in his bag. Then, waving goodbye to his mother and sister, he set off down the road from the village. After walking for a mile, he reached the highway where there was a hamlet with a bus stop. A number of villagers were waiting patiently for a bus. It was an hour late but they were used to that. As long as it arrived safely and got them to their destination, they would be content. They were patient people.

And although Bisnu wasn't quite so patient, he too had learnt how to wait—for late buses and late monsoons.

II

Along the valley and over the mountains went the little bus with its load of frail humans. A little misjudgement on the part of the driver, and they would all be dashed to pieces on the rocks far below.

'How tiny we are,' thought Bisnu, looking up at the towering peaks and the immensity of the sky. 'Each of us no more than a raindrop... And I wish we had a few raindrops!'

There were still fires burning to the north but the road went south, where there were no forests anyway, just bare brown hillsides. Down near the river there were small paddy fields but unfortunately rivers ran downhill and not uphill, and there was no inexpensive way in which the water could be brought up the steep slopes to the fields that depended on rainfall.

Bisnu stared out of the bus window at the river running far below. On either bank huge boulders lay exposed, for the level of the water had fallen considerably during the past few months. 'Why are there no trees here?' he asked aloud, and received the attention of a fellow passenger, an old man in the next seat who had been keeping up a relentless dry coughing. Even though it was a warm day, he wore a woollen cap and had an old muffler wrapped about his neck.

'There were trees here once,' he said. 'But the contractors took the deodars for furniture and houses. And the pines were tapped to death for resin. And the oaks were stripped of their leaves to feed the cattle—you can still see a few tree skeletons if you look hard—and the bushes that remained were finished off by the goats!'

'When did all this happen?' asked Bisnu.

'A few years ago. And it's still happening in other areas, although it's forbidden now to cut trees. The only forests that remain are in remote places where there are no roads.' A fit of coughing came over him, but he had found a good listener and was eager to continue. 'The road helps you and me to get about but it also makes it easier for others to do mischief. Rich men from the cities come here and buy up what they want—land, trees, people!'

'What takes you to Mussoorie, Uncle?' asked Bisnu politely. He always addressed elderly people as uncle or aunt.

'I have a cough that won't go away. Perhaps they can do something for it at the hospital in Mussoorie. Doctors don't like coming to villages, you know—there's no money to be made in villages. So we must go to the doctors in the towns. I had a brother who could not be cured in Mussoorie. They told him to go to Delhi. He sold his buffaloes and went to Delhi, but there they told him it was too late to do anything. He died on the way back. I won't go to Delhi. I don't wish to die amongst strangers.'

'You'll get well, Uncle,' said Bisnu.

'Bless you for saying so. And you—what takes you to the big town?'

'Looking for work—we need money at home.'

'It is always the same. There are many like you who must go out in search of work. But don't be led astray. Don't let your friends persuade you to go to Bombay to become a film star! It is better to be hungry in your village than to be hungry on the streets of Bombay. I had a nephew who went to Bombay. The smugglers put him to work selling afeem (opium) and now he is in jail. Keep away from the big cities, boy. Earn your money and go home.'

'I'll do that, Uncle. My mother and sister will expect me to return before the summer season is over.'

The old man nodded vigorously and began coughing again. Presently he dozed off. The interior of the bus smelt of tobacco smoke and petrol fumes and as a result Bisnu had a headache. He kept his face near the open window to get as much fresh air as possible, but the dust kept getting into his mouth and eyes.

Several dusty hours later the bus got into Mussoorie, honking its horn furiously at everything in sight. The passengers, looking dazed, got down and went their different ways. The old man trudged off to the hospital.

Bisnu had to start looking for a job straightaway. He needed a lodging for the night and he could not afford even the cheapest of hotels. So he went from one shop to another, and to all the little restaurants and eating places, asking for work—anything in exchange for a bed, a meal, and a minimum wage. A boy at one of the sweet shops told him there was a job at the Picture Palace, one of the town's three cinemas. The hill station's main road was crowded with people, for the season was just starting. Most of them were tourists who had come up from Delhi and other large towns.

The street lights had come on, and the shops were lighting up, when Bisnu presented himself at the Picture Palace.

III

The man who ran the cinema's tea stall had just sacked the previous helper for his general clumsiness. Whenever he engaged a new boy (which was fairly often) he started him off with the warning: 'I will be keeping a record of all the cups and plates you break, and their cost will be deducted from your salary at the end of the month.'

As Bisnu's salary had been fixed at fifty rupees a month, he would have to be very careful if he were going to receive any of it.

'In my first month,' said Chittru, one of the three tea stall boys, 'I broke six cups and five saucers, and my pay came to three rupees! Better be careful!'

Bisnu's job was to help prepare the tea and samosas, serve these refreshments to the public during intervals in the film, and later wash up the dishes. In addition to his salary, he was allowed to drink as much tea as he wanted or could hold in his stomach. But the sugar supply was kept to a minimum.

Bisnu went to work immediately and it was not long before he was as well-versed in his duties as the other two tea boys, Chittru and Bali. Chittru was an easy-going, lazy boy who always tried to place the brunt of his work on someone else's shoulders. But he was generous and lent Bisnu five rupees during the first week. Bali, besides being a tea boy, had the enviable job of being the poster boy. As the cinema was closed during the mornings, Bali would be busy either pushing the big poster board around Mussoorie, or sticking posters on convenient walls.

'Posters are very useful,' he claimed. 'They prevent old walls from falling down.'

Chittru had relatives in Mussoorie and slept at their house. But both Bisnu and Bali were on their own and had to sleep at the cinema. After the last show the hall was locked up, so they could not settle down in the expensive seats as they would have liked! They had to sleep on a dirty mattress in the foyer, near the ticket office, where they were often at the mercy of icy Himalayan winds.

Bali made things more comfortable by setting his poster board at an angle to the wall, which gave them a little alcove where they could sleep protected from the wind. As they had only one blanket each, they placed their blankets together and rolled themselves into a tight warm ball.

During shows, when Bisnu took the tea around, there was nearly always someone who would be rude and offensive. Once when he spilt some tea on a college student's shoes, he received a hard kick on the shin. He complained to the tea stall owner, but his employer said, 'The customer is always right. You should have got out of the way in time!'

As he began to get used to this life, Bisnu found himself taking an interest in some of the regular customers.

There was, for instance, the large gentleman with the soup-strainer moustache, who drank his tea from the saucer. As he drank, his lips worked like a suction pump, and the tea, after a brief agitation in the saucer, would disappear in a matter of seconds. Bisnu often wondered if there was something lurking in the forests of that gentleman's upper lip, something that would suddenly spring out and fall upon him! The boys took great pleasure in exchanging anecdotes about the peculiarities of some of the customers.

Bisnu had never seen such bright, painted women before. The girls in his village, including his sister Puja, were good-looking and often sturdy; but they did not use perfumes or make-up like these more prosperous women from the towns of the plains. Wearing expensive clothes and jewellery, they never gave Bisnu more than a brief, bored glance. Other women were more inclined to notice him, favouring him with kind words and a small tip when he took away the cups and plates. He found he could make a few rupees a month in tips; and when he received his first month's pay, he was able to send some of it home.

Chittru accompanied him to the post office and helped him to fill in the money order form. Bisnu had been to the village school, but be wasn't used to forms and official paperwork. As Chittru had been in the town for a while, he knew all about them, even though he could just about read and write.

Walking back to the cinema, Chittru said, 'We can make more money at the limestone quarries.'

'All right, let's try them,' said Bisnu.

'Not now,' said Chittru, who enjoyed the busy season in the hill station. 'After the season—after the monsoon.'

But there was still no monsoon to speak of, just an occasional drizzle which did little to clear the air of the dust that blew up from the plains. Bisnu wondered how his mother and sister were faring at home. A wave of homesickness swept over him. The hill station, with all its glitter, was just a pretty gift box with nothing inside.

One day in the cinema Bisnu saw the old man who had been with him on the bus. He greeted him like a long lost friend. At first the old man did not recognize the boy, but when Bisnu asked him if he had recovered from his illness, the old man remembered, and said, 'So you are still in Mussoorie, boy. That is good. I thought you might have gone down to Delhi to make more money.' He added that he was a little better and that he was undergoing a course of treatment at the hospital. Bisnu brought him a cup of tea and refused to take any money for it; it could be included in his own quota of free tea. When the show was over, the old man went his way and Bisnu did not see him again.

In September, the town began to get empty. The taps were running dry or giving out just a trickle of muddy water. A thick mist lay over the mountain for days on end, but there was no rain. When the mists cleared, an autumn wind came whispering through the deodars.

At the end of the month the manager of the Picture Palace

gave everyone a week's notice, a week's pay, and announced that the cinema would be closing for the winter.

IV

Bali said, 'I'm going to Delhi to find work. I'll come back next summer. What about you, Bisnu, why don't you come with me? It's easier to find work in Delhi.'

'I'm staying with Chittru,' said Bisnu. 'We may work at the quarries.'

'I like the big towns,' said Bali. 'I like shops and people and lots of noise. I will never go back to my village. There is no money there, no fun.'

Bali made a bundle of his things and set out for the bus stand. Bisnu bought himself a pair of cheap shoes, for his old ones had fallen to pieces. With what was left of his money, he sent another money order home. Then he and Chittru set out for the limestone quarries, an eight-mile walk from Mussoorie.

They knew they were nearing the quarries when they saw clouds of limestone dust hanging in the air. The dust hid the next mountain from view. When they did see the mountain, they found that the top of it was missing—blasted away by dynamite to enable the quarries to get at the rich strata of limestone rock below the surface.

The skeletons of a few trees remained on the lower slopes. Almost everything else had gone—grass, flowers, shrubs, birds, butterflies, grasshoppers, ladybirds. A rock lizard popped its head out of a crevice to look at the intruders. Then, like some prehistoric survivor, it scuttled back into its underground shelter. 'I used to come here when I was small,' announced Chittru cheerfully.

'Were the quarries here then?'

'Oh, no. My friends and I—we used to come for the strawberries. They grew all over this mountain. Wild strawberries, but very tasty.'

'Where are they now?' asked Bisnu, looking around at the devastated hillside.

'All gone,' said Chittru. 'Maybe there are some on the next mountain.'

Even as they approached the quarries, a blast shook the hillside. Chittru pulled Bisnu under an overhanging rock to avoid the shower of stones that pelted down on the road. As the dust enveloped them, Bisnu had a fit of coughing. When the air cleared a little, they saw the limestone dump ahead of them.

Chittru, who was older and bigger than Bisnu, was immediately taken on as a labourer; but the quarry foreman took one look at Bisnu and said, 'You're too small. You won't be able to break stones or lift those heavy rocks and load them into the trucks. Be off, boy. Find something else to do.'

He was offered a job in the labourers' canteen, but he'd had enough of making tea and washing dishes. He was about to turn around and walk back to Mussoorie when he felt a heavy hand descend on his shoulder. He looked up to find a grey-bearded, turbanned Sikh looking down at him in some amusement.

'I need a cleaner for my truck,' he said. 'The work is easy, but the hours are long!'

Bisnu responded immediately to the man's gruff but jovial manner.

'What will you pay?' he asked.

'Fifteen rupees a day, and you'll get food and a bed at the depot.'

'As long as I don't have to cook the food,' said Bisnu.

The truck driver laughed. 'You might prefer to do so, once you've tasted the depot food. Are you coming on my truck?

Make up your mind.'

'I'm your man,' said Bisnu; and waving goodbye to Chittru, he followed the Sikh to his truck.

V

A horn blared, shattering the silence of the mountains, and the truck came round a bend in the road. A herd of goats scattered left and right.

The goatherds cursed as a cloud of dust enveloped them, and then the truck had left them behind and was rattling along the bumpy, unmetalled road to the quarries.

At the wheel of the truck, stroking his grey moustache with one hand, sat Pritam Singh. It was his own truck. He had never allowed anyone else to drive it. Every day he made two trips to the quarries, carrying truckloads of limestone back to the depot at the bottom of the hill. He was paid by the trip and he was always anxious to get in two trips every day. Sitting beside him was Bisnu, his new cleaner. In less than a month Bisnu had become an experienced hand at looking after trucks, riding in them, and even sleeping in them. He got on well with Pritam, the grizzled, fifty-year-old Sikh, who boasted two well off sons—one a farmer in Punjab, the other a wine merchant in far-off London. He could have gone to live with either of them, but his sturdy independence kept him on the road in his battered, old truck.

Pritam pressed hard on his horn. Now there was no one on the road—neither beast nor man—but Pritam was fond of the sound of his horn and liked blowing it. He boasted that it was the loudest horn in northern India. Although it struck terror into the hearts of all who heard it—for it was louder than the trumpeting of an elephant—it was music to Pritam's ears.

Pritam treated Bisnu as an equal and a friendly banter had grown between them during their many trips together.

'One more year on this bone-breaking road,' said Pritam, 'and then I'll sell my truck and retire.'

'But who will buy such a shaky old truck?' asked Bisnu. 'It will retire before you do!'

'Now don't be insulting, boy. She's only twenty years old—there are still a few years left in her!' And as though to prove it he blew the horn again. Its strident sound echoed and re-echoed down the mountain gorge. A pair of wildfowl burst from the bushes and fled to more silent regions.

Pritam's thoughts went to his dinner. 'Haven't had a good meal for days.'

'Haven't had a good meal for weeks,' said Bisnu, although in fact he looked much healthier than when he had worked at the cinema's tea stall.

'Tonight I'll give you a dinner in a good hotel. Tandoori chicken and rice pulao.'

He sounded his horn again as though to put a seal on his promise. Then he slowed down, because the road had become narrow and precipitous, and trotting ahead of them was a train of mules.

As the horn blared, one mule ran forward, another ran backward. One went uphill, another went downhill. Soon there were mules all over the place. Pritam cursed the mules and the mule drivers cursed Pritam; but he had soon left them far behind.

Along this range, all the hills were bare and dry. Most of the forest had long since disappeared.

'Are your hills as bare as these?' asked Pritam. 'No, we still have some trees,' said Bisnu. 'Nobody has started blasting the hills as yet. In front of our house there is a walnut tree which gives us two baskets of walnuts every year. And there is an apricot tree. But it was a bad year for fruit. There was no rain. And the stream is too far away.'

'It will rain soon,' said Pritam. 'I can smell rain. It is coming from the north. The winter will be early.'

'It will settle the dust.'

Dust was everywhere. The truck was full of it. The leaves of the shrubs and the few trees were thick with it. Bisnu could feel the dust under his eyelids and in his mouth. And as they approached the quarries, the dust increased. But it was a different kind of dust now—whiter, stinging the eyes, irritating the nostrils.

They had been blasting all morning.

'Let's wait here,' said Pritam, bringing the truck to a halt. They sat in silence, staring through the windscreen at the scarred cliffs a little distance down the road. There was a sharp crack of explosives and the hillside blossomed outwards. Earth and rocks hurtled down the mountain.

Bisnu watched in awe as shrubs and small trees were flung into the air. It always frightened him—not so much the sight of the rocks bursting asunder, as the trees being flung aside and destroyed. He thought of the trees at home—the walnut, the chestnuts, the pines—and wondered if one day they would suffer the same fate, and whether the mountains would all become a desert like this particular range. No trees, no grass, no water—only the choking dust of mines and quarries.

VI

Pritam pressed hard on his horn again to let the people at the site know that he was approaching. He parked outside a small shed where the contractor and the foreman were sipping cups of tea. A short distance away, some labourers, Chittru among then, were hammering at chunks of rock, breaking them up into manageable pieces. A pile of stones stood ready for loading; while the rock that had just been blasted lay scattered about the hillside.

'Come and have a cup of tea,' called out the contractor.

'I can't hang about all day,' said Pritam. 'There's another trip to make—and the days are getting shorter. I don't want to be driving by night.'

But he sat down on a bench and ordered two cups of tea from the stall. The foreman strolled over to the group of labourers and told them to start loading. Bisnu let down the grid at the back of the truck. Then, to keep himself warm, he began helping Chittru and the men with the loading.

'Don't expect to be paid for helping,' said Sharma, the contractor, for whom every rupee spent was a rupee off his profits.

'Don't worry,' said Bisnu. 'I don't work for contractors, I work for friends.'

'That's right,' called out Pritam. 'Mind what you say to Bisnu—he's no one's servant!'

Sharma wasn't happy until there was no space left for a single stone. Then Bisnu had his cup of tea and three of the men climbed on the pile of stones in the open truck.

'All right, let's go!' said Pritam. 'I want to finish early today, Bisnu and I are having a big dinner!'

Bisnu jumped in beside Pritam, banging the door shut. It never closed properly unless it was slammed really hard. But it opened at a touch.

'This truck is held together with sticking plaster,' joked Pritam.

He was in good spirits. He started the engine, and blew his horn just as he passed the foreman and the contractor.

'They are deaf in one ear from the blasting,' said Pritam.

'I'll make them deaf in the other ear!'

The labourers were singing as the truck swung round the sharp bends of the winding road. The door beside Bisnu rattled on its hinges. He was feeling quite dizzy.

'Not too fast,' he said.

'Oh,' said Pritam. 'About my driving?'

'It's just today,' said Bisnu uneasily.

'You're getting old,' said Pritam. 'And since when did you become nervous?'

'It's a feeling, that's all.'

'That's your trouble.'

'I suppose so,' said Bisnu.

Pritam was feeling young, exhilarated. He drove faster. As they swung round a bend, Bisnu looked out of his window.

All he saw was the sky above and the valley below. They were very near the edge; but it was usually like that on this narrow mountain road.

After a few more hairpin bends, the road descended steeply to the valley. Just then a stray mule ran into the middle of the road. Pritam swung the steering wheel over to the right to avoid the mule, but here the road turned sharply to the left. The truck went over the edge.

As it tipped over, hanging for a few seconds on the edge of the cliff, the labourers leapt from the back of the truck. It pitched forward, and as it struck a rock outcrop, the loose door burst open. Bisnu was thrown out.

The truck hurtled forward, bouncing over the rocks, turning over on its side and rolling over twice before coming to rest against the trunk of a scraggly old oak tree. But for the tree, the truck would have plunged several hundred feet down to the bottom of the gorge.

Two of the labourers sat on the hillside, stunned and badly

shaken. The third man had picked himself up and was running back to the quarry for help.

Bisnu had landed in a bed of nettles. He was smarting all over, but he wasn't really hurt; the nettles had broken his fall. His first impulse was to get up and run back to the road. Then he realized that Pritam was still in the truck.

Bisnu skidded down the steep slope, calling out, 'Pritam Uncle, are you all right?'

There was no answer.

VII

When Bisnu saw Pritam's arm and half his body jutting out of the open door of the truck, he feared the worst. It was a strange position, half in and half out. Bisnu was about to turn away and climb back up the hill, when he noticed that Pritam had opened a bloodied and swollen eye. It looked straight up at Bisnu.

'Are you alive?' whispered Bisnu, terrified.

'What do you think?' muttered Pritam. He closed his eye again. When the contractor and his men arrived, it took them almost an hour to get Pritam Singh out of the wreckage of the truck, and another hour to get him to the hospital in the next big town. He had broken bones, fractured ribs, and a dislocated shoulder. But the doctors said he was repairable—which was more than could be said for the truck.

'So the truck's finished,' said Pritam, between groans when Bisnu came to see him after a couple of days. 'Now I'll have to go home and live with my son. And what about you, boy? I can get you a job on a friend's truck.'

'No,' said Bisnu, 'I'll be going home soon.'

'And what will you do at home?'

'I'll work on my land. It's better to grow things on the land, than to blast things out of it.'

They were silent for some time.

'There is something to be said for growing things,' said Pritam. 'But for that tree, the truck would have finished up at the foot of the mountain, and I wouldn't be here, all bandaged up and talking to you. It was the tree that saved me. Remember that, boy.'

'I'll remember, and I won't forget the dinner you promised me, either.'

It snowed during Bisnu's last night at the quarries. He slept on the floor with Chittru, in a large shed meant for the labourers. The wind blew the snowflakes in at the entrance; it whistled down the deserted mountain pass. In the morning Bisnu opened his eyes to a world of dazzling whiteness. The snow was piled high against the walls of the shed, and they had some difficulty getting out. Bisnu joined Chittru at the tea stall, drank a glass of hot, sweet tea, and ate two stale buns. He said goodbye to Chittru and set out on the long march home. The road would be closed to traffic because of the heavy snow, and he would have to walk all the way.

He trudged over the hills all day, stopping only at small villages to take refreshment. By nightfall he was still ten miles from home.

But he had fallen in with other travellers, and with them he took shelter at a small inn. They built a fire and crowded around it, and each man spoke of his home and fields and all were of the opinion that the snow and rain had come just in time to save the winter crops. Someone sang, and another told a ghost story. Feeling at home already, Bisnu fell asleep listening to their tales. In the morning they parted and went their different ways. It was almost noon when Bisnu reached his village. The fields were covered with snow and the mountain stream was in spate. As he climbed the terraced fields to his house, he heard the sound of barking, and his mother's big black mastiff came bounding towards him over the snow. The dog jumped on him and licked his arms and then went bounding back to the house to tell the others.

Puja saw him from the courtyard and ran indoors shouting, 'Bisnu has come, my brother has come!'

His mother ran out of the house, calling, 'Bisnu, Bisnu!'

Bisnu came walking through the fields, and he did not hurry, he did not run; he wanted to savour the moment of his return, with his mother and sister smiling, waiting for him in front of the house.

There was no need to hurry now. He would be with them for a long time, and the manager of the Picture Palace would have to find someone else for the summer season... It was his home, and these were his fields! Even the snow was his. When the snow melted he would clear the fields, and nourish them, and make them rich.

He felt very big and very strong as he came striding over the land he loved.

The Good Earth

As with many who love gardens, I have never really had enough space in which to create a proper garden of my own. A few square feet of rocky hillside has been the largest patch at my disposal. All that I managed to grow on it were daisies—and they'd probably have grown there anyway. Still, they made for a charmingly dappled hillside throughout the summer, especially on full-moon nights when the flowers were at their most radiant.

For the past few years, here in Mussoorie, I have had to live in two small rooms on the second floor of a tumbledown building which has no garden space at all. All the same, it has a number of ever-widening cracks in which wild sorrels, dandelions, thorn apples and nettles all take root and thrive. You could, I suppose, call it a wild wall-garden. Not that I am deprived of flowers. I am better off than most city dwellers because I have only to walk a short way out of the hill station to see (or discover) a variety of flowers in their wild state; and wild flowers are rewarding, because the best ones are often the most difficult to find.

But I have always had this dream of possessing a garden of my own. Not a very formal garden—certainly not the 'stately home' type, with its pools and fountains and neat hedges as described in such detail by Bacon in his essay 'Of Gardens'. Bacon had a methodical mind, and he wanted a methodical garden. I like a garden to be a little untidy, unplanned, full of surprises—rather like my own muddled mind, which gives even me a few surprises at times.

My grandmother's garden in Dehra, in north India, for example; Grandmother liked flowers, and she didn't waste space on lawns and hedges. There was plenty of space at the back of the house for shrubs and fruit trees, but the front garden was a maze of flower beds of all shapes and sizes, and everything that could grow in Dehra (a fertile valley) was grown in them—masses of sweet peas, petunias, antirrhinum, poppies, phlox, and larkspur; scarlet poinsettia leaves draped the garden walls, while purple and red bougainvillea climbed the porch; geraniums of many hues mounted the veranda steps; and, indoors, vases full of cut flowers gave the rooms a heady fragrance. I suppose it was this garden of my childhood that implanted in my mind the permanent vision of a perfect garden so that, whenever I am worried or down in the dumps, I close my eyes and conjure up a picture of this lovely place, where I am wandering through forests of cosmos and banks of rambling roses. It soothes the agitated mind.

I remember an aunt who sometimes came to stay with my grandmother, and who had an obsession about watering the flowers. She would be at it morning and evening, an old and rather lopsided watering-can in her frail hands. To everyone's amazement, she would water the garden in all weathers, even during the rains.

'But it's just been raining, Aunt,' I would remonstrate. 'Why are you watering the garden?'

'The rain comes from above,' she would reply. 'This is from me. They expect me at this time, you know.'

Grandmother died when I was still a boy, and the garden soon passed into other hands. I've never done well enough to be able to acquire something like it. And there's no point in getting sentimental about the past.

Yes, I'd love to have a garden of my own—spacious and gracious, and full of everything that's fragrant and flowering. But if I don't succeed, never mind—I've still got the dream.

I wouldn't go so far as to say that a garden is the answer to all problems, but it's amazing how a little digging and friendly dialogue with the good earth can help reactivate us when we grow sluggish.

Before I moved into my present home which has no space for a garden, I had, as I've said, a tiny patch on a hillside, where I grew some daisies. Whenever I was stuck in the middle of a story or an essay, I would go into my tiny hillside garden and get down to the serious business of transplanting or weeding or pruning or just plucking off dead blooms, and in no time at all I was struck with a notion of how to proceed with the stalled story, reluctant essay, or unresolved poem.

Not all gardeners are writers, but you don't have to be a writer to benefit from the goodness of your garden. Baldev, who heads a large business corporation in Delhi, tells me that he wouldn't dream of going to his office unless he'd spent at least half an hour in his garden that morning. If you can start the day by looking at the dew on your antirrhinums, he tells me, you can face the stormiest of board meetings.

Or take Cyril, an old friend.

When I met him, he was living in a small apartment on the first floor of a building that looked over a steep, stony precipice. The house itself appeared to be built on stilts, although these turned out to be concrete pillars. Altogether an ugly edifice. 'Poor Cyril,' I thought. 'There's no way *he* can have a garden.'

I couldn't have been more wrong. Cyril's rooms were surrounded by a long veranda that allowed in so much sunlight and air, resulting in such a profusion of leaf and flower, that at first I thought I was back in one of the greenhouses at Kew Gardens, where I used to wander during a lonely sojourn in London.

Cyril found a chair for me among the tendrils of a climbing ivy, while a coffee table materialized from behind a plant. By the time I had recovered enough from taking in my arboreal surroundings, I discovered that there were at least two other guests—one concealed behind a tree-sized philodendron, the other apparently embedded in a pot of begonias.

Cyril, of course, was an exception. We cannot all have sunny verandas; nor would I show the same tolerance as he does towards the occasional caterpillar on my counterpane. But he was a happy man until his landlord, who lived below, complained that water was cascading down through the ceiling.

'Fix the ceiling,' said Cyril, and went back to watering his plants. It was the end of a beautiful tenant–landlord relationship.

So let us move on to the washerwoman who lives down the road, a little distance from my own abode. She and her family live at the subsistence level. They have one square meal at midday, and they keep the leftovers for the evening. But the steps to their humble quarters are brightened by geraniums potted in large tin cans, all ablaze with several shades of flower.

Hard as I try, I cannot grow geraniums to match hers. Does she scold her plants the way she scolds her children? Maybe I'm not firm enough with my geraniums. Or has it something to do with the washing? Anyway, her abode certainly looks more attractive than some of the official residences here in Mussoorie.

Some gardeners like to specialize in particular flowers, but specialization has its dangers. My friend, Professor Saili, an ardent admirer of the nature poetry of William Wordsworth, decided he would have his own field of nodding daffodils, and planted daffodil bulbs all over his front yard. The following spring, after much waiting, he was rewarded by the appearance of a solitary daffodil that looked like a railway passenger who had gotten off at the wrong station. This year he is specializing in 'easy-to-grow' French marigolds. They grow easily enough in France, I'm sure; but the professor is discovering that they are stubborn growers on our stony Himalayan soil.

Not everyone in this hill station has a lovely garden. Some palatial homes and spacious hotels are approached through forests of weeds, clumps of nettle, and dead or dying rose bushes. The owners are often plagued by personal problems that prevent them from noticing the state of their gardens. Loveless lives, unloved gardens.

On the other hand, there was Annie Powell who, at the age of ninety, was up early every morning to water her lovely garden. Watering-can in hand, she would move methodically from one flower bed to the next, devotedly giving each plant a sprinkling. She said she loved to see leaves and flowers sparkling with fresh water, it gave her a new lease of life every day.

And there were my maternal grandparents, whose home in Dehra in the valley was surrounded by a beautiful, well-kept garden. How I wish I had been old enough to prevent that lovely home from passing into other hands. But no one can take away our memories.

Grandfather looked after the orchard, Grandmother looked after the flower garden. Like all people who have lived together for many years, they had the occasional disagreement.

Grandfather would proceed to sulk on a bench beneath the jackfruit tree while, at the other end of the garden, Grandmother would start clipping a hedge with more than her usual vigour. Silently, imperceptibly, they would make their way towards the centre of the garden, where the flower beds gave way to a vegetable patch. This was neutral ground. My cousins and I looked on like UN observers. And there among the cauliflowers, conversation would begin again, and the quarrel would be forgotten. There's nothing like home-grown vegetables for bringing two people together.

Red roses for young lovers. French beans for long-standing relationships!

On Fairy Hill

Those little green lights that I used to see twinkling away on Pari Tibba—there had to be a scientific explanation for them. I was sure of that. After dark we see or hear many things that seem mysterious and irrational. And then, by the clear light of day, we find that the magic and the mystery have an explanation after all.

I saw those lights occasionally, late at night, when I walked home from the town to my little cottage at the edge of the forest. They moved too fast to be torches or lanterns carried by people. And as there were no roads on Pari Tibba, they could not have been cycle or cart lamps. Someone told me there was phosphorus in the rocks and that this probably accounted for the luminous glow emanating from the hillside late at night. Possibly, but I was not convinced.

My encounter with the little people happened by the light of day.

One morning early in April, purely on an impulse, I decided to climb to the top of Pari Tibba and look around for myself. It was springtime in the Himalayan foothills. The sap was rising—in the trees, in the grass, in the wild flowers, in my own veins. I took the path through the oak forest, down to the little stream at the foot of the hill, and then up the steep slope of Pari Tibba, Hill of Fairies.

It was quite a scramble to get to the top. The path ended

at the stream at the bottom of the slope. I had to clutch at brambles and tufts of grass to make the ascent. Fallen pine needles, slippery underfoot, made it difficult to get a foothold. But finally I made it to the top—a grassy plateau fringed by pines and a few wild medlar trees now clothed in white blossom.

It was a pretty spot. And as I was hot and sweaty, I removed most of my clothing and lay down under a medlar to rest. The climb had been quite tiring. But a fresh breeze soon revived me. It made a soft humming sound in the pines. And the grass, sprinkled with yellow buttercups, buzzed with the sound of crickets and grasshoppers.

After some time, I stood up and surveyed the scene. To the north, Landour with its rusty red-roofed cottages; to the south, the wide valley and a silver stream flowing towards the Ganga. To the west were rolling hills, patches of forest and a small village tucked into a fold of the mountain.

Disturbed by my presence, a barking deer ran across the clearing and down the opposite slope. A band of long-tailed blue magpies rose from the oak trees, glided across the knoll and settled in another copse of oaks.

I was alone, alone with the wind and the sky. It had probably been months, possibly years, since any human had passed that way. The soft lush grass looked most inviting. I lay down again on the sun-warmed sward. Pressed and bruised by my weight, the catmint and clover in the grass gave out a soft fragrance. A ladybird climbed up my leg and began to explore my body. A swarm of white butterflies fluttered around me.

I slept.

I have no idea how long I slept. When I awoke, it was to experience an unusual soothing sensation all over my limbs, as though they were being gently stroked with rose petals.

All lethargy gone, I opened my eyes to find a little girl—or was it a woman?—about two inches tall, sitting cross-legged on my chest and studying me intently. Her hair fell in long black tresses. Her skin was the colour of honey. Her firm little breasts were like tiny acorns. She held a buttercup, which was larger than her hand, and she was stroking my skin with it.

I was tingling all over. A sensation of sensual joy surged through my limbs.

A tiny boy—man?—also naked, now joined the elfin girl, and they held hands and looked into my eyes, smiling. Their teeth were like little pearls, their lips soft petals of apricot blossom. Were these the nature spirits, the flower fairies I had often dreamt of?

I raised my head, and saw that there were scores of little people all over me. The delicate and gentle creatures were exploring my legs, arms and body with caressing gestures. Some of them were laving me with dew or pollen or some other soft essence. I closed my eyes again. Waves of pure physical pleasure swept over me. I had never known anything like it. It was endless, all-embracing. My limbs turned to water. The sky revolved around me, and I must have fainted.

When I came to, perhaps an hour later, the little people had gone. The fragrance of honeysuckle lingered in the air. A deep rumble overhead made me look up. Dark clouds had gathered, threatening rain. Had the thunder frightened them away to their abode beneath the rocks and roots? Or had they simply tired of sporting with an unknown newcomer? Mischievous they were; for when I looked around for my clothes I could not find them anywhere.

A wave of panic surged through me. I ran here and there, looking behind shrubs and tree trunks, but to no avail. My clothes had disappeared, along with the fairies—if indeed they were fairies!

It began to rain. Large drops cannoned off the dry rocks. Then it hailed, and soon the slope was covered with ice. There was no shelter. Naked, I clambered down as far as the stream. There was no one to see me—except for a wild mountain goat speeding away in the opposite direction. Gusts of wind slashed rain and hail across my face and body. Panting and shivering, I took shelter beneath an overhanging rock until the storm had passed. By then it was almost dusk, and I was able to ascend the path to my cottage without encountering anyone, apart from a band of startled langoors who chattered excitedly on seeing me.

I couldn't stop shivering, so I went straight to bed. I slept a deep, dreamless sleep through the afternoon, evening and night, and woke up next morning with a high fever.

Mechanically I dressed, made myself some breakfast and tried to get through the morning's chores. When I took my temperature, I found it was one hundred four. So I swallowed a Brufen and went back to bed.

There I lay till late afternoon, when the postman's knocking woke me. I left my letters unopened on my desk—breaking a sacrosanct ritual—and returned to my bed.

The fever lasted almost a week and left me weak and feeble. I couldn't have climbed Pari Tibba again even if I'd wanted to. But I reclined on my window seat and looked at the clouds drifting over that bleak hill. Desolate it seemed, and yet strangely inhabited. When it grew dark, I waited for those little green fairy lights to appear; but these, it seemed, were now to be denied to me.

And so I returned to my desk, my typewriter, my newspaper articles and correspondence. It was a lonely period in my life. My marriage hadn't worked out: my wife, fond of high society and averse to living with an unsuccessful writer in a remote cottage in the woods, was pursuing her own, more successful career in Mumbai. I had always been rather half-hearted in my approach to making money, whereas she had always wanted more and more of it. She left me—left me with my books and my dreams…

Had it all been a dream, that strange episode on Pari Tibba? Had a too-active imagination conjured up those aerial spirits, those siddhas of the upper air? Or were they underground people, living deep within the bowels of the hill? If I was going to preserve my sanity, I knew I had better get on with the more mundane aspects of living—going into town to buy groceries, mending the leaking roof, paying the electricity bill, plodding up to the post office and remembering to deposit the odd cheque that came my way. All the routine things that made life so dull and dreary.

The truth is, what we commonly call life is not really living at all. The regular and settled ways which we accept as the course of life are really the curse of life. They tie us down to the trivial and monotonous, and we will do almost anything to get away, ideally for a more exalted and fulfilling existence, but if that is not possible, for a few hours of forgetfulness in alcohol, drugs, forbidden sex or even golf. So it would give me great joy to go underground with the fairies. Those little people who have sought refuge in Mother Earth from mankind's killing ways are as vulnerable as butterflies and flowers. All things beautiful are easily destroyed.

I am sitting at my window in the gathering dark, penning these stray thoughts, when I see them coming—hand-in-hand, walking on a swirl of mist, suffused with all the radiant colours of the rainbow. For a rainbow has formed a bridge for them from Pari Tibba to the edge of my window.

I am ready to go with them to their secret lairs or to the

upper air—far from the stifling confines of the world in which we toil…

Come, fairies, carry me away, to experience again the perfection I did that summer's day!

In Grandfather's Garden

Though the house and grounds of our home in Dehra were Grandfather's domain—where he kept an odd assortment of pets—the magnificent old banyan tree was mine, chiefly because Grandfather, at the age of sixty-five, could no longer climb it. Grandmother used to tease him about this, and would speak of a certain Countess of Desmond, an Englishwoman who lived to the age of 117, and would have lived longer if she hadn't fallen while climbing an apple tree. The spreading branches of the banyan tree, which curved to the ground and took root again, forming a maze of arches, gave me endless pleasure. The tree was older than the house, older than Grandfather, as old as the town of Dehra, nestling in a valley at the foot of the Himalayas.

My first friend and familiar was a small grey squirrel. Arching his back and sniffing into the air, he seemed at first to resent my invasion of his privacy. But when he found that I did not arm myself with a catapult or air-gun, he became friendlier. And when I started leaving him pieces of cake and biscuit, he grew bolder, and finally became familiar enough to take food from my hands.

Before long he was delving into my pockets and helping himself to whatever he could find. He was a very young squirrel, and his friends and relatives probably thought him headstrong and foolish for trusting a human.

In the spring, when the banyan tree was full of small red figs, birds of all kinds would flock into its branches, the red-bottomed bulbul, cheerful and greedy; gossiping rosy-pastors; and parrots and crows, squabbling with each other all the time. During the fig season, the banyan tree was the noisiest place on the road.

Halfway up the tree I had built a small platform on which I would often spend the afternoons when it wasn't too hot. I could read there, propping myself up against the bole of the tree with the cushions taken from the drawing room. *Treasure Island*, Huck Finn, the Mowgli stories, and detective novels made up my bag of very mixed reading.

When I didn't want to read, I could look down through the banyan leaves at the world below, at Grandmother hanging up or taking down the washing, at the cook quarrelling with a fruit vendor, or at Grandfather grumbling at the hardy Indian marigold, which insisted on springing up all over his very English garden. Usually nothing very exciting happened while I was in the banyan tree, but on one particular afternoon I had enough excitement to last me through the summer.

That was the time I saw a mongoose and a cobra fight to death in the garden, while I sat directly above them in the banyan tree.

It was an April afternoon. The warm breezes of approaching summer had sent everyone, including Grandfather, indoors. I was feeling drowsy myself and was wondering if I should go to the pond behind the house for a swim, when I saw a huge black cobra gliding out of a clump of cacti and making for some cooler part of the garden. At the same time a mongoose (whom I had often seen) emerged from the bushes and went straight for the cobra.

In a clearing beneath the tree, in bright sunshine, they came face to face.

The cobra knew only too well that the grey mongoose, three feet long, was a superb fighter, clever and aggressive. But the cobra was a skilful and experienced fighter, too. He could move swiftly and strike with the speed of light, and the sacs behind his long, sharp fangs were full of deadly venom.

It was to be a battle of champions.

Hissing defiance, his forked tongue darting in and out, the cobra raised three of his six feet off the ground, and spread his broad, spectacled hood. The mongoose bushed his tail. The long hair on his spine stood up (in the past, the very thickness of his hair had saved him from bites that would have been fatal to others).

Though the combatants were unaware of my presence in the banyan tree, they soon became aware of the arrival of two other spectators. One was a mynah, and the other a jungle crow (not the wily urban crow). They had seen these preparations for battle, and had settled on the cactus to watch the outcome. Had they been content only to watch, all would have been well with both of them.

The cobra stood on the defensive, swaying slowly from side to side, trying to mesmerize the mongoose into making a false move. The mongoose knew the power of his opponent's glassy, twinkling eyes, and refused to meet them. Instead, he fixed his gaze at a point just below the cobra's hood, and opened the attack.

Moving forward quickly until he was just within the cobra's reach, he made a feint to one side. Immediately the cobra struck. His great hood came down so swiftly that I thought nothing could save the mongoose. But the little fellow jumped neatly to one side, and darted in as swiftly as the cobra, biting the snake on the back and darting away again out of reach.

The moment the cobra struck, the crow and the mynah hurled themselves at him, only to collide heavily in mid-air. Shrieking at each other, they returned to the cactus plant.

A few drops of blood glistened on the cobra's back.

The cobra struck again and missed. Again the mongoose sprang aside, jumped in and bit. Again the birds dived at the snake, bumped into each other instead, and returned shrieking to the safety of the cactus.

The third round followed the same course as the first but with one dramatic difference. The crow and the mynah, still determined to take part in the proceedings, dived at the cobra, but this time they missed each other as well as their mark. The mynah flew on and reached its perch, but the crow tried to pull up in mid-air and turn back. In the second that it took him to do this, the cobra whipped his head back and struck with great force, his snout thudding against the crow's body.

I saw the bird flung nearly twenty feet across the garden, where, after fluttering about for a while, it lay still. The mynah remained on the cactus plant, and when the snake and the mongoose returned to the fray, it very wisely refrained from interfering again!

The cobra was weakening, and the mongoose, walking fearlessly up to it, raised himself on his short legs, and with a lightning snap had the big snake by the snout. The cobra writhed and lashed about in a frightening manner, and even coiled itself about the mongoose, but all to no avail. The little fellow hung grimly on, until the snake had ceased to struggle. He then smeared along its quivering length, gripping it round the hood, and dragging it into the bushes.

The mynah dropped cautiously to the ground, hopped about, peered into the bushes from a safe distance, and then, with a shrill cry of congratulation, flew away.

When I had also made a cautious descent from the tree and returned to the house, I told Grandfather of the fight I had seen. He was pleased that the mongoose had won. He had encouraged it to live in the garden, to keep away the snakes, and fed it regularly with scraps from the kitchen. He had never tried taming it, because a wild mongoose was more useful than a domesticated one.

From the banyan tree I often saw the mongoose patrolling the four corners of the garden, and once I saw him with an egg in his mouth and knew he had been in the poultry house; but he hadn't harmed the birds, and I knew Grandmother would forgive him for stealing as long as he kept the snakes away.

The banyan tree was also the setting for what we were to call the Strange Case of the Grey Squirrel and the White Rat.

The white rat was Grandfather's—he had bought it from the bazaar for four annas—but I would often take it with me into the banyan tree, where it soon struck up a friendship with one of the squirrels. They would go off together on little excursions among the roots and branches of the old tree.

Then the squirrel started building a nest. At first she tried building it in my pockets, and when I went indoors and changed my clothes I would find straw and grass falling out. Then one day Grandmother's knitting was missing. We hunted for it everywhere but without success.

Next day I saw something glinting in the hole in the banyan tree and, going up to investigate, saw that it was the end of Grandmother's steel knitting needle. On looking further, I discovered that the hole was crammed with knitting. And amongst the wool were three baby squirrels—all of them white!

Grandfather had never seen white squirrels before, and we gazed at them in wonder. We were puzzled for some time, but when I mentioned the white rat's frequent visits to the tree, Grandfather told me that the rat must be the father. Rats and squirrels were related to each other, he said, and so it was quite possible for them to have offspring—in this case, white squirrels!

The Tunnel

It was almost noon, and the jungle was very still, very silent. Heat waves shimmered along the railway embankment where it cut a path through the tall evergreen trees. The railway lines were two straight black serpents disappearing into the tunnel in the hillside.

Suraj stood near the cutting, waiting for the midday train. It wasn't a station, and he wasn't catching a train. He was waiting so that he could watch the steam engine come roaring out of the tunnel.

He had cycled out of Dehra and taken the jungle path until he had come to a small village. He had left the cycle there, and walked over a low scrub-covered hill and down to the tunnel exit.

Now he looked up. He had heard, in the distance, the shrill whistle of the engine. He couldn't see anything, because the train was approaching from the other side of the hill; but presently a sound like distant thunder issued from the tunnel, and he knew the train was coming through.

A second or two later, the steam engine shot out of the tunnel, snorting and puffing like some green, black and gold dragon, some beautiful monster out of Suraj's dreams. Showering sparks left and right, it roared a challenge to the jungle.

Instinctively, Suraj stepped back a few paces. Waves of hot steam struck him in the face. Even the trees seemed to flinch from the noise and heat. And then the train had gone, leaving only a plume of smoke to drift lazily over the tall shisham trees.

The jungle was still again. No one moved.

Suraj turned from his contemplation of the drifting smoke and began walking along the embankment towards the tunnel.

The tunnel grew darker as he walked further into it. When he had gone about twenty yards it became pitch dark. Suraj had to turn and look back at the opening to reassure himself that there was still daylight outside. Ahead of him, the tunnel's other opening was just a small round circle of light.

The tunnel was still full of smoke from the train, but it would be several hours before another train came through. Till then, the cutting belonged to the jungle again.

Suraj didn't stop, because there was nothing to do in the tunnel and nothing to see. He had simply wanted to walk through, so that he would know what the inside of a tunnel was really like. The walls were damp and sticky. A bat flew past. A lizard scuttled between the lines.

Coming straight from the darkness into the light, Suraj was dazzled by the sudden glare and put a hand up to shade his eyes. He looked up at the tree-covered hillside and thought he saw something moving between the trees.

It was just a flash of orange and gold, and a long swishing tail. It was there between the trees for a second or two, and then it was gone.

About fifteen metres from the entrance to the tunnel stood the watchman's hut. Marigolds grew in front of the hut, and at the back there was a small vegetable patch. It was the watchman's duty to inspect the tunnel and keep it clear of obstacles. Every day, before the train came through, he would walk the length of the tunnel. If all was well, he would return to his hut and take a nap. If something was wrong, he would walk back up the line and wave a red flag and the engine driver would slow down. At night, the watchman lit an oil lamp and made a similar inspection of the tunnel. Of course, he would not stop the train if there was a porcupine on the line. But if there was any danger to the train, he'd go back up the line and wave his lamp to the approaching engine. If all was well, he'd hang his lamp at the door of his hut and go to sleep.

He was just settling down on his cot for an afternoon nap when he saw the boy emerge from the tunnel. He waited until Suraj was only a metre or so away and then said: 'Welcome, welcome. I don't often have visitors. Sit down for a while, and tell me why you were inspecting my tunnel.'

'Is it your tunnel?' asked Suraj.

'It is,' said the watchman. 'It is truly my tunnel, since no one else will have anything to do with it. I have only lent it to the Government.'

Suraj sat down on the edge of the cot.

'I wanted to see the train come through,' he said. 'And then, when it had gone, I thought I'd walk through the tunnel.'

'And what did you find in it?'

'Nothing. It was very dark. But when I came out, I thought I saw an animal—up on the hill—but I'm not sure, it moved off very quickly.'

'It was a leopard you saw,' said the watchman. 'My leopard.'

'Do you own a leopard too?'

'I do.'

'And do you lend it to the Government?'

'I do not.'

'Is it dangerous?'

'No, it's a leopard that minds its own business. It comes to this range for a few days every month.'

'Have you been here a long time?' asked Suraj.

'Many years. My name is Sunder Singh.'

'My name's Suraj.'

'There is one train during the day. And there is one train during the night. Have you seen the night mail come through the tunnel?'

'No. At what time does it come?'

'About nine o'clock, if it isn't late. You could come and sit here with me, if you like. And after it has gone, instead of going to sleep I will take you home.'

'I'll ask my parents,' said Suraj. 'Will it be safe?'

'Of course. It is safer in the jungle than in the town. Nothing happens to me out here. But last month, when I went into town, I was almost run over by a bus.'

Sunder Singh yawned and stretched himself out on the cot. 'And now I am going to take a nap, my friend. It is too hot to be up and about in the afternoon.'

'Everyone goes to sleep in the afternoon,' complained Suraj. 'My father lies down as soon as he's had his lunch.'

'Well, the animals also rest in the heat of the day. It is only the tribe of boys who cannot, or will not, rest.'

Sunder Singh placed a large banana leaf over his face to keep away the flies, and was soon snoring gently. Suraj stood up, looking up and down the railway tracks. Then he began walking back to the village.

The following evening, towards dusk, as the flying foxes swooped silently out of the trees, Suraj made his way to the watchman's hut.

It had been a long hot day, but now the earth was cooling, and a light breeze was moving through the trees. It carried with it the scent of mango blossoms, the promise of rain.

Sunder Singh was waiting for Suraj. He had watered his small garden, and the flowers looked cool and fresh. A kettle was boiling on a small oil stove.

'I am making tea,' he said. 'There is nothing like a glass of hot tea while waiting for a train.'

They drank their tea, listening to the sharp notes of the tailorbird and the noisy chatter of the seven sisters.

As the brief twilight faded, most of the birds fell silent. Sunder Singh lit his oil lamp and said it was time for him to inspect the tunnel. He moved off towards the tunnel, while Suraj sat on the cot, sipping his tea. In the dark, the trees seemed to move closer to him. And the nightlife of the forest was conveyed on the breeze—the sharp call of a barking deer, the cry of a fox, the quaint *tonk-tonk* of a nightjar. There were some sounds that Suraj didn't recognize—sounds that came from the trees, creakings and whisperings, as though the trees were coming to life, stretching their limbs in the dark, shifting a little, flexing their fingers.

Sunder Singh stood inside the tunnel, trimming his lamp. The night sounds were familiar to him and he did not give them much thought; but something else—a padded footfall, a rustle of dry leaves—made him stand still for a few seconds, peering into the darkness. Then, humming softly to himself, he returned to where Suraj was waiting. Ten minutes remained for the night mail to arrive.

As Sunder Singh sat down on the cot beside Suraj, a new sound reached both of them quite distinctly—a rhythmic sawing sound, as of someone cutting through the branch of a tree.

'What's that?' whispered Suraj.

'It's the leopard,' said Sunder Singh. 'I think it's in the tunnel.'

'The train will soon be here,' said Suraj.

'Yes, my friend. And if we don't drive the leopard out of the tunnel, it will be run over and killed. I can't let that happen.'

'But won't it attack us if we try to drive it out?' asked Suraj, beginning to share the watchman's concern.

'Not this leopard. It knows me well. We have seen each other many times. It has a weakness for goats and stray dogs, but it will not harm us. Even so, I'll take my axe with me. You stay here, Suraj.'

'No, I'm coming with you. It will be better than sitting here alone in the dark!'

'All right, but stay close behind me. And remember, there is nothing to fear.'

Raising his lamp, Sunder Singh advanced into the tunnel, shouting at the top of his voice to try and scare away the animal. Suraj followed close behind; but he found he was unable to do any shouting. His throat was quite dry.

They had gone about twenty paces into the tunnel when the light from the lamp fell upon the leopard. It was crouching between the tracks, only five metres away from them. It was not a very big leopard, but it looked lithe and sinewy. Baring its teeth and snarling, it went down on its belly, tail twitching.

Suraj and Sunder Singh both shouted together. Their voices rang through the tunnel. And the leopard, uncertain as to how many terrifying humans were there in the tunnel with him, turned swiftly and disappeared into the darkness.

To make sure that it had gone, Sunder Singh and Suraj walked the length of the tunnel. When they returned to the entrance, the rails were beginning to hum. They knew the train was coming.

Suraj put his hand to one of the rails and felt its tremor. He heard the distant rumble of the train. And then the engine came round the bend, hissing at them, scattering sparks into the darkness, defying the jungle as it roared through the steep sides of the cutting. It charged straight at the tunnel, and into it, thundering past Suraj like the beautiful dragon of his dreams.

And when it had gone, the silence returned and the forest

seemed to breathe, to live again. Only the rails still trembled with the passing of the train.

They trembled again to the passing of the same train, almost a week later, when Suraj and his father were both travelling in it.

Suraj's father was scribbling in a notebook, doing his accounts. Suraj sat at an open window staring out at the darkness. His father was going to Delhi on a business trip and had decided to take the boy along. ('I don't know where he gets to, most of the time,' he'd complained. 'I think it's time he learnt something about my business.')

The night mail rushed through the forest with its hundreds of passengers. The carriage wheels beat out a steady rhythm on the rails. Tiny flickering lights came and went, as they passed small villages on the fringe of the jungle.

Suraj heard the rumble as the train passed over a small bridge. It was too dark to see the hut near the cutting, but he knew they must be approaching the tunnel. He strained his eyes looking out into the night; and then, just as the engine let out a shrill whistle, Suraj saw the lamp.

He couldn't see Sunder Singh, but he saw the lamp, and he knew that his friend was out there.

The train went into the tunnel and out again; it left the jungle behind and thundered across the endless plains.

Suraj stared out at the darkness, thinking of the lonely cutting in the forest and the watchman with the lamp who would always remain a firefly for those travelling thousands as he lit up the darkness for steam engines and leopards.

The Blue Umbrella

I

'Neelu! Neelu!' cried Binya.

She scrambled barefoot over the rocks, ran over the short summer grass, up and over the brow of the hill, all the time calling 'Neelu, Neelu!' Neelu—Blue—was the name of the blue-grey cow. The other cow, which was white, was called Gori, meaning Fair One. They were fond of wandering off on their own, down to the stream or into the pine forest, and sometimes they came back by themselves and sometimes they stayed away—almost deliberately, it seemed to Binya.

If the cows didn't come home at the right time, Binya would be sent to fetch them. Sometimes her brother, Bijju, went with her, but these days he was busy preparing for his exams and didn't have time to help with the cows.

Binya liked being on her own, and sometimes she allowed the cows to lead her into some distant valley, and then they would all be late coming home. The cows preferred having Binya with them, because she let them wander. Bijju pulled them by their tails if they went too far.

Binya belonged to the mountains, to this part of the Himalayas known as Garhwal. Dark forests and lonely hilltops held no terrors for her. It was only when she was in the market town, jostled by the crowds in the bazaar, that she felt rather nervous and lost. The town, five miles from the village, was also a pleasure resort for tourists from all over India.

Binya was probably ten. She may have been nine or even eleven, she couldn't be sure because no one in the village kept birthdays; but her mother told her she'd been born during a winter when the snow had come up to the windows, and that was just over ten years ago, wasn't it? Two years later, her father had died, but his passing had made no difference to their way of life. They had three tiny terraced fields on the side of the mountain, and they grew potatoes, onions, ginger, beans, mustard and maize: not enough to sell in the town, but enough to live on.

Like most mountain girls, Binya was quite sturdy, fair of skin, with pink cheeks and dark eyes and her black hair tied in a pigtail. She wore pretty glass bangles on her wrists, and a necklace of glass beads. From the necklace hung a leopard's claw. It was a lucky charm, and Binya always wore it. Bijju had one, too, only his was attached to a string.

Binya's full name was Binyadevi, and Bijju's real name was Vijay, but everyone called them Binya and Bijju. Binya was two years younger than her brother.

She had stopped calling for Neelu; she had heard the cowbells tinkling, and knew the cows hadn't gone far. Singing to herself, she walked over fallen pine needles into the forest glade on the spur of the hill. She heard voices, laughter, the clatter of plates and cups, and stepping through the trees, she came upon a party of picnickers.

They were holidaymakers from the plains. The women were dressed in bright saris, the men wore light summer shirts and the children had pretty new clothes. Binya, standing in the shadows between the trees, went unnoticed; for some time she watched the picnickers, admiring their clothes, listening to their unfamiliar accents and gazing rather hungrily at the sight of all their food. And then her gaze came to rest on a bright blue umbrella, a frilly thing for women, which lay open on the grass beside its owner.

Now Binya had seen umbrellas before, and her mother had a big black umbrella which nobody used anymore because the field rats had eaten holes in it, but this was the first time Binya had seen such a small, dainty, colourful umbrella and she fell in love with it. The umbrella was like a flower, a great blue flower that had sprung up on the dry brown hillside.

She moved forward a few paces so that she could see the umbrella better. As she came out of the shadows into the sunlight, the picnickers saw her.

'Hello, look who's here!' exclaimed the older of the two women. 'A little village girl!'

'Isn't she pretty?' remarked the other. 'But how torn and dirty her clothes are!' It did not seem to bother them that Binya could hear and understand everything they said about her.

'They're very poor in the hills,' said one of the men.

'Then let's give her something to eat.' And the older woman beckoned to Binya to come closer.

Hesitantly, nervously, Binya approached the group.

Normally she would have turned and fled, but the attraction was the pretty blue umbrella. It had cast a spell over her, drawing her forward almost against her will.

'What's that on her neck?' asked the younger woman.

'A necklace of sorts.'

'It's a pendant—see, there's a claw hanging from it!'

'It's a tiger's claw,' said the man beside her. (He had never seen a tiger's claw.) 'A lucky charm. These people wear them to keep away evil spirits.' He looked to Binya for confirmation, but Binya said nothing.

'Oh, I want one too!' said the woman, who was obviously his wife.

'You can't get them in shops.'

'Buy hers, then. Give her two or three rupees, she's sure to need the money.'

The man, looking slightly embarrassed but anxious to please his young wife, produced a two-rupee note and offered it to Binya, indicating that he wanted the pendant in exchange. Binya put her hand to the necklace, half afraid that the excited woman would snatch it away from her. Solemnly she shook her head.

The man then showed her a five-rupee note, but again Binya shook her head.

'How silly she is!' exclaimed the young woman.

'It may not be hers to sell,' said the man. 'But I'll try again. How much do you want—what can we give you?' And he waved his hand towards the picnic things scattered about on the grass.

Without any hesitation Binya pointed to the umbrella.

'My umbrella!' exclaimed the young woman. 'She wants my umbrella. What cheek!'

'Well, you want her pendant, don't you?'

'That's different.'

'Is it?'

The man and his wife were beginning to quarrel with each other.

'I'll ask her to go away,' said the older woman.

'We're making such fools of ourselves.'

'But I want the pendant!' cried the other, petulantly.

And then, on an impulse, she picked up the umbrella and held it out to Binya.

'Here, take the umbrella!'

Binya removed her necklace and held it out to the young woman, who immediately placed it around her own neck. Then

Binya took the umbrella and held it up. It did not look so small in her hands; in fact, it was just the right size.

She had forgotten about the picnickers, who were busy examining the pendant. She turned the blue umbrella this way and that, looked through the bright blue silk at the pulsating sun, and then, still keeping it open, turned and disappeared into the forest glade.

II

Binya seldom closed the blue umbrella. Even when she had it in the house, she left it lying open in a corner of the room. Sometimes Bijju snapped it shut, complaining that it got in the way. She would open it again a little later. It wasn't beautiful when it was closed.

Whenever Binya went out—whether it was to graze the cows, or fetch water from the spring, or carry milk to the little tea shop on the Tehri road—she took the umbrella with her. That patch of sky blue silk could always be seen on the hillside.

Old Ram Bharosa (Ram the Trustworthy) kept the tea shop on the Tehri road. It was a dusty, un-metalled road. Once a day, the Tehri bus stopped near his shop and passengers got down to sip hot tea or drink a glass of curd. He kept a few bottles of Coca-Cola too, but as there was no ice, the bottles got hot in the sun and so were seldom opened. He also kept sweets and toffees, and when Binya or Bijju had a few coins to spare, they would spend them at the shop. It was only a mile from the village.

Ram Bharosa was astonished to see Binya's blue umbrella.

'What have you there, Binya?' he asked.

Binya gave the umbrella a twirl and smiled at Ram Bharosa. She was always ready with her smile, and would willingly have lent it to anyone who was feeling unhappy.

'That's a lady's umbrella,' said Ram Bharosa. 'That's only for memsahibs. Where did you get it?'

'Someone gave it to me—for my necklace.'

'You exchanged it for your lucky claw!'

Binya nodded.

'But what do you need it for? The sun isn't hot enough, and it isn't meant for the rain. It's just a pretty thing for rich ladies to play with!'

Binya nodded and smiled again. Ram Bharosa was quite right; it was just a beautiful plaything. And that was exactly why she had fallen in love with it.

'I have an idea,' said the shopkeeper. 'It's no use to you, that umbrella. Why not sell it to me? I'll give you five rupees for it.'

'It's worth fifteen,' said Binya.

'Well, then, I'll give you ten.'

Binya laughed and shook her head.

'Twelve rupees?' said Ram Bharosa, but without much hope.

Binya placed a five-paise coin on the counter.

'I came for a toffee,' she said.

Ram Bharosa pulled at his drooping whiskers, gave Binya a wry look, and placed a toffee in the palm of her hand. He watched Binya as she walked away along the dusty road. The blue umbrella held him fascinated, and he stared after it until it was out of sight.

The villagers used this road to go to the market town. Some used the bus, a few rode on mules and most people walked. Today, everyone on the road turned their heads to stare at the girl with the bright blue umbrella.

Binya sat down in the shade of a pine tree. The umbrella, still open, lay beside her. She cradled her head in her arms, and presently she dozed off. It was that kind of day, sleepily warm and summery.

And while she slept, a wind sprang up.

It came quietly, swishing gently through the trees, humming softly. Then it was joined by other random gusts, bustling over the tops of the mountains. The trees shook their heads and came to life. The wind fanned Binya's cheeks. The umbrella stirred on the grass.

The wind grew stronger, picking up dead leaves and sending them spinning and swirling through the air. It got into the umbrella and began to drag it over the grass. Suddenly it lifted the umbrella and carried it about six feet from the sleeping girl. The sound woke Binya.

She was on her feet immediately, and then she was leaping down the steep slope. But just as she was within reach of the umbrella, the wind picked it up again and carried it further downhill.

Binya set off in pursuit. The wind was in a wicked, playful mood. It would leave the umbrella alone for a few moments but as soon as Binya came near, it would pick up the umbrella again and send it bouncing, floating, dancing away from her.

The hill grew steeper. Binya knew that after twenty yards it would fall away in a precipice. She ran faster. And the wind ran with her, ahead of her, and the blue umbrella stayed up with the wind.

A fresh gust picked it up and carried it to the very edge of the cliff. There it balanced for a few seconds, before toppling over, out of sight.

Binya ran to the edge of the cliff. Going down on her hands and knees, she peered down the cliff face. About a hundred feet below, a small stream rushed between great boulders. Hardly anything grew on the cliff face—just a few stunted bushes, and, halfway down, a wild cherry tree growing crookedly out of the rocks and hanging across the chasm. The umbrella had stuck in the cherry tree.

Binya didn't hesitate. She may have been timid with strangers, but she was at home on a hillside. She stuck her bare leg over the edge of the cliff and began climbing down. She kept her face to the hillside, feeling her way with her feet, only changing her handhold when she knew her feet were secure. Sometimes she held on to the thorny bilberry bushes, but she did not trust the other plants, which came away very easily.

Loose stones rattled down the cliff. Once on their way, the stones did not stop until they reached the bottom of the hill; and they took other stones with them, so that there was soon a cascade of stones, and Binya had to be very careful not to start a landslide.

As agile as a mountain goat, she did not take more than five minutes to reach the crooked cherry tree. But the most difficult task remained—she had to crawl along the trunk of the tree, which stood out at right angles from the cliff. Only by doing this could she reach the trapped umbrella.

Binya felt no fear when climbing trees. She was proud of the fact that she could climb them as well as Bijju. Gripping the rough cherry bark with her toes, and using her knees as leverage, she crawled along the trunk of the projecting tree until she was almost within reach of the umbrella. She noticed with dismay that the blue cloth was torn in a couple of places.

She looked down, and it was only then that she felt afraid. She was right over the chasm, balanced precariously about eighty feet above the boulder-strewn stream. Looking down, she felt quite dizzy. Her hands shook, and the tree shook too. If she slipped now, there was only onc direction in which she could fall—down, down, into the depths of that dark and shadowy ravine.

There was only one thing to do; concentrate on the patch

of blue just a couple of feet away from her. She did not look down or up, but straight ahead, and willing herself forward, she managed to reach the umbrella.

She could not crawl back with it in her hands. So, after dislodging it from the forked branch in which it had stuck, she let it fall, still open, into the ravine below.

Cushioned by the wind, the umbrella floated serenely downwards, landing in a thicket of nettles.

Binya crawled back along the trunk of the cherry tree. Twenty minutes later, she emerged from the nettle clump, her precious umbrella held aloft. She had nettle stings all over her legs, but she was hardly aware of the smarting. She was as immune to nettles as Bijju was to bees.

III

About four years previously, Bijju had knocked a hive out of an oak tree, and had been badly stung on the face and legs. It had been a painful experience. But now, if a bee stung him, he felt nothing at all: he had been immunized for life!

He was on his way home from school. It was two o'clock and he hadn't eaten since six in the morning. Fortunately, the kingora bushes—the bilberries—were in fruit, and already Bijju's lips were stained purple with the juice of the wild, sour fruit.

He didn't have any money to spend at Ram Bharosa's shop, but he stopped there anyway to look at the sweets in their glass jars.

'And what will you have today?' asked Ram Bharosa.

'No money,' said Bijju.

'You can pay me later.'

Bijju shook his head. Some of his friends had taken sweets on credit, and at the end of the month they had found they'd eaten more sweets than they could possibly pay for! As a result, they'd had to hand over to Ram Bharosa some of their most treasured possessions—such as a curved knife for cutting grass or a small hand-axe or a jar for pickles or a pair of earrings—and these had become the shopkeeper's possessions and were kept by him or sold in his shop.

Ram Bharosa had set his heart on having Binya's blue umbrella, and so naturally he was anxious to give credit to either of the children, but so far neither had fallen into the trap.

Bijju moved on, his mouth full of Kingora berries. Halfway home, he saw Binya with the cows. It was late evening, and the sun had gone down, but Binya still had the umbrella open. The two small rents had been stitched up by her mother.

Bijju gave his sister a handful of berries. She handed him the umbrella while she ate the berries.

'You can have the umbrella until we get home,' she said. It was her way of rewarding Bijju for bringing her the wild fruit.

Calling 'Neelu! Gori!' Binya and Bijju set out for home, followed at some distance by the cows.

It was dark before they reached the village, but Bijju still had the umbrella open.

◆

Most of the people in the village were a little envious of Binya's blue umbrella. No one else had ever possessed one like it. The schoolmaster's wife thought it was quite wrong for a poor cultivator's daughter to have such a fine umbrella while she, a second-class BA, had to make do with an ordinary black one. Her husband offered to have their old umbrella dyed blue; she gave him a scornful look, and loved him a little less than before. The pujari, who looked after the temple, announced that he would buy a multi-coloured umbrella the next time he was in the town. A few days later he returned looking annoyed and grumbling that they weren't available except in Delhi. Most people consoled themselves by saying that Binya's pretty umbrella wouldn't keep out the rain, if it rained heavily; that it would shrivel in the sun, if the sun was fierce; that it would collapse in a wind, if the wind was strong; that it would attract lightning, if lightning fell near it; and that it would prove unlucky, if there was any ill luck going about. Secretly, everyone admired it.

Unlike the adults, the children didn't have to pretend. They were full of praise for the umbrella. It was so light, so pretty, so bright a blue! And it was just the right size for Binya. They knew that if they said nice things about the umbrella, Binya would smile and give it to them to hold for a little while—just a very little while!

Soon it was the time of the monsoon. Big black clouds kept piling up, and thunder rolled over the hills.

Binya sat on the hillside all afternoon, waiting for the rain. As soon as the first big drop of rain came down, she raised the umbrella over her head. More drops, big ones, came pattering down. She could see them through the umbrella silk, as they broke against the cloth.

And then there was a cloudburst, and it was like standing under a waterfall. The umbrella wasn't really a rain umbrella, but it held up bravely. Only Binya's feet got wet. Rods of rain fell around her in a curtain of shivered glass.

Everywhere on the hillside people were scurrying for shelter. Some made for a charcoal burner's hut, others for a mule-shed, or Ram Bharosa's shop. Binya was the only one who didn't run. This was what she'd been waiting for—rain on her umbrella—and she wasn't in a hurry to go home. She didn't mind getting her feet wet. The cows didn't mind getting wet either.

Presently she found Bijju sheltering in a cave. He would have enjoyed getting wet, but he had his schoolbooks with him and he couldn't afford to let them get spoilt. When he saw Binya, he came out of the cave and shared the umbrella. He was a head taller than his sister, so he had to hold the umbrella for her, while she held his books.

The cows had been left far behind.

'Neelu, Neelu!' called Binya.

'Gori!' called Bijju.

When their mother saw them sauntering home through the driving rain, she called out: 'Binya! Bijju! Hurry up, and bring the cows in! What are you doing out there in the rain?'

'Just testing the umbrella,' said Bijju.

IV

The rains set in, and the sun only made brief appearances. The hills turned a lush green. Ferns sprang up on walls and tree trunks. Giant lilies reared up like leopards from the tall grass. A white mist coiled and uncoiled as it floated up from the valley. It was a beautiful season, except for the leeches.

Every day, Binya came home with a couple of leeches fastened to the flesh of her bare legs. They fell off by themselves just as soon as they'd had their thimbleful of blood, but you didn't know they were on you until they fell off, and then, later, the skin became very sore and itchy. Some of the older people still believed that to be bled by leeches was a remedy for various ailments. Whenever Ram Bharosa had a headache, he applied a leech to his throbbing temple.

Three days of incessant rain had flooded out a number of small animals who lived in holes in the ground. Binya's mother suddenly found the roof full of field rats. She had to drive them out; they ate too much of her stored-up wheat flour and rice.

Bijju liked lifting up large rocks to disturb the scorpions who were sleeping beneath. And snakes came out to bask in the sun.

Binya had just crossed the small stream at the bottom of the hill when she saw something gliding out of the bushes and coming towards her. It was a long black snake. A clatter of loose stones frightened it. Seeing the girl in its way, it rose up, hissing, prepared to strike. The forked tongue darted out, the venomous head lunged at Binya.

Binya's umbrella was open as usual. She thrust it forward, between herself and the snake, and the snake's hard snout thudded twice against the strong silk of the umbrella. The reptile then turned and slithered away over the wet rocks, disappearing into a clump of ferns.

Binya forgot about the cows and ran all the way home to tell her mother how she had been saved by the umbrella. Bijju had to put away his books and go out to fetch the cows. He carried a stout stick, in case he met with any snakes.

◆

First the summer sun, and now the endless rain, meant that the umbrella was beginning to fade a little. From a bright blue it had changed to a light blue. But it was still a pretty thing, and tougher than it looked, and Ram Bharosa still desired it. He did not want to sell it; he wanted to own it. He was probably the richest man in the area—so why shouldn't he have a blue umbrella? Not a day passed without his getting a glimpse of Binya and the umbrella; and the more he saw the umbrella, the more he wanted it.

The schools closed during the monsoon, but this didn't mean that Bijju could sit at home doing nothing. Neelu and Gori were providing more milk than was required at home, so Binya's mother was able to sell a kilo of milk every day: half a kilo to the schoolmaster, and half a kilo (at reduced rate) to the temple pujari. Bijju had to deliver the milk every morning.

Ram Bharosa had asked Bijju to work in his shop during the holidays, but Bijju didn't have time—he had to help his mother with the ploughing and the transplanting of the rice seedlings. So Ram Bharosa employed a boy from the next village, a boy called Rajaram. He did all the washing-up, and ran various errands. He went to the same school as Bijju, but the two boys were not friends.

One day, as Binya passed the shop, twirling her blue umbrella, Rajaram noticed that his employer gave a deep sigh and began muttering to himself.

'What's the matter, Babuji?' asked the boy.

'Oh, nothing,' said Ram Bharosa. 'It's just a sickness that has come upon me. And it's all due to that girl Binya and her wretched umbrella.'

'Why, what has she done to you?'

'Refused to sell me her umbrella! There's pride for you. And I offered her ten rupees.'

'Perhaps, if you gave her twelve...'

'But it isn't new any longer. It isn't worth eight rupees now. All the same, I'd like to have it.'

'You wouldn't make a profit on it,' said Rajaram.

'It's not the profit I'm after, wretch! It's the thing itself. It's the beauty of it!'

'And what would you do with it, Babuji? You don't visit anyone—you're seldom out of your shop. Of what use would it be to you?'

'Of what use is a poppy in a cornfield? Of what use is a rainbow? Of what use are you, numbskull? Wretch! I, too, have a soul. I want the umbrella, because—because I want its beauty to be mine!'

Rajaram put the kettle on to boil, began dusting the counter, all the time muttering: 'I'm as useful as an umbrella,' and then, after a short period of intense thought, said: 'What will you give me, Babuji, if I get the umbrella for you?'

'What do you mean?' asked the old man.

'You know what I mean. What will you give me?'

'You mean to steal it, don't you, you wretch? What a delightful child you are! I'm glad you're not my son or my enemy. But look, everyone will know it has been stolen, and then how will I be able to show off with it?'

'You will have to gaze upon it in secret,' said Rajaram with a chuckle. 'Or take it into Tehri, and have it coloured red! That's your problem. But tell me, Babuji, do you want it badly enough to pay me three rupees for stealing it without being seen?'

Ram Bharosa gave the boy a long, sad look. 'You're a sharp boy,' he said. 'You'll come to a bad end. I'll give you two rupees.'

'Three,' said the boy.

'Two,' said the old man.

'You don't really want it, I can see that,' said the boy.

'Wretch!' said the old man. 'Evil one! Darkener of my doorstep! Fetch me the umbrella, and I'll give you three rupees.'

V

Binya was in the forest glade where she had first seen the umbrella. No one came there for picnics during the monsoon. The grass was always wet and the pine needles were slippery underfoot. The tall trees shut out the light, and poisonous-looking mushrooms, orange and purple, sprang up everywhere. But it was a good place for porcupines, who seemed to like the mushrooms, and Binya was searching for porcupine quills.

The hill people didn't think much of porcupine quills, but

far away in southern India, the quills were valued as charms and sold at a rupee each. So Ram Bharosa paid a tenth of a rupee for each quill brought to him, and he in turn sold the quills at a profit to a trader from the plains.

Binya had already found five quills, and she knew there'd be more in the long grass. For once, she'd put her umbrella down. She had to put it aside if she was to search the ground thoroughly.

It was Rajaram's chance.

He'd been following Binya for some time, concealing himself behind trees and rocks, creeping closer whenever she became absorbed in her search. He was anxious that she should not see him and be able to recognize him later.

He waited until Binya had wandered some distance from the umbrella. Then, running forward at a crouch, he seized the open umbrella and dashed off with it.

But Rajaram had very big feet. Binya heard his heavy footsteps and turned just in time to see him as he disappeared between the trees. She cried out, dropped the porcupine quills, and gave chase.

Binya was swift and sure-footed, but Rajaram had a long stride. All the same, he made the mistake of running downhill. A long-legged person is much faster going uphill than down. Binya reached the edge of the forest glade in time to see the thief scrambling down the path to the stream. He had closed the umbrella so that it would not hinder his flight.

Binya was beginning to gain on the boy. He kept to the path, while she simply slid and leapt down the steep hillside. Near the bottom of the hill the path began to straighten out, and it was here that the long-legged boy began to forge ahead again.

Bijju was coming home from another direction. He had a bundle of sticks which he'd collected for the kitchen fire. As he reached the path, he saw Binya rushing down the hill as though all the mountain spirits in Garhwal were after her.

'What's wrong?' he called. 'Why are you running?'

Binya paused only to point at the fleeing Rajaram.

'My umbrella!' she cried. 'He has stolen it!'

Bijju dropped his bundle of sticks, and ran after his sister. When he reached her side, he said, 'I'll soon catch him!' and went sprinting away over the lush green grass. He was fresh, and he was soon well ahead of Binya and gaining on the thief.

Rajaram was crossing the shallow stream when Bijju caught up with him. Rajaram was the taller boy, but Bijju was much stronger. He flung himself at the thief, caught him by the legs, and brought him down in the water. Rajaram got to his feet and tried to drag himself away, but Bijju still had him by a leg. Rajaram overbalanced and came down with a great splash. He had let the umbrella fall. It began to float away on the current. Just then Binya arrived, flushed and breathless, and went dashing into the stream after the umbrella.

Meanwhile, a tremendous fight was taking place. Locked in fierce combat, the two boys swayed together on a rock, tumbled on to the sand, rolled over and over the pebbled bank until they were again thrashing about in the shallows of the stream. The magpies, bulbuls and other birds were disturbed, and flew away with cries of alarm.

Covered with mud, gasping and spluttering, the boys groped for each other in the water. After five minutes of frenzied struggle, Bijju emerged victorious.

Rajaram lay flat on his back on the sand, exhausted, while Bijju sat astride him, pinning him down with his arms and legs.

'Let me get up!' gasped Rajaram. 'Let me go—I don't want your useless umbrella!'

'Then why did you take it?' demanded Bijju. 'Come on—tell me why!'

'It was that skinflint Ram Bharosa,' said Rajaram.

'He told me to get it for him. He said if I didn't fetch it, I'd lose my job.'

◆

By early October, the rains were coming to an end. The leeches disappeared. The ferns turned yellow, and the sunlight on the green hills was mellow and golden, like the limes on the small tree in front of Binya's home. Bijju's days were happy ones as he came home from school, munching on roasted corn. Binya's umbrella had turned a pale milky blue, and was patched in several places, but it was still the prettiest umbrella in the village, and she still carried it with her wherever she went.

The cold, cruel winter wasn't far off, but somehow October seems longer than other months, because it is a kind month: the grass is good to be upon, the breeze is warm and gentle and pine-scented. That October, everyone seemed contented—everyone, that is, except Ram Bharosa.

The old man had by now given up all hope of ever possessing Binya's umbrella. He wished he had never set eyes on it. Because of the umbrella, he had suffered the tortures of greed, the despair of loneliness. Because of the umbrella, people had stopped coming to his shop!

Ever since it had become known that Ram Bharosa had tried to have the umbrella stolen, the village people had turned against him. They stopped trusting the old man; instead of buying their soap and tea and matches from his shop, they preferred to walk an extra mile to the shops near the Tehri bus stand. Who would have dealings with a man who had sold his soul for an umbrella? The children taunted him, twisted his name around. From 'Ram the Trustworthy' he became 'Trusty Umbrella Thief'.

The old man sat alone in his empty shop, listening to the eternal hissing of his kettle and wondering if anyone would ever again step in for a glass of tea. Ram Bharosa had lost his own appetite, and ate and drank very little. There was no money coming in. He had his savings in a bank in Tehri, but it was a terrible thing to have to dip into them! To save money, he had dismissed the blundering Rajaram. So he was left without any company. The roof leaked and the wind got in through the corrugated tin sheets, but Ram Bharosa didn't care.

Bijju and Binya passed his shop almost every day. Bijju went by with a loud but tuneless whistle. He was one of the world's whistlers; cares rested lightly on his shoulders. But, strangely enough, Binya crept quietly past the shop, looking the other way, almost as though she was in some way responsible for the misery of Ram Bharosa.

She kept reasoning with herself, telling herself that the umbrella was her very own, and that she couldn't help it if others were jealous of it. But had she loved the umbrella too much? Had it mattered more to her than people mattered? She couldn't help feeling that, in a small way, she was the cause of the sad look on Ram Bharosa's face ('His face is a yard long,' said Bijju) and the ruinous condition of his shop. It was all due to his own greed, no doubt, but she didn't want him to feel too bad about what he'd done, because it made her feel bad about herself; and so she closed the umbrella whenever she came near the shop, opening it again only when she was out of sight.

One day towards the end of October, when she had ten paise in her pocket, she entered the shop and asked the old man for a toffee.

She was Ram Bharosa's first customer in almost two weeks. He looked suspiciously at the girl. Had she come to taunt him, to flaunt the umbrella in his face? She had placed her coin on the counter. Perhaps it was a bad coin. Ram Bharosa picked it up and bit it; he held it up to the light; he rang it on the ground. It was a good coin. He gave Binya the toffee.

Binya had already left the shop when Ram Bharosa saw the closed umbrella lying on his counter. There it was, the blue umbrella he had always wanted, within his grasp at last! He had only to hide it at the back of his shop, and no one would know that he had it, no one could prove that Binya had left it behind.

He stretched out his trembling, bony hand, and took the umbrella by the handle. He pressed it open. He stood beneath it, in the dark shadows of his shop, where no sun or rain could ever touch it.

'But I'm never in the sun or in the rain,' he said aloud. 'Of what use is an umbrella to me?'

And he hurried outside and ran after Binya.

'Binya, Binya!' he shouted. 'Binya, you've left your umbrella behind!'

He wasn't used to running, but he caught up with her, held out the umbrella, saying, 'You forgot it—the umbrella!'

In that moment it belonged to both of them.

But Binya didn't take the umbrella. She shook her head and said, 'You keep it. I don't need it anymore.'

'But it's such a pretty umbrella!' protested Ram Bharosa. 'It's the best umbrella in the village.'

'I know,' said Binya. 'But an umbrella isn't everything.'

And she left the old man holding the umbrella, and went tripping down the road, and there was nothing between her and the bright blue sky.

VI

Well, now that Ram Bharosa has the blue umbrella—a gift from Binya, as he tells everyone—he is sometimes persuaded to go out into the sun or the rain, and as a result he looks much healthier. Sometimes he uses the umbrella to chase away pigs or goats. It is always left open outside the shop, and anyone who wants to borrow it may do so; and so in a way it has become everyone's umbrella. It is faded and patchy, but it is still the best umbrella in the village.

People are visiting Ram Bharosa's shop again. Whenever Bijju or Binya stop for a cup of tea, he gives them a little extra milk or sugar. They like their tea sweet and milky.

A few nights ago, a bear visited Ram Bharosa's shop. There had been snow on the higher ranges of the Himalayas, and the bear had been finding it difficult to obtain food; so it had come lower down, to see what it could pick up near the village. That night it scrambled on to the tin roof of Ram Bharosa's shop, and made off with a huge pumpkin which had been ripening on the roof. But in climbing off the roof, the bear had lost a claw.

Next morning Ram Bharosa found the claw just outside the door of his shop. He picked it up and put it in his pocket. A bear's claw was a lucky find.

A day later, when he went into the market town, he took the claw with him, and left it with a silversmith, giving the craftsman certain instructions. The silversmith made a locket for the claw, then he gave it a thin silver chain. When Ram Bharosa came again, he paid the silversmith ten rupees for his work.

The days were growing shorter, and Binya had to be home a little earlier every evening. There was a hungry leopard at large, and she couldn't leave the cows out after dark.

She was hurrying past Ram Bharosa's shop when the old man called out to her.

'Binya, spare a minute! I want to show you something.'

Binya stepped into the shop.

'What do you think of it?' asked Ram Bharosa, showing her the silver pendant with the claw.

'It's so beautiful,' said Binya, just touching the claw and the silver chain.

'It's a bear's claw,' said Ram Bharosa. 'That's even luckier than a leopard's claw. Would you like to have it?'

'I have no money,' said Binya.

'That doesn't matter. You gave me the umbrella, I give you the claw! Come, let's see what it looks like on you.'

He placed the pendant on Binya, and indeed it looked very beautiful on her.

Ram Bharosa says he will never forget the smile she gave him when she left the shop.

She was halfway home when she realized she had left the cows behind.

'Neelu, Neelu!' she called. 'Oh, Gori!'

There was a faint tinkle of bells as the cows came slowly down the mountain path.

In the distance she could hear her mother and Bijju calling for her.

She began to sing. They heard her singing, and knew she was safe and near.

She walked home through the darkening glade, singing of the stars, and the trees stood still and listened to her, and the mountains were glad.

Things I Love Most

Sea-shells. They are among my earliest memories. I was five years old, walking barefoot along the golden sands of a Kathiawar beach, collecting shells and cowries and taking them home to fill up an old trunk. Some of these shells have remained with me through the years. I still have one which I place against my ear to listen to the distant music of the Arabian Sea.

A jackfruit tree. It stood outside my grandfather's house in Dehra Dun: it was easy to climb and generous with its shade and in its trunk was a large hole where I kept my marbles, sweets, prohibited books and other treasures.

I have always liked the smell of certain leaves, perhaps even more than the scent of flowers. Crushed geranium and chrysanthemum leaves, mint and myrtle, lime and neem trees after the rain, and the leaves of ginger, marigolds and nasturtiums.

Of course, there were other smells which as a boy I especially liked—the smells of pillau and kofta, curry, hot jalebis, roast chicken and fried prawns. But these are smells loved most by gourmets (and most boys) and are not as personal as the smell of leaves and grass.

I have always liked trains and railway stations. I like eating at railway stations—hot gram, peanut, puris, oranges.

As a boy, I travelled to Shimla on a little train that crawls round and through the mountains. In March, the Dowers on the rhododendron trees provided splashes of red against the dark green of the hills. Sometimes there would be snow on the ground to add to the contrast.

What else do I love and remember of the hills? Smells again. The smells of fallen pine needles, cow-dung smoke, spring, rain, bruised grass, the pure cold water of mountain streams, the depth and blue-ness of the sky.

In the hills, I have loved forests. In the plains, I have loved single trees. A lone tree on a wide, flat plain—even if it is a thin, crooked, nondescript tree—gains beauty and nobility from its isolation, from the precarious nature of its existence.

Of course, I have had my favourites among trees. The banyan, with its great branches spreading to form roots and intricate passageways. The peepul with its beautiful heart-shaped leaves catching the breeze and fluttering even on the stillest of days. It is always cool under a peepul. The Jacaranda and gulmohar bursting into blossom with the coming of summer. The cherries, peaches and apricots flowering in the hills—the tall, handsome chestnuts and the whispering deodars.

Deodars have often inspired me to poetry. One day I wrote:

Trees of God, we call them. Planted there when the world
was young.
The first trees
Their fingers pointing to the stars,
Older than the cedars of Lebanon.
Several of these trees were cut down recently and I was
furious
They cut them down last spring
With quick and efficient tools,
The sap was rising still.

The trees bled,
Slaughtered
To make furniture for tools.

And which flower is most redolent of India? Not for me the lotus or the water-lily but the simple marigold, fresh, golden, dew-drenched, kissed by the morning sun.

The smell of the sea. I lived with it for over a year in the Channel Islands, I liked the sea mist and liked the fierce gales that swept across the islands in the winter.

Later, there were the fogs of London; I did not like them but they made me think of Dickens, and I walked to Wapping and the East India Dock Road and watched the barges on the Thames, I had my favourite pub and my favourite fish-and-chips shop. There were always children flying kites from Primrose Hill or sailing boats in the ponds on Hampstead Heath.

Once we visited the gardens at Kew and in a hot-house, moist and smelling of the tropics, I remembered the East and some of the simple things I had known—a field of wheat, a stack of sugar-cane, a cow at rest and a boy sleeping in the shade of a long, red-fingered poinsettia. And I knew I would go home to India.

In the Garden of My Dreams

The cosmos has all the genius of simplicity. The plant stands tall and erect; its foliage is uncomplicated, its inflorescence are bold, fresh, cheerful. Any flower, from a rose to a rhododendron, can be complicated. The cosmos is splendidly simple.

No wonder it takes its name from the Greek 'cosmos', meaning the universe as an ordered whole—the sum total of experience! For this unpretentious flower does seem to sum it all up: perfection without apparent striving for it, the artistry of the South American footballer! Needless to say, it came from tropical America.

And growing it is no trouble. A handful of seeds thrown in a waste patch or on a grassy hill slope, and a few months later there they are, en masse, doing their samba in the sunshine. They are almost wild, but not quite. They need very little attention, but if you take them too much for granted they will go away the following year. Simple they may be, but not insensitive. They need plenty of space. And as my own small apartment cannot accommodate them, they definitely belong to my dream garden.

My respect for the cosmos goes back to my childhood when I wandered into what seemed like a forest of these flowers, all twice my height (I must have been five at the time) but looking down on me in the friendliest way, their fine feathery foliage giving off a faint aroma. Now when I find them flowering on the Himalayan hillsides in mellow October sunshine, they are like old friends and I greet them accordingly, pressing my face to their petals.

Not everyone likes the cosmos. I have met some upper-class ladies (golf club members) who complain that it gives them hay fever, and they use this as an excuse to root out all cosmos from their gardens. I expect they are just being snobbish. There are other flowers which give off just as much pollen dust.

I have noticed the same snobbishness in regard to marigolds, especially the smaller Indian variety. 'Cultivated' people won't cultivate these humble but attractive flowers. Is it because they are used for making garlands? Or because they are not delicately scented? Or because they are so easily grown in the backyards of homes?

My grandparents once went to war with each other over the marigold. Grandfather had grown a few in one corner of the garden. Just as they began flowering, they vanished—Granny had removed them overnight! There was a row, and my grandparents did not speak to each other for several days. Then, by calling them 'French' marigolds, Grandfather managed to reintroduce them to the garden. Granny liked the idea of having something 'French' in her garden. Such is human nature!

Sometimes a wildflower can put its more spectacular garden cousins to shame. I am thinking now of the Commelina, which I discover in secret places after the rains have passed. Its bright sky-blue flowers take my breath away. It has a sort of unguarded innocence that is beyond corruption.

Wild roses give me more pleasure than the sophisticated domestic variety. On a walk in the Himalayan foothills I have encountered a number of these shrubs and climbers—the ineptly named Dog Rose, sparkling white in summer; the Sweet Briar with its deep pink petals and bright red rosehips; the Trailing

Rose, found in shady places; and the wild Raspberry (the fruit more attractive than the flower) which belongs to the same family.

A sun-lover, I like plenty of yellow on the hillsides and in gardens—sunflowers, Californian poppies, winter jasmine, St John's Wort, buttercups, wild strawberries, mustard in bloom... But if you live in a hot place, you might prefer cooling blues and soft purples—forget-me-not, bluebells, cornflowers, lavender. I'd go far for a sprig of sweetly-scented lavender. To many older people the word lavender is charm; it seems to recall the plaintive strain of once familiar music—

> Lavender blue, dilly dilly,
> Lavender green,
> When I am king, dilly dilly,
> You'll be my queen.

This tame-looking, blue-green, stiff, sticky, and immovable shrub holds as much poetry and romance in its wiry arms as would fill a large book.

Most cultivated flowers were originally wild, and many take their names from the botanists who first 'tamed' them. Thus, the dahlia is named after Mr Dahl, a Swede; the rudbeckia after Rudbeck, a Dutchman; the zinnia after Dr Zinn, a German; and the lobelia after Monsieur Lobel, a Flemish physician. They and others brought to Europe many of the flowers found growing wild in tropical America, Asia and Africa.

But I am no botanist. I prefer to be the butterfly, perfectly happy in going from flower to flower in search of nectar.

A Village in Garhwal

I wake to what sounds like the din of a factory buzzer, but is in fact the music of a single vociferous cicada in the lime tree near my window.

Through the open window, I focus on a pattern of small, glossy lime leaves; then through them I see the mountains, the Himalayas, striding away into an immensity of sky.

'In a thousand ages of the gods I could not tell thee of the glories of Himachal.' So confessed a Sanskrit poet at the dawn of Indian history and he came closer than anyone else to capturing the spell of the Himalayas. The sea has had Conrad and Stevenson and Masefield, but the mountains continue to defy the written word. We have climbed their highest peaks and crossed their most difficult passes, but still they keep their secrets and their reserve; they remain remote, mysterious, spirit-haunted.

No wonder then, that the people who live on the mountain slopes in the mist-filled valleys of Garhwal have long since learned humility, patience and a quiet resignation. Deep in the crouching mist lie their villages, while climbing the mountain slopes are forests of rhododendron, spruce and deodar, soughing in the wind from the ice-bound passes. Pale women plough, they laugh at the thunder as their men go down to the plains for work; for little grows on the beautiful mountains in the north wind.

When I think of Manjari village in Garhwal I see a small river, a tributary of the Ganga, rushing along the bottom of a steep, rocky valley. On the banks of the river and on the terraced hills above, there are small fields of corn, barley, mustard, potatoes and onions. A few fruit trees grow near the village. Some hillsides are rugged and bare, just masses of quartz or granite. On hills exposed to wind, only grass and small shrubs are able to obtain a foothold.

This landscape is typical of Garhwal, one of India's most northerly regions with its massive snow ranges bordering on Tibet. Although thinly populated, it does not provide much of a living for its people. Most Garhwali cultivators are poor, some are very poor. 'You have beautiful scenery,' I observed after crossing the first range of hills.

'Yes,' said my friend, 'but we cannot eat the scenery.'

And yet these are cheerful people, sturdy and with wonderful powers of endurance. Somehow they manage to wrest a precarious living from the unhelpful, calcinated soil. I am their guest for a few days.

My friend Gajadhar has brought me to his home, to his village above the little Nayar River. We took a train into the foothills and then we took a bus and finally, made dizzy by the hairpin bends devised in the last century by a brilliantly diabolical road-engineer, we alighted at the small hill station of Lansdowne, chief recruiting centre for the Garhwal Regiment.

Lansdowne is just over 6,000 feet high. From there we walked, covering twenty-five miles between sunrise and sunset, until we came to Manjari village, clinging to the terraced slopes of a very proud, very permanent mountain.

And this is my fourth morning in the village.

Other mornings I was woken by the throaty chuckles of the red-billed blue magpies, as they glided between oak trees and medlars; but today the cicada has drowned all birdsong. It is a little out of season for cicadas but perhaps this sudden warm spell in late September has deceived him into thinking it is mating season again.

Early though it is I am the last to get up. Gajadhar is exercising in the courtyard, going through an odd combination of Swedish exercises and yoga. He has a fine physique with the sturdy legs that most Garhwalis possess. I am sure he will realize his ambition of joining the Indian army as a cadet. His younger brother Chakradhar, who is slim and fair with high cheekbones, is milking the family's buffalo. Normally, he would be on his long walk to school, five miles distant; but this is a holiday, so he can stay at home and help with the household chores.

His mother is lighting a fire. She is a handsome woman, even though her ears, weighed down by heavy silver earrings, have lost their natural shape. Garhwali women usually invest their savings in silver ornaments. And at the time of marriage it is the boy's parents who make a gift of land to the parents of an attractive girl; a dowry system in reverse. There are fewer women than men in the hills and their good looks and sturdy physique give them considerable status among the menfolk.

Chakradhar's father is a corporal in the Indian army and is away for most of the year.

When Gajadhar marries, his wife will stay in the village to help his mother and younger brother look after the fields, house, goats and buffalo. Gajadhar will see her only when he comes home on leave. He prefers it that way; he does not think a simple hill girl should be exposed to the sophisticated temptations of the plains.

The village is far above the river and most of the fields depend on rainfall. But water must be fetched for cooking, washing and drinking. And so, after a breakfast of hot sweet milk and thick chapattis stuffed with minced radish, the brothers and I set off down the rough track to the river.

The sun has climbed the mountains but it has yet to reach the narrow valley. We bathe in the river. Gajadhar and Chakradhar dive off a massive rock; but I wade in circumspectly, unfamiliar with the river's depths and currents. The water, a milky blue, has come from the melting snows; it is very cold. I bathe quickly and then dash for a strip of sand where a little sunshine has split down the mountainside in warm, golden pools of light. At the same time the song of the whistling thrush emerges like a dark secret from the wooded shadows.

A little later, buckets filled we toil up the steep mountain. We must go by a better path this time if we are not to come tumbling down with our buckets of water. As we climb we are mocked by a barbet which sits high up in a spruce calling feverishly in its monotonous mournful way.

'We call it the mewli bird.' says Gajadhar. 'There is a story about it. People say that the souls of men who have suffered injuries in the law courts of the plains and who have died of their disappointments, transmigrate into the mewli birds. That is why the birds are always crying *un-nee-ow, un-nee-ow,* which means "injustice, injustice!"'

The path leads us past a primary school, a small temple, and a single shop in which it is possible to buy salt, soap and a few other necessities. It is also the post office. And today it is serving as a lock-up.

The villagers have apprehended a local thief, who specializes in stealing jewellery from women while they are working in the fields. He is awaiting escort to the Lansdowne police station, and the shop-keeper-cum-postmaster-cum-constable brings him out for us to inspect. He is a mild-looking fellow, clearly shy of the small crowd that has gathered round him. I wonder how he manages to deprive the strong hill-women of their jewellery; it could not be by force! In any case crimes of violence are rare in

Garhwal; and robbery too, is uncommon for the simple reason that there is very little to rob.

The thief is rather glad of my presence, as it distracts attention from him. Strangers seldom come to Manjari. The crowd leaves him, turns to me, eager to catch a glimpse of the stranger in its midst. The children exclaim, point at me with delight, chatter among themselves. I might be a visitor from another planet instead of just an itinerant writer from the plains.

The postman has yet to arrive. The mail is brought in relays from Lansdowne. The Manjari postman who has to cover eight miles and delivers letters at several small villages on his route, should arrive around noon. He also serves as a newspaper, bringing the villagers news of the outside world. Over the years he has acquired a reputation for being highly inventive, sometimes creating his own news; so much so that when he told the villagers that men had landed on the moon, no one believed him. There are still a few sceptics.

Gajadhar has been walking out of the village every day, anxious to meet the postman. He is expecting a letter giving the results of his army entrance examination. If he is successful he will be called for an interview. And then, if he is accepted, he will be trained as an officer-cadet. After two years he will become a second lieutenant. His father, after twelve years in the army, is still only a corporal. But his father never went to school. There were no schools in the hills during the father's youth.

The Manjari school is only up to Class 5 and it has about forty pupils. If these children (most of them boys) want to study any further, then, like Chakradhar, they must walk the five miles to the high school at the next big village.

'Don't you get tired walking ten miles every day?' I ask Chakradhar.

'I am used to it,' he says. 'I like walking.'

I know that he only has two meals a day—one at seven in the morning when he leaves home and the other at six or seven in the evening when he returns from school—and I ask him if he does not get hungry on the way.

'There is always the wild fruit,' he replies.

It appears that he is an expert on wild fruit: the purple berries of the thorny bilberry bushes ripening in May and June; wild strawberries like drops of blood on the dark green monsoon grass; small sour cherries and tough medlars in the winter months. Chakradhar's strong teeth and probing tongue extract whatever tang or sweetness lies hidden in them. And in March there are the rhododendron flowers. His mother makes them into jam. But Chakradhar likes them as they are: he places the petals on his tongue and chews till the sweet juice trickles down his throat.

He has never been ill.

'But what happens when someone is ill?' I ask, knowing that in Manjari there are no medicines, no dispensary or hospital.

'He goes to bed until he is better,' says Gajadhar. 'We have a few home remedies. But if someone is very sick, we carry the person to the hospital at Lansdowne.' He pauses as though wondering how much he should say, then shrugs and says: 'Last year my uncle was very ill. He had a terrible pain in his stomach. For two days he cried out with the pain. So we made a litter and started out for Lansdowne. We had already carried him fifteen miles when he died. And then we had to carry him back again.'

Some of the villages have dispensaries managed by compounders but the remoter areas of Garhwal are completely without medical aid. To the outsider, life in the Garhwal hills may seem idyllic and the people simple. But the Garhwali is far from being simple and his life is one long struggle, especially if he happens to be living in a high altitude village snowbound for four months in the year, with cultivation coming to a standstill and people having to manage with the food gathered and stored during the summer months.

Fortunately, the clear mountain air and the simple diet keep the Garhwalis free from most diseases, and help them recover from the more common ailments. The greatest dangers come from unexpected disasters, such as an accident with an axe or scythe, or an attack by a wild animal. A few years back, several Manjari children and old women were killed by a man-eating leopard. The leopard was finally killed by the villagers who hunted it down with spears and axes. But the leopard that sometimes prowls round the village at night looking for a stray dog or goat slinks away at the approach of a human.

I do not see the leopard but at night I am woken by a rumbling and thumping on the roof. I wake Gajadhar and ask him what is happening.

'It is only a bear,' he says.

'Is it trying to get in?'

'No, it's been in the cornfield and now it's after the pumpkins on the roof.'

A little later, when we look out of the small window, we see a black bear making off like a thief in the night, a large pumpkin held securely to his chest.

At the approach of winter when snow covers the higher mountains the brown and black Himalayan bears descend to lower altitudes in search of food. Because they are short-sighted and suspicious of anything that moves, they can be dangerous; but, like most wild animals, they will avoid men if they can and are aggressive only when accompanied by their cubs.

Gajadhar advises me to run downhill if chased by a bear. He says that bears find it easier to run uphill than downhill.

I am not interested in being chased by a bear, but the following night Gajadhar and I stay up to try and prevent the bear from depleting his cornfield. We take up our position on a highway promontory of rock, which gives us a clear view of the moonlit field.

A little after midnight, the bear comes down to the edge of the field but he is suspicious and has probably smelt us. He is, however, hungry; and so, after standing up as high as possible on his hind legs and peering about to see if the field is empty, he comes cautiously out of the forest and makes his way towards the corn.

When about halfway, his attention is suddenly attracted by some Buddhist prayer-flags which have been strung up recently between two small trees by a band of wandering Tibetans. On spotting the flags the bear gives a little grunt of disapproval and begins to move back into the forest; but the fluttering of the little flags is a puzzle that he feels he must make out (for a bear is one of the most inquisitive animals); so after a few backward steps, he again stops and watches them.

Not satisfied with this, he stands on his hind legs looking at the flags, first at one side and then at the other. Then seeing that they do not attack him and so not appear dangerous, he makes his way right up to the flags taking only two or three steps at a time and having a good look before each advance. Eventually, he moves confidently up to the flags and pulls them all down. Then, after careful examination of the flags, he moves into the field of corn.

But Gajadhar has decided that he is not going to lose any more corn, so he starts shouting, and the rest of the village wakes up and people come out of their houses beating drums and empty kerosene tins.

Deprived of his dinner, the bear makes off in a bad temper.

He runs downhill and at a good speed too; and I am glad that I am not in his path just then. Uphill or downhill, an angry bear is best given a very wide berth.

For Gajadhar, impatient to know the result of his army entrance examination, the following day is a trial of his patience.

First, we hear that there has been a landslide and that the postman cannot reach us. Then, we hear that although there has been a landslide, the postman has already passed the spot in safety. Another alarming rumour has it that the postman disappeared with the landslide. This is soon denied. The postman is safe. It was only the mailbag that disappeared.

And then, at two in the afternoon, the postman turns up. He tells us that there was indeed a landslide but that it took place on someone else's route. Apparently, a mischievous urchin who passed him on the way was responsible for all the rumours. But we suspect the postman of having something to do with them…

Gajadhar has passed his examination and will leave with me in the morning. We have to be up early in order to reach Lansdowne before dark. But Gajadhar's mother insists on celebrating her son's success by feasting her friends and neighbours. There is a partridge (a present from a neighbour who had decided that Gajadhar will make a fine husband for his daughter), and two chickens: rich fare for folk whose normal diet consists mostly of lentils, potatoes and onions.

After dinner, there are songs, and Gajadhar's mother sings of the homesickness of those who are separated from their loved ones and their home in the hills. It is an old Garhwali folk-song:

> 'Oh, mountain-swift, you are from my father's home;
> Speak, oh speak, in the courtyard of my parents,
> My mother will hear you; She will send my brother to fetch me.

A grain of rice alone in the cooking pot cries,
"I wish I could get out!"
Likewise I wonder: "Will I ever reach my father's house?"'

The hookah is passed round and stories are told. Tales of ghosts and demons mingle with legends of ancient kings and heroes. It is almost midnight by the time the last guest has gone. Chakradhar approaches me as I am about to retire for the night.

'Will you come again?' he asks.

'Yes, I'll come again,' I reply. 'If not next year, then the year after. How many years are left before you finish school?'

'Four.'

'Four years. If you walk ten miles a day for four years, how many miles will that make?'

'Four thousand and six hundred miles,' says Chakradhar after a moment's thought, 'but we have two months' holiday each year. That means I'll walk about 12,000 miles in four years.'

The moon has not yet risen. Lanterns swing in the dark.

The lanterns flit silently over the hillside and go out one by one. This Garhwali day, which is just like any other day in the hills, slips quietly into the silence of the mountains.

I stretch myself out on my cot. Outside the small window the sky is brilliant with stars. As I close my eyes, someone brushes against the lime tree, brushing its leaves; and the fresh fragrance of limes comes to me on the night air, making the moment memorable for all time.

Getting Granny's Glasses

Granny could hear the distant roar of the river and smell the pine needles beneath her feet, and feel the presence of her grandson, Mani; but she couldn't see the river or the trees; and of her grandson she could only make out his fuzzy hair, and sometimes, when he was very close, his blackberry eyes and the gleam of his teeth when he smiled.

Granny wore a pair of old glasses; she'd been wearing them for well over ten years, but her eyes had grown steadily weaker, and the glasses had grown older and were now scratched and spotted, and there was very little she could see through them. Still, they were better than nothing. Without them, everything was just a topsy-turvy blur.

Of course, Granny knew her way about the house and the fields, and on a clear day she could see the mountains—the mighty Himalayan snow peaks—striding away into the sky; but it was felt by Mani and his father that it was high time Granny had her eyes tested and got herself new glasses.

'Well, you know we can't get them in the village,' said Granny.

Mani said, 'You'll have to go to the eye hospital in Mussoorie. That's the nearest town.'

'But that's a two-day journey,' protested Granny. 'First I'd have to walk to Nain Market, twelve miles at least, spend the night there at your Uncle's place, and then catch a bus for the rest of the journey! You know how I hate buses. And it's ten years since I walked all the way to Mussoorie. That was when I had these glasses made.'

'Well, it's still there,' said Mani's father.

'What is still there?'

'Mussoorie.'

'And the eye hospital?'

'That too.'

'Well, my eyes are not too bad, really,' said Granny, looking for excuses. She did not feel like going far from the village; in particular, she did not want to be parted from Mani. He was eleven and quite capable of looking after himself, but Granny had brought him up ever since his mother had died when he was only a year old. She was his Nani (maternal grandmother), and had cared for boy and father, and cows and hens and household, all these years, with great energy and devotion.

'I can manage quite well,' she said. As long as I can see what's right in front of me, there's no problem. I know you got a ball in your hand, Mani; please don't bounce it off the cow.'

'It's not a ball, Granny; it's an apple.'

'Oh, is it?' said Granny, recovering quickly from her mistake. 'Never mind, just don't bounce it off the cow. And don't eat too many apples!'

'Now listen,' said Mani's father sternly, 'I know you don't want to go anywhere. But we're not sending you off on your own. I'll take you to Mussoorie.'

'And leave Mani here by himself? How could you even think of doing that?'

'Then I'll take you to Mussoorie,' said Mani eagerly. 'We can leave Father on his own, can't we? I've been to Mussoorie before, with my school friends. I know where we can stay. But—' He paused a moment and looked doubtfully from his father to his grandmother. 'You wouldn't be able to walk all the way to Nain, would you, Granny?'

'Of course I can walk,' said Granny. 'I may be going blind, but there's nothing wrong with my legs!'

That was true enough. Only day before they'd found Granny in the walnut tree, tossing walnuts, not very accurately, into a large basket on the ground.

'But you're seventy, Granny.'

'What has that got to do with it? And besides, it's downhill to Nain.'

'And uphill coming back.'

'Uphill's easier!' said Granny.

Now that she knew Mani might be accompanying her, she was more than ready to make the journey.

The monsoon rains had begun, and in front of the small stone house a cluster of giant dahlias reared their heads. Mani had seen them growing in Nain and had brought some bulbs home. 'These are big flowers, Granny,' he'd said. 'You'll be able to see them better.'

She could indeed see the dahlias, splashes of red and yellow against the old stone of the cottage walls.

Looking at them now, Granny said, 'While we're in Mussoorie, we'll get some seeds and bulbs. And a new bell for the white cow. And a pullover for your father. And shoes for you. Look, there's nothing much left of the ones you're wearing.'

'Now just a minute,' said Mani's father. 'Are you going there to get your eyes tested, or are you going on a shopping expedition? I've got only a hundred rupees to spare. You'll have to manage with that.'

'We'll manage,' said Mani. 'We'll sleep at the bus shelter.'

'No, we won't,' said Granny. 'I've got fifty rupees of my own. We'll stay at a hotel!'

Early next morning, in a light drizzle, Granny and Mani set out on the path to Nain.

Mani carried a small bedding roll on his shoulder; Granny carried a large cloth shopping bag and an umbrella. The path went through fields and around the brow of the hill and then began to wind here and there, up and down and around, as though it had a will of its own and no intention of going anywhere in particular. Travellers new to the area often left the path, because they were impatient or in a hurry, and thought there were quicker, better ways of reaching their destinations. Almost immediately they found themselves lost. For it was a wise path and a good path, and had found the right way of crossing the mountains after centuries of trial and error.

'Whenever you feel tired, we'll take a rest,' said Mani.

'We've only just started out,' said Granny. 'We'll rest when you're hungry!'

They walked at a steady pace, without talking too much. A flock of parrots whirled overhead, flashes of red and green against the sombre sky. High in a spruce tree a barbet called monotonously. But there were no other sounds, except for the hiss and gentle patter of the rain.

Mani stopped to pick wild blackberries from a bush. Granny wasn't fond of berries and didn't slacken her pace. Mani had to run to catch up with her. Soon his lips were purple with the juice from the berries.

The rain stopped and the sun came out. Below them, the light green of the fields stood out against the dark green of the forests, and the hills were bathed in golden sunshine.

Mani ran ahead.

'Can you see all right, Granny?' he called.

'I can see the path and I can see your white shirt. That's enough for now.'

'Well, watch out, there are some mules coming down the road.'

Granny stepped aside to allow the mules to pass. They clattered by, the mule-driver urging them on with a romantic song; but the last mule veered toward Granny and appeared to be heading straight for her. Granny saw it just in time. She knew that mules and ponies always preferred going around objects, if they could see what lay ahead of them, so she held out her open umbrella and the mule cantered round it without touching her.

Granny and Mani ate their light meal on the roadside, in the shade of a whispering pine, and drank from a spring a little further down the path.

By late afternoon they were directly above Nain.

'We're almost there,' said Mani. 'I can see the temple near Uncle's house.'

'I can't see a thing,' said Granny.

'That's because of the mist. There's a thick mist coming up the valley.'

It started raining heavily as they entered the small market town on the banks of the river. Granny's umbrella was leaking badly. But they were soon drying themselves in Uncle's house, and drinking glasses of hot sweet milky tea.

Mani got up early the next morning and ran down the narrow street to bathe in the river. The swift but shallow mountain river was a tributary of the sacred Ganges, and its waters were held sacred too. As the sun rose, people thronged the steps leading down to the river, to bathe or pray or float flower offerings downstream.

As Mani dressed, he heard the blare of a bus horn. There was only one bus to Mussoorie. He scampered up the slope, wondering if they'd miss it. But Granny was waiting for him at the bus stop. She had already bought their tickets.

The motor road followed the course of the river, which thundered a hundred feet below. The bus was old and rickety, and rattled so much that the passengers could barely hear themselves speaking.

One of them was pointing to a spot below, where another bus had gone off the road a few weeks back, resulting in many casualties.

The driver appeared to be unaware of the accident. He drove at some speed, and whenever he went round a bend, everyone in the bus was thrown about. In spite of all the noise and confusion, Granny fell asleep; her head resting against Mani's shoulder.

Suddenly the bus came to a grinding halt. People were thrown forward in their seats. Granny's glasses fell off and had to be retrieved from the folds of someone else's umbrella.

'What's happening?' she asked. 'Have we arrived?'

'No, something is blocking the road,' said Mani.

'It's a landslide!' exclaimed someone, and all the passengers put their heads out of the windows to take a look.

It was a big landslide. Sometime in the night, during the heavy rain, earth and trees and bushes had given way and come crashing down, completely blocking the road. Nor was it over yet. Debris was still falling. Mani saw rocks hurtling down the hill and into the river.

'Not a suitable place for a bus stop,' observed Granny, who couldn't see a thing.

Even as she spoke, a shower of stones and small rocks came clattering down on the roof of the bus. Passengers cried out in alarm. The driver began reversing, as more rocks came crashing down.

'I never did trust motor roads,' said Granny.

The driver kept backing until they were well away from the

landslide. Then everyone tumbled out of the bus. Granny and Mani were the last to get down.

They were told that it would take days to clear the road, and most of the passengers decided to return to Nain with the bus. But a few bold spirits agreed to walk to Mussoorie, taking a shortcut up the mountain which would bypass the landslide.

'It's only ten miles from here by the footpath,' said one of them. 'A stiff climb, but we can make it by evening.'

Mani looked at Granny. 'Shall we go back?'

'What's ten miles?' said Granny. 'We did that yesterday.'

So they started climbing a narrow path, little more than a goat-track, which went steeply up the mountainside. But there was much huffing and puffing, and pausing for breath and by the time they got to the top of the mountain Granny and Mani were on their own. They could see a few stragglers far below; the rest had retreated to Nain.

Granny and Mani stood on the summit of the mountain. They had it all to themselves. Their village was hidden by the range to the north. Far below rushed the river. Far above circled a golden eagle.

In the distance, on the next mountain, the houses of Mussoorie were white specks on the dark green hillside.

'Did you bring any food from Uncle's house?' asked Mani.

'Naturally,' said Granny. 'I knew you'd soon be hungry. There are pakoras and buns, and peaches from Uncle's garden.'

'Good!' said Mani, forgetting his tiredness. 'We'll eat as we go along. There's no need to stop.'

'Eating or walking?'

'Eating, of course. We'll stop when you're tired, Granny.'

'Oh, I can walk forever,' said Granny, laughing. 'I've been doing it all my life. And one day I'll just walk over the mountains and into the sky. But not if it's raining. This umbrella leaks badly.'

Down again they went, and up the next mountain, and over bare windswept hillsides, and up through a dark gloomy deodar forest. And then just as it was getting dark, they saw the lights of Mussoorie twinkling ahead of them.

As they came nearer, the lights increased, until presently they were in a brightly lit bazaar, swallowed up by crowds of shoppers, strollers, tourists and merrymakers. Mussoorie seemed a very jolly sort of place for those who had money to spend. Jostled in the crowd, Granny kept one hand firmly on Mani's shoulder so that she did not lose him.

They asked around for the cheapest hotel. But there were no cheap hotels. So they spent the night in a dharamsala adjoining the temple, where other pilgrims had taken shelter.

Next morning, at the eye hospital, they joined a long queue of patient patients. The eye specialist, a portly man in a suit and tie who himself wore glasses, dealt with the patients in a brisk but kind manner. After an hour's wait, Granny's turn came.

The doctor took one horrified look at Granny's glasses and dropped them in a wastebasket. Then he fished them out and placed them on his desk and said, 'On second thought, I think I'll send them to a museum. You should have changed your glasses years ago. They've probably done more harm than good.'

He examined Granny's eyes with a strong light, and said, 'Your eyes are very weak, but you're not going blind. We'll fit you up with a stronger pair of glasses.' Then he placed her in front of a board covered with letters in English and Hindi, large and small, and asked Granny if she could make them out.

'I can't even see the board,' said Granny.

'Well, can you see me?' asked the doctor.

'Some of you,' said Granny.

'I want you to see all of me,' said the doctor, and he balanced a wire frame on Granny's nose and began trying out different lenses.

Suddenly Granny could see much better. She saw the board and the biggest letters on it.

'Can you see me now?' asked the doctor.

'Most of you,' said Granny. And then added, by way of being helpful: 'There's quite a lot of you to see.'

'Thank you,' said the doctor. 'And now turn around and tell me if you can see your grandson.'

Granny turned, and saw Mani clearly for the first time in many years.

'Mani!' she exclaimed, clapping her hands with joy. 'How nice you look! What a fine boy I've brought up! But you do need a haircut. And a wash. And buttons on your shirt. And a new pair of shoes. Come along to the bazaar!'

'First have your new glasses made,' said Mani, laughing. 'Then we'll go for shopping!'

A day later they were in a bus again, although no one knew how far it would be able to go. Sooner or later they would have to walk.

Granny had a window seat, and Mani sat beside her. He had new shoes and Granny had a new umbrella and they had also bought a thick woollen Tibetan pullover for Mani's father. And seeds and bulbs and a cowbell.

As the bus moved off, Granny looked eagerly out of the window. Each bend in the road opened up new vistas for her, and she could see many things that she hadn't seen for a long time—distant villages, people working in the fields, milkmen on the road, two dogs rushing along beside the bus, monkeys in the trees, and, most wonderful of all, a rainbow in the sky.

She couldn't see perfectly, of course, but she was very pleased with the improvement.

'What a large cow!' she remarked, pointing at a beast grazing on the hillside.

'It's not a cow, Granny,' said Mani. 'It's a buffalo.'

Granny was not to be discouraged. 'Anyway, I saw it,' she insisted.

While most of the people on the bus looked weary and bored, Granny continued to gaze out of the window, discovering new sights.

Mani watched for some time and listened to her excited chatter. Then his head began to nod. It dropped against Granny's shoulder, and remained there, comfortably supported. The bus swerved and jolted along the winding mountain road, but Mani was fast asleep.

Sita and the River

In the middle of the big river, the river that began in the mountains and ended in the sea, was a small island. The river swept round the island, sometimes clawing at its banks, but never going right over it. It was over twenty years since the river had flooded the island, and at that time no one had lived there. But for the last ten years a small hut had stood there, a mud-walled hut with a sloping thatched roof. The hut had been built into a huge rock, so only three of the walls were mud, and the fourth was rock.

Goats grazed on the short grass which grew on the island, and on the prickly leaves of thorn bushes. A few hens followed them about. There was a melon patch and a vegetable patch.

In the middle of the island stood a peepul tree. It was the only tree there.

Even during the Great Flood, when the island had been under water, the tree had stood firm.

It was an old tree. A seed had been carried to the island by a strong wind some fifty years back, had found shelter between two rocks, had taken root there, and had sprung up to give shade and shelter to a small family; and Indians love peepul trees, especially during the hot summer months when the heart-shaped leaves catch the least breath of air and flutter eagerly, fanning those who sit beneath.

A sacred tree, the peepul: the abode of spirits, good and bad.

'Don't yawn when you are sitting beneath the tree,' Grandmother used to warn Sita. 'And if you must yawn, always snap your fingers in front of your mouth. If you forget to do that, a spirit might jump down your throat!'

'And then what will happen?' asked Sita.

'It will probably ruin your digestion,' said Grandfather, who wasn't much of a believer in spirits.

The peepul had a beautiful leaf, and Grandmother likened it to the body of the mighty god Krishna—broad at the shoulders, then tapering down to a very slim waist.

It was an old tree, and an old man sat beneath it.

He was mending a fishing net. He had fished in the river for ten years, and he was a good fisherman. He knew where to find the slim silver Chilwa fish and the big beautiful Mahseer and the long-moustached Singhara; he knew where the river was deep and where it was shallow; he knew which baits to use—which fish liked worms and which liked gram. He had taught his son to fish, but his son had gone to work in a factory in a city, nearly a hundred miles away. He had no grandson; but he had a granddaughter, Sita, and she could do all the things a boy could do, and sometimes she could do them better. She had lost her mother when she was very small. Grandmother had taught her all the things a girl should know, and she could do these as well as most girls. But neither of her grandparents could read or write, and as a result Sita couldn't read or write either.

There was a school in one of the villages across the river, but Sita had never seen it. There was too much to do on the island.

While Grandfather mended his net, Sita was inside the hut, pressing her Grandmother's forehead, which was hot with fever. Grandmother had been ill for three days and could not eat. She had been ill before, but she had never been so bad. Grandfather had brought her some sweet oranges from the market in the nearest town, and she could suck the juice from the oranges, but she couldn't eat anything else.

She was younger than Grandfather, but because she was sick, she looked much older. She had never been very strong.

When Sita noticed that Grandmother had fallen asleep, she tiptoed out of the room on her bare feet and stood outside.

The sky was dark with monsoon clouds. It had rained all night, and in a few hours it would rain again. The monsoon rains had come early, at the end of June. Now it was the middle of July, and already the river was swollen. Its rushing sound seemed nearer and more menacing than usual.

Sita went to her grandfather and sat down beside him beneath the peepul tree.

'When you are hungry, tell me,' she said, 'and I will make the bread.'

'Is your grandmother asleep?'

'She sleeps. But she will wake soon, for she has a deep pain.'

The old man stared out across the river, at the dark green of the forest, at the grey sky, and said, 'Tomorrow, if she is not better, I will take her to the hospital at Shahganj. There they will know how to make her well. You may be on your own for a few days—but you have been on your own before...'

Sita nodded gravely; she had been alone before, even during the rainy season. Now she wanted Grandmother to get well, and she knew that only Grandfather had the skill to take the small dugout boat across the river when the current was so strong. Someone would have to stay behind to look after their few possessions.

Sita was not afraid of being alone, but she did not like the look of the river. That morning, when she had gone down to fetch water, she had noticed that the level had risen. Those rocks which were normally spattered with the droppings of snipe and curlew and other waterbirds had suddenly disappeared.

They disappeared every year—but not so soon, surely?

'Grandfather, if the river rises, what will I do?'

'You will keep to the high ground.'

'And if the water reaches the high ground?'

'Then take the hens into the hut, and stay there.'

'And if the water comes into the hut?'

'Then climb into the peepul tree. It is a strong tree. It will not fall. And the water cannot rise higher than the tree!'

'And the goats, Grandfather?'

'I will be taking them with me, Sita. I may have to sell them to pay for good food and medicines for your grandmother. As for the hens, if it becomes necessary, put them on the roof. But do not worry too much'—and he patted Sita's head—'the water will not rise as high. I will be back soon, remember that.'

'And won't Grandmother come back?'

'Yes, of course, but they may keep her in the hospital for some time.'

◆

Towards evening, it began to rain again—big pellets of rain, scarring the surface of the river. But it was warm rain, and Sita could move about in it. She was not afraid of getting wet, she rather liked it. In the previous month, when the first monsoon shower had arrived, washing the dusty leaves of the tree and bringing up the good smell of the earth, she had exulted in it, had run about shouting for joy. She was used to it now, and indeed a little tired of the rain, but she did not mind getting wet. It was steamy indoors, and her thin dress would soon dry in the heat from the kitchen fire.

She walked about barefooted, barelegged. She was very sure on her feet; her toes had grown accustomed to gripping all kinds of rocks, slippery or sharp. And though thin, she was surprisingly strong.

Black hair, streaming across her face. Black eyes. Slim brown arms. A scar on her thigh—when she was small, visiting her mother's village, a hyena had entered the house where she was sleeping, fastened on to her leg and tried to drag her away, but her screams had roused the villagers and the hyena had run off.

She moved about in the pouring rain, chasing the hens into a shelter behind the hut. A harmless brown snake, flooded out of its hole, was moving across the open ground. Sita picked up a stick, scooped the snake up, and dropped it between a cluster of rocks. She had no quarrel with snakes. They kept down the rats and the frogs. She wondered how the rats had first come to the island—probably in someone's boat, or in a sack of grain. Now it was a job to keep their numbers down.

When Sita finally went indoors, she was hungry. She ate some dried peas and warmed up some goat's milk.

Grandmother woke once and asked for water, and Grandfather held the brass tumbler to her lips.

◆

It rained all night.

The roof was leaking, and a small puddle formed on the floor. They kept the kerosene lamp alight. They did not need the light, but somehow it made them feel safer.

The sound of the river had always been with them, although they were seldom aware of it; but that night they noticed a change in its sound. There was something like a moan, like a wind in the tops of tall trees and a swift hiss as the water swept round the rocks and carried away pebbles. And sometimes there was a rumble, as loose earth fell into the water.

Sita could not sleep.

She had a rag doll, made with Grandmother's help out of bits of old clothing. She kept it by her side every night. The doll was someone to talk to, when the nights were long and sleep elusive. Her grandparents were often ready to talk—and Grandmother, when she was well, was a good storyteller—but sometimes Sita wanted to have secrets, and though there were no special secrets in her life, she made up a few, because it was fun to have them. And if you have secrets, you must have a friend to share them with, a companion of one's own age. Since there were no other children on the island, Sita shared her secrets with the rag doll whose name was Mumta.

Grandfather and Grandmother were asleep, though the sound of Grandmother's laboured breathing was almost as persistent as the sound of the river.

'Mumta,' whispered Sita in the dark, starting one of her private conversations. 'Do you think Grandmother will get well again?'

Mumta always answered Sita's questions, even though the answers could only be heard by Sita.

'She is very old,' said Mumta.

'Do you think the river will reach the hut?' asked Sita.

'If it keeps raining like this, and the river keeps rising, it will reach the hut.'

'I am a little afraid of the river, Mumta. Aren't you afraid?'

'Don't be afraid. The river has always been good to us.'

'What will we do if it comes into the hut?'

'We will climb onto the roof.'

'And if it reaches the roof?'

'We will climb the peepul tree. The river has never gone higher than the peepul tree.'

As soon as the first light showed through the little skylight, Sita got up and went outside. It wasn't raining hard, it was drizzling, but it was the sort of drizzle that could continue for days, and it probably meant that heavy rain was falling in the hills where the river originated.

Sita went down to the water's edge. She couldn't find her favourite rock, the one on which she often sat dangling her feet in the water, watching the little Chilwa fish swim by. It was still there, no doubt, but the river had gone over it.

She stood on the sand, and she could feel the water oozing and bubbling beneath her feet.

The river was no longer green and blue and flecked with white, but a muddy colour.

She went back to the hut. Grandfather was up now. He was getting his boat ready.

Sita milked the goat. Perhaps it was the last time she would milk it.

◆

The sun was just coming up when Grandfather pushed off in the boat. Grandmother lay in the prow. She was staring hard at Sita, trying to speak, but the words would not come. She raised her hand in a blessing.

Sita bent and touched her grandmother's feet, and then Grandfather pushed off. The little boat—with its two old people and three goats—riding swiftly on the river, moved slowly, very slowly, towards the opposite bank. The current was so swift now that Sita realized the boat would be carried about half a mile downstream before Grandfather could get it to dry land.

It bobbed about on the water, getting smaller and smaller, until it was just a speck on the broad river.

And suddenly Sita was alone.

There was a wind, whipping the raindrops against her face; and there was the water, rushing past the island; and there was the distant shore, blurred by rain; and there was the small hut; and there was the tree.

Sita got busy. The hens had to be fed. They weren't bothered about anything except food. Sita threw them handfuls of coarse grain and potato peelings and peanut shells.

Then she took the broom and swept out the hut, lit the charcoal burner, warmed some milk and thought, 'Tomorrow there will be no milk…' She began peeling onions. Soon her eyes started smarting and, pausing for a few moments and glancing round the quiet room, she became aware again that she was alone. Grandfather's hookah pipe stood by itself in one corner. It was a beautiful old hookah, which had belonged to Sita's great-grandfather. The bowl was made out of a coconut encased in silver. The long winding stem was at least four feet in length. It was their most valuable possession. Grandmother's sturdy Shisham-wood walking stick stood in another comer.

Sita looked around for Mumta, found the doll beneath the cot, and placed her within sight and hearing.

Thunder rolled down from the hills. BOOM—BOOM—BOOM…

'The gods of the mountains are angry,' said Sita. 'Do you think they are angry with me?'

'Why should they be angry with you?' asked Mumta.

'They don't have to have a reason for being angry. They are angry with everything, and we are in the middle of everything. We are so small—do you think they know we are here?'

'Who knows what the gods think?'

'But I made you,' said Sita, 'and I know you are here.'

'And will you save me if the river rises?'

'Yes, of course. I won't go anywhere without you, Mumta.'

Sita couldn't stay indoors for long. She went out, taking Mumta with her, and stared out across the river, to the safe land on the other side. But was it safe there? The river looked much wider now. Yes, it had crept over its banks and spread far across the flat plain. Far away, people were driving their cattle through waterlogged, flooded fields, carrying their belongings in bundles on their heads or shoulders, leaving their homes, making for the high land. It wasn't safe anywhere.

She wondered what had happened to Grandfather and Grandmother. If they had reached the shore safely, Grandfather would have to engage a bullock cart, or a pony-drawn carriage, to get Grandmother to the district town, five or six miles away, where there was a market, a court, a jail, a cinema and a hospital.

She wondered if she would ever see Grandmother again. She had done her best to look after the old lady, remembering the times when Grandmother had looked after her, had gently touched her fevered brow and had told her stories—stories about the gods: about the young Krishna, friend of birds and animals, so full of mischief, always causing confusion among the other gods; and Indra, who made the thunder and lightning; and Vishnu, the preserver of all good things, whose steed was a great white bird; and Ganesh, with the elephant's head; and Hanuman, the monkey-god, who helped the young Prince Rama in his war with the King of Ceylon. Would Grandmother return to tell her more about them, or would she have to find out for herself?

The island looked much smaller now. In parts, the mud banks had dissolved quickly, sinking into the river. But in the middle of the island there was rocky ground, and the rocks would never crumble, they could only be submerged. In a space in the middle of the rocks grew the tree.

Sita climbed into the tree to get a better view. She had climbed the tree many times and it took her only a few seconds to reach the higher branches. She put her hand to her eyes to shield them from the rain, and gazed upstream.

There was water everywhere. The world had become one vast river. Even the trees on the forested side of the river looked as though they had grown from the water, like mangroves. The sky was banked with massive, moisture-laden clouds. Thunder rolled down from the hills and the river seemed to take it up with a hollow booming sound.

Something was floating down with the current, something big and bloated. It was closer now, and Sita could make out the bulky object—a drowned buffalo, being carried rapidly downstream.

So the water had already inundated the villages further upstream. Or perhaps the buffalo had been grazing too close to the rising river.

Sita's worst fears were confirmed when, a little later, she saw planks of wood, small trees and bushes, and then a wooden bedstead, floating past the island.

How long would it take for the river to reach her own small hut?

As she climbed down from the tree, it began to rain more heavily. She ran indoors, shooing the hens before her. They flew into the hut and huddled under Grandmother's cot. Sita thought it would be best to keep them together now. And having them with her took away some of the loneliness.

There were three hens and a cock bird. The river did not bother them. They were interested only in food, and Sita kept them happy by throwing them a handful of onion skins.

She would have liked to close the door and shut out the swish of the rain and the boom of the river, but then she would have no way of knowing how fast the water rose.

She took Mumta in her arms, and began praying for the rain to stop and the river to fall. She prayed to the god Indra, and, just in case he was busy elsewhere, she prayed to other gods too. She prayed for the safety of her grandparents and for her own safety. She put herself last but only with great difficulty.

She would have to make herself a meal. So she chopped up some onions, fried them, then added turmeric and red chilli powder and stirred until she had everything sizzling; then she added a tumbler of water, some salt, and a cup of one of the cheaper lentils. She covered the pot and allowed the mixture to simmer.

Doing this took Sita about ten minutes. It would take at least half an hour for the dish to be ready.

When she looked outside, she saw pools of water amongst the rocks and near the tree. She couldn't tell if it was rain water or overflow from the river.

She had an idea.

A big tin trunk stood in a corner of the room. It had belonged to Sita's mother. There was nothing in it except a cotton-filled quilt, for use during the cold weather. She would stuff the trunk with everything useful or valuable, and weigh it down so that it wouldn't be carried away, just in case the river came over the island.

Grandfather's hookah went into the trunk. Grandmother's walking stick went in too. So did a number of small tins containing the spices used in cooking—nutmeg, caraway seed, cinnamon, coriander and pepper—a bigger tin of flour and a tin of raw sugar. Even if Sita had to spend several hours in the tree, there would be something to eat when she came down again.

A clean white cotton shirt of Grandfather's, and Grandmother's only spare sari also went into the trunk. Never mind if they got stained with yellow curry powder! Never mind if they got to smell of salted fish, some of that went in too.

Sita was so busy packing the trunk that she paid no attention to the lick of cold water at her heels. She locked the trunk, placed the key high on the rock wall, and turned to give her attention to the lentils. It was only then that she discovered that she was walking about on a watery floor.

She stood still, horrified by what she saw. The water was oozing over the threshold, pushing its way into the room.

Sita was filled with panic. She forgot about her meal and everything else. Darting out of the hut, she ran splashing through ankle-deep water towards the safety of the peepul tree. If the tree hadn't been there, such a well-known landmark, she might have floundered into deep water, into the river.

She climbed swiftly into the strong arms of the tree, made herself secure on a familiar branch, and thrust the wet hair away from her eyes.

◆

She was glad she had hurried. The hut was now surrounded by water. Only the higher parts of the island could still be seen—a few rocks, the big rock on which the hut was built, a hillock on which some thorny bilberry bushes grew.

The hens hadn't bothered to leave the hut. They were probably perched on the cot now.

Would the river rise still higher? Sita had never seen it like this before. It swirled around her, stretching in all directions.

More drowned cattle came floating down. The most unusual things went by on the water—an aluminium kettle, a cane chair, a tin of tooth powder, an empty cigarette packet, a wooden slipper, a plastic doll…

A doll!

With a sinking feeling, Sita remembered Mumta.

Poor Mumta! She had been left behind in the hut. Sita, in her hurry, had forgotten her only companion.

Well, thought Sita, if I can be careless with someone I've

made, how can I expect the gods to notice me, alone in the middle of the river?

The waters were higher now, the island fast disappearing.

Something came floating out of the hut.

It was an empty kerosene tin, with one of the hens perched on top. The tin came bobbing along on the water, not far from the tree, and was then caught by the current and swept into the river. The hen still managed to keep its perch.

A little later, the water must have reached the cot because the remaining hens flew up to the rock ledge and sat huddled there in the small recess.

The water was rising rapidly now, and all that remained of the island was the big rock that supported the hut, the top of the hut itself and the peepul tree.

It was a tall tree with many branches and it seemed unlikely that the water could ever go right over it. But how long would Sita have to remain there? She climbed a little higher, and as she did so, a jet-black jungle crow settled in the upper branches, and Sita saw that there was a nest in them—a crow's nest, an untidy platform of twigs wedged in the fork of a branch.

In the nest were four blue-green, speckled eggs. The crow sat on them and cawed disconsolately. But though the crow was miserable, its presence brought some cheer to Sita. At least she was not alone. Better to have a crow for company than no one at all.

Other things came floating out of the hut—a large pumpkin; a red turban belonging to Grandfather, unwinding in the water like a long snake; and then—Mumta!

The doll, being filled with straw and wood-shavings, moved quite swiftly on the water and passed close to the peepul tree. Sita saw it and wanted to call out, to urge her friend to make for the tree, but she knew that Mumta could not swim—the doll could only float, travel with the river, and perhaps be washed ashore many miles downstream.

The tree shook in the wind and the rain. The crow cawed and flew up, circled the tree a few times and returned to the nest. Sita clung to her branch.

The tree trembled throughout its tall frame. To Sita it felt like an earthquake tremor; she felt the shudder of the tree in her own bones.

The river swirled all around her now. It was almost up to the roof of the hut. Soon the mud walls would crumble and vanish. Except for the big rock and some trees far, far away, there was only water to be seen.

For a moment or two Sita glimpsed a boat with several people in it moving sluggishly away from the ruins of a flooded village, and she thought she saw someone pointing towards her, but the river swept them on and the boat was lost to view.

The river was very angry; it was like a wild beast, a dragon on the rampage, thundering down from the hills and sweeping across the plain, bringing with it dead animals, uprooted trees, household goods and huge fish choked to death by the swirling mud.

The tall old peepul tree groaned. Its long, winding roots clung tenaciously to the earth from which the tree had sprung many, many years ago. But the earth was softening, the stones were being washed away. The roots of the tree were rapidly losing their hold.

The crow must have known that something was wrong, because it kept flying up and circling the tree, reluctant to settle in it and reluctant to fly away. As long as the nest was there, the crow would remain, flapping about and cawing in alarm.

Sita's wet cotton dress clung to her thin body. The rain ran down from her long black hair. It poured from every leaf of the tree. The crow, too, was drenched and groggy.

The tree groaned and moved again. It had seen many monsoons. Once before, it had stood firm while the river had swirled around its massive trunk. But it had been young then.

Now, old in years and tired of standing still, the tree was ready to join the river.

With a flurry of its beautiful leaves, and a surge of mud from below, the tree left its place in the earth, and, tilting, moved slowly forward, turning a little from side to side, dragging its roots along the ground. To Sita, it seemed as though the river was rising to meet the sky. Then the tree moved into the main current of the river, and went a little faster, swinging Sita from side to side. Her feet were in the water but she clung tenaciously to her branch.

◆

The branches swayed, but Sita did not lose her grip. The water was very close now. Sita was frightened. She could not see the extent of the flood or the width of the river. She could only see the immediate danger—the water surrounding the tree.

The crow kept flying around the tree. The bird was in a terrible rage. The nest was still in the branches, but not for long… The tree lurched and twisted slightly to one side, and the nest fell into the water. Sita saw the eggs go one by one.

The crow swooped low over the water, but there was nothing it could do. In a few moments, the nest had disappeared.

The bird followed the tree for about fifty yards, as though hoping that something still remained in the tree. Then, flapping its wings, it rose high into the air and flew across the river until it was out of sight.

Sita was alone once more. But there was no time for feeling lonely. Everything was in motion—up and down and sideways and forwards. 'Any moment,' thought Sita, 'the tree will turn right over and I'll be in the water!'

She saw a turtle swimming past—a great river turtle, the kind that feeds on decaying flesh. Sita turned her face away. In the distance, she saw a flooded village and people in flat-bottomed boats but they were very far away.

Because of its great size, the tree did not move very swiftly on the river. Sometimes, when it passed into shallow water, it stopped, its roots catching in the rocks; but not for long—the river's momentum soon swept it on.

At one place, where there was a bend in the river, the tree struck a sandbank and was still.

Sita felt very tired. Her arms were aching and she was no longer upright. With the tree almost on its side, she had to cling tightly to her branch to avoid falling off. The grey weeping sky was like a great shifting dome.

She knew she could not remain much longer in that position. It might be better to try swimming to some distant rooftop or tree. Then she heard someone calling. Craning her neck to look upriver, she was able to make out a small boat coming directly towards her.

The boat approached the tree. There was a boy in the boat who held on to one of the branches to steady himself, giving his free hand to Sita.

She grasped it, and slipped into the boat beside him.

The boy placed his bare foot against the tree trunk and pushed away.

The little boat moved swiftly down the river. The big tree was left far behind. Sita would never see it again.

◆

She lay stretched out in the boat, too frightened to talk. The boy looked at her, but he did not say anything, he did not even smile. He lay on his two small oars, stroking smoothly, rhythmically, trying to keep from going into the middle of the river. He wasn't strong enough to get the boat right out of the swift current, but he kept trying.

A small boat on a big river—a river that had no boundaries but which reached across the plains in all directions. The boat moved swiftly on the wild waters, and Sita's home was left far behind.

The boy wore only a loincloth. A sheathed knife was knotted into his waistband. He was a slim, wiry boy, with a hard flat belly; he had high cheekbones, strong white teeth. He was a little darker than Sita.

'You live on the island,' he said at last, resting on his oars and allowing the boat to drift a little, for he had reached a broader, more placid stretch of the river. 'I have seen you sometimes. But where are the others?'

'My grandmother was sick,' said Sita, 'so Grandfather took her to the hospital in Shahganj.'

'When did they leave?'

'Early this morning.'

Only that morning—and yet it seemed to Sita as though it had been many mornings ago.

'Where have you come from?' she asked. She had never seen the boy before.

'I come from…' he hesitated, '…near the foothills. I was in my boat, trying to get across the river with the news that one of the villages was badly flooded, but the current was too strong. I was swept down past your island. We cannot fight the river, we must go wherever it takes us.'

'You must be tired. Give me the oars.'

'No. There is not much to do now, except keep the boat steady.'

He brought in one oar, and with his free hand he felt

under the seat where there was a small basket. He produced two mangoes, and gave one to Sita.

They bit deep into the ripe fleshy mangoes, using their teeth to tear the skin away. The sweet juice trickled down their chins. The flavour of the fruit was heavenly—truly this was the nectar of the gods! Sita hadn't tasted a mango for over a year. For a few moments she forgot about the flood—all that mattered was the mango!

The boat drifted, but not so swiftly now, for as they went further away across the plains, the river lost much of its tremendous force.

'My name is Krishan,' said the boy. 'My father has many cows and buffaloes, but several have been lost in the flood.'

'I suppose you go to school,' said Sita.

'Yes, I am supposed to go to school. There is one not far from our village. Do you have to go to school?'

'No—there is too much work at home.'

It was no use wishing she was at home—home wouldn't be there any more—but she wished, at that moment, that she had another mango.

Towards evening, the river changed colour. The sun, low in the sky, emerged from behind the clouds, and the river changed slowly from grey to gold, from gold to a deep orange, and then, as the sun went down, all these colours were drowned in the river, and the river took on the colour of the night.

The moon was almost at the full and Sita could see across the river, to where the trees grew on its banks.

'I will try to reach the trees,' said the boy, Krishan. 'We do not want to spend the night on the water, do we?'

And so he pulled for the trees. After ten minutes of strenuous rowing, he reached a turn in the river and was able to escape the pull of the main current.

Soon they were in a forest, rowing between tall evergreens.

◆

They moved slowly now, paddling between the trees, and the moon lighted their way, making a crooked silver path over the water.

'We will tie the boat to one of these trees,' said Krishan. 'Then we can rest. Tomorrow we will have to find our way out of the forest.'

He produced a length of rope from the bottom of the boat, tied one end to the boat's stern and threw the other end over a stout branch which hung only a few feet above the water. The boat came to rest against the trunk of the tree.

It was a tall, sturdy toon tree—the Indian mahogany—and it was quite safe, for there was no rush of water here; besides, the trees grew close together, making the earth firm and unyielding.

But the denizens of the forest were on the move. The animals had been flooded out of their holes, caves and lairs, and were looking for shelter and dry ground.

Sita and Krishan had barely finished tying the boat to the tree when they saw a huge python gliding over the water towards them. Sita was afraid that it might try to get into the boat; but it went past them, its head above water, its great awesome length trailing behind, until it was lost in the shadows.

Krishan had more mangoes in the basket, and he and Sita sucked hungrily on them while they sat in the boat.

A big sambur stag came thrashing through the water. He did not have to swim; he was so tall that his head and shoulders remained well above the water. His antlers were big and beautiful.

'There will be other animals,' said Sita. 'Should we climb into the tree?'

'We are quite safe in the boat,' said Krishan. 'The animals

are interested only in reaching dry land. They will not even hunt each other. Tonight, the deer are safe from the panther and the tiger. So lie down and sleep, and I will keep watch.'

Sita stretched herself out in the boat and closed her eyes, and the sound of the water lapping against the sides of the boat soon lulled her to sleep. She woke once, when a strange bird called overhead. She raised herself on one elbow, but Krishan was awake, sitting in the prow, and he smiled reassuringly at her. He looked blue in the moonlight, the colour of the young god Krishna, and for a few moments Sita was confused and wondered if the boy was indeed Krishna; but when she thought about it, she decided that it wasn't possible. He was just a village boy and she had seen hundreds like him—well, not exactly like him; he was different, in a way she couldn't explain to herself...

And when she slept again, she dreamt that the boy and Krishna were one, and that she was sitting beside him on a great white bird which flew over mountains, over the snow peaks of the Himalayas, into the cloud-land of the gods. There was a great rumbling sound, as though the gods were angry about the whole thing, and she woke up to this terrible sound and looked about her, and there in the moonlit glade, up to his belly in water, stood a young elephant, his trunk raised as he trumpeted his predicament to the forest—for he was a young elephant, and he was lost, and he was looking for his mother.

He trumpeted again, and then lowered his head and listened. And presently, from far away, came the shrill trumpeting of another elephant. It must have been the young one's mother, because he gave several excited trumpet calls, and then went stamping and churning through the flood water towards a gap in the trees. The boat rocked in the waves made by his passing.

'It's all right now,' said Krishan. 'You can go to sleep again.'

'I don't think I will sleep now,' said Sita.

'Then I will play my flute for you,' said the boy, 'and the time will pass more quickly.'

From the bottom of the boat he took a flute, and putting it to his lips, he began to play. The sweetest music that Sita had ever heard came pouring from the little flute, and it seemed to fill the forest with its beautiful sound. And the music carried her away again, into the land of dreams, and they were riding on the bird once more, Sita and the blue god, and they were passing through clouds and mist, until suddenly the sun shot out through the clouds. And at the same moment, Sita opened her eyes and saw the sun streaming through the branches of the toon tree, its bright green leaves making a dark pattern against the blinding blue of the sky.

Sita sat up with a start, rocking the boat. There were hardly any clouds left. The trees were drenched with sunshine.

The boy Krishan was fast asleep in the bottom of the boat. His flute lay in the palm of his half-open hand. The sun came slanting across his bare brown legs. A leaf had fallen on his upturned face, but it had not woken him, it lay on his cheek as though it had grown there.

Sita did not move again. She did not want to wake the boy. It didn't look as though the water had gone down, but it hadn't risen, and that meant the flood had spent itself.

The warmth of the sun, as it crept up Krishan's body, woke him at last. He yawned, stretched his limbs, and sat up beside Sita.

'I'm hungry,' he said with a smile.

'So am I,' said Sita.

'The last mangoes,' he said, and emptied the basket of its last two mangoes.

After they had finished the fruit, they sucked the big seeds until these were quite dry. The discarded seeds floated well on the water. Sita had always preferred them to paper boats.

'We had better move on,' said Krishan.

He rowed the boat through the trees, and then for about an hour they were passing through the flooded forest, under the dripping branches of rain-washed trees. Sometimes they had to use the oars to push away vines and creepers. Sometimes drowned bushes hampered them. But they were out of the forest before noon.

Now the water was not very deep and they were gliding over flooded fields. In the distance, they saw a village. It was on high ground. In the old days, people had built their villages on hilltops, which gave them a better defence against bandits and invading armies. This was an old village, and though its inhabitants had long ago exchanged their swords for pruning forks, the hill on which it stood now protected it from the flood.

The people of the village—long-limbed, sturdy Jats—were generous, and gave the stranded children food and shelter. Sita was anxious to find her grandparents, and an old farmer who had business in Shahganj offered to take her there. She was hoping that Krishan would accompany her, but he said he would wait in the village, where he knew others would soon be arriving, his own people among them.

'You will be all right now,' said Krishan. 'Your grandfather will be anxious for you, so it is best that you go to him as soon as you can. And in two or three days, the water will go down and you will be able to return to the island.'

'Perhaps the island has gone forever,' said Sita.

As she climbed into the farmer's bullock cart, Krishan handed her his flute.

'Please keep it for me,' he said. 'I will come for it one day.' And when he saw her hesitate, he added, his eyes twinkling, 'It is a good flute!'

◆

It was slow going in the bullock cart. The road was awash, the wheels got stuck in the mud, and the farmer, his grown son and Sita had to keep getting down to heave and push in order to free the big wooden wheels. They were still in a foot or two of water. The bullocks were bespattered with mud, and Sita's legs were caked with it.

They were a day and a night in the bullock cart before they reached Shahganj; by that time, Sita, walking down the narrow bazaar of the busy market town, was hardly recognizable.

Grandfather did not recognize her. He was walking stiffly down the road, looking straight ahead of him, and would have walked right past the dusty, dishevelled girl if she had not charged straight at his thin, shaky legs and clasped him around the waist.

'Sita!' he cried, when he had recovered his wind and his balance. 'But how are you here? How did you get off the island? I was so worried—it has been very bad these last two days…'

'Is Grandmother all right?' asked Sita.

But even as she spoke, she knew that Grandmother was no longer with them. The dazed look in the old man's eyes told her as much. She wanted to cry, not for Grandmother, who could suffer no more, but for Grandfather, who looked so helpless and bewildered; she did not want him to be unhappy. She forced back her tears, took his gnarled and trembling hand, and led him down the crowded street. And she knew, then, that it would be on her shoulder that Grandfather would have to lean in the years to come.

They returned to the island after a few days, when the river was no longer in spate. There was more rain, but the worst was over. Grandfather still had two of the goats; it had not been necessary to sell more than one.

He could hardly believe his eyes when he saw that the tree had disappeared from the island—the tree that had seemed as permanent as the island, as much a part of his life as the river itself. He marvelled at Sita's escape. 'It was the tree that saved you,' he said.

'And the boy,' said Sita.

'Yes, and the boy.'

She thought about the boy, and wondered if she would ever see him again. But she did not think too much, because there was so much to do.

For three nights they slept under a crude shelter made out of jute bags. During the day, she helped Grandfather rebuild the mud hut. Once again, they used the big rock as a support.

The trunk which Sita had packed so carefully had not been swept off the island, but the water had got into it, and the food and clothing had been spoilt. But Grandfather's hookah had been saved, and, in the evenings, after their work was done and they had eaten the light meal which Sita prepared, he would smoke with a little of his old contentment, and tell Sita about other floods and storms which he had experienced as a boy.

Sita planted a mango seed in the same spot where the peepul tree had stood. It would be many years before it grew into a big tree, but Sita liked to imagine sitting in its branches one day, picking the mangoes straight from the tree, and feasting on them all day. Grandfather was more particular about making a vegetable garden and putting down peas, carrots, gram and mustard.

One day, when most of the hard work had been done and the new hut was almost ready, Sita took the flute which had been given to her by the boy, and walked down to the water's edge and tried to play it. But all she could produce were a few broken notes, and even the goats paid no attention to her music.

Sometimes, Sita thought she saw a boat coming down the river and she would run to meet it; but usually there was no boat, or if there was, it belonged to a stranger or to another fisherman. And so she stopped looking out for boats. Sometimes she thought she heard the music of a flute, but it seemed very distant and she could never tell where the music came from.

Slowly, the rains came to an end. The flood waters had receded, and in the villages people were beginning to till the land again and sow crops for the winter months. There were cattle fairs and wrestling matches. The days were warm and sultry. The water in the river was no longer muddy, and one evening Grandfather brought home a huge Mahseer fish and Sita made it into a delicious curry.

◆

Grandfather sat outside the hut, smoking his hookah. Sita was at the far end of the island, spreading clothes on the rocks to dry. One of the goats had followed her. It was the friendlier of the two, and often followed Sita about the island. She had made it a necklace of coloured beads.

She sat down on a smooth rock, and, as she did so, she noticed a small bright object in the sand near her feet. She stooped and picked it up. It was a little wooden toy—a coloured peacock—that must have come down on the river and been swept ashore on the island. Some of the paint had rubbed off, but for Sita, who had no toys, it was a great find. Perhaps it would speak to her, as Mumta had spoken to her.

As she held the toy peacock in the palm of her hand, she thought she heard the flute music again, but she did not look up. She had heard it before, and she was sure that it was all in her mind.

But this time the music sounded nearer, much nearer. There was a soft footfall in the sand. And, looking up, she saw the boy, Krishan; standing over her.

'I thought you would never come,' said Sita.

'I had to wait until the rains were over. Now that I am free, I will come more often. Did you keep my flute?'

'Yes, but I cannot play it properly. Sometimes it plays by itself, I think, but it will not play for me!'

'I will teach you how to play it,' said Krishan.

He sat down beside her, and they cooled their feet in the water, which was clear now, reflecting the blue of the sky. You could see the sand and the pebbles of the riverbed.

'Sometimes the river is angry, and sometimes it is kind,' said Sita.

'We are part of the river,' said the boy. 'We cannot live without it.'

It was a good river, deep and strong, beginning in the mountains and ending in the sea. Along its banks, for hundreds of miles, lived millions of people, and Sita was only one small girl among them, and no one had ever heard of her, no one knew her—except for the old man, the boy, and the river.